Praise for Essence Bestselling Author Monica F. Anderson

When A Sistah's FED UP

"…an engaging debut novel with the perfect balance of well-developed characters, honest dialogue, and Dr. Moes' trademark brand of humor!"
Victoria Christopher Murray, National Bestselling Author

"The storyline was excellent and the plot was so wonderful that it left me wanting more..."
Pamela Bolden, Literary Critic

"...an intriguing tale, with well-developed characters and plenty of suspense."
Cheryl Smith, Editor-at-Large Dallas Weekly

Sinphony

"Anderson does a wonderful job at developing characters especially detailing people we would hate…people we would love…even a few that would leave us wondering. Anderson continues to work her magic with words. Glad she has come back to romance."
Deltareviewer, Literary Critic

Success Is A Side Effect: Leadership, Relationships, and Selective Amnesia
"A mix of you-go-girl optimism and no-nonsense straight talk…A counterpoint to the idea that success means excelling at everything…A practical guide for women on how to find happiness and boost self-worth."
Kirkus Reviews

"A master class in corporate ascension from a trusted mentor delivered with humor and candor. These are insights your manager won't tell you and your mother may not know."
Boyd, Writer, Editor

I Stand Accused
"*I Stand Accused* is cleverly written, crisp and witty. It transcends time while simultaneously introducing readers to a refreshing literary voice."
Bestselling Author Victor McGlothin

"The story is told in alternating sequences between present and past in such vivid language that long after the murder is solved and you have closed the book, the scenes will haunt you."
Bestselling Author Evelyn Palfrey

ALSO BY MONICA F. ANDERSON

FICTION

I Stand Accused

When A Sistah's FED UP

Sinphony

NONFICTION

Mom, Are We There Yet?

Black English Vernacular: From Ain't to Yo Mama

Success Is A Side Effect

ANTHOLOGIES

Misadventures of Moms and Disasters of Dads

So How was Your Date?: Dating Chronicles

Kente Cloth: Southwest Voices of the African Diaspora

Kente Cloth: African American Voices In Texas

ACKNOWLEDGMENTS

Acknowledgment and many thanks to the friends, family, and professionals who worked with me, encouraged me and inspired me during this process. With the numerous challenges that occurred between my last novel and this one, I could not have successfully reached this goal without your unwavering support. God bless you.

Rhonda McKnight (editor), Tony Anderson, A.C. Anderson, Dr. Gladys Jenkins, Jimmy Jenkins, Jaye Chase, Lesley Anderson, A'aren Powdrill, Susan Karnes, Timmothy McCann, Anne Boyd, Rosalind Oliphant, Sheryl Grace and the DFW Metro Authors Group, Dr. Akshay Thusu, Ed Gray, Dr. Partha Mukherji, Dr. Karla Frazier, Dr. Marie Holliday, Tiena and Mario Hall, Dr. Jeanine Thomas, Dr. Michael Jacques, Adesewa Faleti, Marie Brown (Baylor University Black Alumni), Renita and Anthony Price, Zeta Phi Beta Sorority, Inc (Psi Zeta and Kappa Zeta Chapters, especially), Phi Beta Sigma Fraternity, Dr. Cathy Hung, Kali Rogers Smith, Dr. Kirsten Trandem, Dr. Quynh Phan, Dr. Kathie Arena, Dr. Michael Wilson, Dr. Ron Bolen, Sistahs in Dentistry Facebook Group, Jill Darden (*Fort Worth Black News*), exceptional librarians in my local Arlington and Grand Prairie, TX branches, and my church family at Oak Cliff Bible Fellowship in Dallas, Texas.

Thank you to every reader and book club who has given me the privilege of sharing my previous publications with the world. I hope you enjoy this one and invite me to your book club discussion. Post and share your reviews!

Remember to like, share, and follow @drmOeanderson on social media. My online connections are so kind. That's where my best ideas have come from during this pandemic. Let's stay safe and stay connected.

Smooches,

mOe

TyMAC BOOKS
Never Close Your Heart
Monica F. Anderson

Printed in the United States of America
First Printing 2020 First Edition 2020

ISBN: 978-0-9786378-4-2

Library of Congress Control Number: 2020917351

10 9 8 7 6 5 4 3 2 1

Contemporary Fiction/Women's Fiction/Family Drama/Christian Fiction/Romance
Cover Design by fastdesign360
Interior Design by PolarBear19325
Author Photograph by ©Dwayne Hills, Austin, Texas

Published in the United States by TyMAC Books

For more information, business or promotional use, quantity discounts, or to book an event, email info@drmoeanderson.com or visit our website at www.drmOeanderson.com.

Never Close Your Heart is dedicated with love and appreciation to my grandchildren Anthony, Apollo, and Aurora Michelle.

The nemesis of love is fear. Fear creeps into you. Builds up walls. Traps you inside yourself...until one day there's nothing left to win or lose. Nothing left, but the thirst for the one drink you don't have.

~Diane Fisher

NEVER CLOSE
YOUR HEART

MONICA F. ANDERSON

CHAPTER 1

A t 6:50 pm, Faith Henry arrived at the scene of her last must-do of what seemed like the longest Tuesday on record. As she exited her car, a crisp wind kissed her cheeks. She inhaled the peculiar scent of late spring hiding summer in its wings. Reluctant to move, she closed the car door and leaned against it embracing the soothing sound of silence.

I just need a minute.

Just one solitary minute when no one has immeasurable expectations of me.

Everything about her day had somehow been both too much and too little. She tried to meditate on a centering thought to calm her anxiety as she started toward her meeting. That didn't last. Four steps later she found herself thinking about work again. She didn't want to become one of those people so obsessed with their career that they thought of nothing else. Maybe it was the hours. She was working too much. She made a mental note to talk to her producer about scheduling.

She marveled at the row of pristine luxury sedans she passed on her way to the massive brick building. A quick bit of mental math gave her a tally of roughly half a million dollars for the eight vehicles, including her Genesis G90 an "almost-fifty-years-old" birthday gift to her well-deserving self. She used the ballpoint of her favorite Waterman pen to press four digits on the keypad and the glass door of the VIP entrance slowly opened with a loud squeak. Despite being in front of a camera lens almost daily, she felt self-conscious, knowing every movement she'd made since driving onto the parking lot was being recorded from multiple angles. She navigated the familiar maze of hallways with practiced ease and arrived at her destination with a minute to spare.

With her arrival, the circle was unbroken. "The Counsel" was convened for their first official session. The room was buzzing with polite chatter and soft chuckles. Upon realizing she was the last to arrive, she quickly occupied the only empty chair and greeted the woman seated on her right: her pastor's wife, First Lady May Bell Carson.

From the sheen of her top knot bun to the flowing hem of her palazzo pants, everything about May Bell's appearance was sophisticated. She wrapped her strong arms around Faith in greeting, then stood. Immediately, the room became quiet and every eye turned in her direction. The respect she received was earned, not bestowed by birth or title. Three decades as the leading lady of a megachurch makes or breaks you. Sister Carson was a *made* woman: formidable and untouchable.

"It's 7 pm. Shall we begin, ladies?" she asked. Seven women of diverse ages and experience had pledged to meet twice a month for three months to provide guidance, instruction, and enlightenment for a young woman who needed every syllable of their collective wisdom. Looking directly at the center of their attention, May Bell smiled and said, "Sloane, since we are here on your behalf, would you please lead us in an opening prayer?"

Faith's heart beat faster. She didn't think that was a good idea, at all. The most useful thing she learned in law school was never ask a question that you don't know the answer to. Asking Sloane, who was Faith's oldest child, to do anything more than making an appearance tonight put their plan at risk of flatlining. Faith had avoided eye contact with Sloane since she entered the room. She finally pushed beyond the overall embarrassment of the circumstances and forced herself to look at the beautiful but angry young woman seated opposite her in the circle of chairs. Faith wished there was a table or some other obstacle between the two of them. Her daughter's rage about being court-ordered to participate in the sessions was palpable. She glared at her mother as if she were a two-headed beast from hell that just ended Netflix and banned online shopping.

Faith was caught between regret and resentment; regret was winning by a slight margin. She wondered if the day would ever come when her daughter appreciated her time as much as she appreciated her money. She hated rarely receiving a "thank you very much" and she hated wanting that little bit of gratitude for her efforts. She pressed her lips into a smile, wordlessly imploring her offspring to be cooperative for once in her self-centered life. When Sloane's nostrils flared, Faith sighed and jerked on the edges of her wig, which suddenly seemed three sizes too small.

Sloane tugged at the hem of her too-short-for-church-skirt and bowed her head. "First of all, Lord. I am thirty years old with a ten-year-old at home who probably needs help with his homework. Please, give these," she paused and licked her upper lip as if the next words she spoke were salty, "women of God or *whoevah* the wisdom to understand that it is what it is and I did what I had to do."

Faith's head snapped up and her eyes flew open as her heart began pounding frantically.

Sloane continued, "Father, anoint them with the discernment to realize it would not be wise to go in on me like I am the only sinner in this room. Oh, ye hypocrites beware! Per the book of Jodeci, Chapter 8, Verse 17, God is not mocked. He knoweth. Bless him! Lord, you showed mercy to the woman in the Bible who was about to be stoned because she was caught in the act of committing adultery with herself." She snapped her finger. "Hmph, so I know you've got me covered. Order my steps up outta here, please."

The initial shock wore off. Faith gripped the edges of her seat like she was preparing for take-off when she saw Tabitha, her niece-in-spirit, wag her finger at Sloane. "Girl, what are you even talking about? The woman Jesus protected from stoning was accused of having sex with a married man. And that's in the Gospel of John, as in John the beloved disciple of Jesus idiot, not Jodeci, the R&B singers!"

Faith felt proud of Tabitha, who was Sloane's age but different in every other way. Then, she saw Sloane's reaction to the sharp rebuke and that pride became wariness. Letting someone else have the last word was not one of Sloane's strengths. Faith looked down and pretended she was invisible. She wanted to publicly disown Sloane but, if she spoke, she might become visible again. She decided to remain cloaked in silence.

"She came here to play," another woman muttered. "This is a serious matter."

Sloane ignored that comment and responded to Tabitha. "First, I got your fool, Cuz. You're too basic to bother. Secondly, it takes two people to commit adultery. The Pharisees brought one person to Jesus. Correct? Where was the man? There is only one sexual so-called sin that lady could commit all by herself. Right? It was hard for a woman back in those days. I understand if she needed to defrost the freezer. Anybody feel me?" She chuckled, but no one seemed to share her sense of humor.

Faith's eyelids fluttered open wide. She recognized the tone of desperation in her daughter's voice and felt the pain of her humiliation. She saw her slouch in the chair and wanted to rescue her as if she were still a little girl.

"I skimmed those chapters so correct me if I'm wrong," Sloane joked weakly, still trying to win The Counsel over with misplaced wit.

Faith knew her daughter too well to be fooled. Sloane's posture and words were at odds. Her expression remained defiant, but Faith knew she felt abandoned, mostly by her.

"Sounds like you skimmed the entire Bible." May Bell's deadpan had that First Lady energy on it.

Faith put her hands over her face. She felt Sloane staring at her. She knew she looked ridiculous playing peek a boo in a room full of adults, but she couldn't stop herself.

The voice screaming in her head sounded like Sloane's inner child…

Oh my God, is Mommy pretending to be invisible again?

Why isn't she defending me?

Mom, help me!!

Why does everyone hate me?

Faith moved her hands to her ears as if that might stop the war of words in her mind. When that didn't work, she looked at each of her companions. Perhaps reality was not as terrible as her imagination. One look at her daughter confirmed that reality was indeed as bad as she was imagining it to be. She saw Sloane tightly cross her legs and fold her arms to dam the tears only her mother could see.

Sloane responded to Tabitha. "You know a bunch of dried-up old men wrote the Bible to make women feel guilty about having sexual desires." She chuckled without mirth and wiggled her dangling foot from side to side. "I mean Jesus was a man. He probably—"

The Counsel detonated when that missile struck their moral target.

"Lord have mercy! Satan done come up in the church with a skirt on." One of the ladies exclaimed.

Everyone but May Bell and Faith jumped to their feet protesting at decibels a coop full of chickens would shush. Faith glanced at May Bell, her long time friend. May Bell was accustomed to Sloane's insatiable need for attention.

"She's been married for ten years. Right?" May Bell whispered thru the din of hell breaking loose.

"Yes," Faith replied, shaking her head. "She's still ashamed of getting pregnant out of wedlock, as if anyone cares these days."

Tabitha was in the red zone, inches from Sloane's face, screaming, "Have you lost your teeny mind? Don't come for my religion! We are in the Lord's house, gurl! And you, my dear, are the only reason we are here instead of at home with our families. The entire state knows you're a vicious animal."

"For the millionth time, I didn't do anything," Sloane said with the weariness of an innocent woman on death row. "Why won't anyone believe me?" She said 'anyone' but she was looking directly at her mother.

Tabitha scoffed, "There were no witnesses to the crime but two people went into the room and you're the only one who was able to walk out. No one in their right mind is going to believe he slipped and fell and a pottery wheel landed on his head." Her lips curled like the spine of Sloane's hunched back. "Sloane Henry Lee, you've been calling me ghetto-fab since we were kids because I didn't wear name brand clothes like you and your brother, but who has a parole officer? It ain't me, Queen, so fall back. You most def haven't used Jesus' name in years so don't start tonight. Blaspheme one more time and see what happens." Tabitha's face was contorted. Her right eye, the one with an off-center pupil, was blinking 90 mph. At that moment, it appeared she needed an intervention more than Sloane.

Faith rose from her chair, instinctively protective of her daughter. She was also worried Tabitha might have a stroke. May Bell caught her wrist. "Stop. Sit down. It's reckoning time," she declared, tightening her grip to restrain Faith. "Let's get it all out."

Sloane snarled and stood toe to toe with her new enemy. She pointed at Tabitha, "I didn't call you ghetto because of that. I called you ghetto because you lack sophistication. Look at you. You can't stunt with a fake Tiffany necklace and cheap bundles of weave. Ratchet is an understatement. You dishonor me." Sloane turned her back to Tabitha and folded her arms.

Sloane was primed to scorch the earth. She retrieved her ever-present iPhone from the back pocket of her skirt. Mocking her cousin, she announced to the room, "Snoop Dogg is calling. He wants his braids back."

Faith watched everyone's focus shift from Sloane to Tabitha's elaborate coiffure of box braids and shea tamed edges. Tabitha deflated. Her righteous indignation melted into humiliation. Her lips trembled as she fought back tears. Faith regretted asking her to join the group. The other women were older, more experienced in verbal boxing. Sloane was a heavyweight when it came to dishing out insults.

Sloane's perfectly manicured index finger bobbed as she pointed at each woman. "Y'all want to be my best life coaches? Well, this is what you're working with, ladies. Come here every session prepared to hear the truth, the whole truth, and allllll the truth. Yours," she placed her finger beneath her chin like the barrel of a handgun, "and mine."

Tabitha's eyes widened and she looked at Faith. They were thinking about the same thing. Faith recalled all the late nights those former ride-or-die cousins had shared. Who knew what "whole truth" might come from the pages of that history? Tabitha hastily returned to her chair, huffing audibly as she plopped onto the cushioned folding chair. She exchanged a sympathetic glance with her Aunt Faith.

The Counsel members murmured bitter nothings to each other. Each one had an axe to grind with Sloane, who had a professional knack for insulting people. They were participating out of loyalty to Faith. Maybe a little jail time would benefit the spoiled Princess of the Dark Side. Sloane sat and casually unlocked her phone as if she intended to make a call or check her email.

Faith's former receptionist, Diamond Sparks, the smallest and most stylishly dressed among them, spoke up. "Turn that damn phone off right now!"

Sloane complied immediately. She had a long history with Diamond Sparks. Something like respect clouded over Sloane's face. She sat up a little straighter.

Diamond's voice was firm. "You don't want none of this smoke, Baby Shark. I may only be a few years older than you, but all my years been in these streets. Church house or not, I will reach through your thick scalp and do CPR on your brain! Ask ya raggedly daddy 'bout me. He's scared of me and you better be, too. Keep my business out yo' mouth." She paused and looked toward Faith for verification.

Faith nodded, thinking her ex-husband, Preston Henry, wasn't exactly afraid of Diamond, but he had a grudging respect for her. During Faith's tenure as mayor of Ulysses, Texas, Diamond was her receptionist. Preston and Diamond often bumped heads, because he was always condescending toward her; insinuating she wasn't well educated or polished enough for the position. She didn't like it one bit, nor did she bite her tongue when she let him know she worked for Faith, not him. She was intelligent enough to hack into a federal database, but dumb enough to get caught. After serving three years behind maximum security prison bars, she had built a thriving multi-media installation company, Triple D's Audio Visual, Inc. She had earned a ton of money and the grudging admiration of many doubters, including Faith's ex-husband.

Diamond continued her rant with a thump to Sloane's forehead. "And don't nevah point your yellow finger in my direction again unless you need an amputation. Add my name to your D-N-F list, honey, because you do NOT want to eff-u-cee-kay with me. Understood?"

Sloane nodded and dropped her phone into her black lambskin Chanel backpack. Faith recognized the extravagant couture gift she had presented to Sloane on her last birthday. She wondered if the way she and Preston always spoiled Sloane was ultimately why they were here. The room was still except for the sound of cars passing by on the boulevard.

Sloane looked cornered. Faith saw her eyes zero in on her next target; the most surprising member of the Counsel.

"Why are you here anyway, Gina?"

When no answer came forth, Sloane turned to Faith. "Mom, why is she here? Seriously, the woman who broke up our family is going to assist in my personal growth? She practically slept with Dad on the altar of this church." Sloane glowered at Gina; the only other attendee as vulnerable as herself. "You broke up my family. There is nothing you could say that I want to hear."

Everyone stared at Gina. Her voice wavered when she spoke, "I...I...I don't want to be here Sloane." She rubbed her hands across the seams of her tight pencil skirt. "Trust me. I couldn't have been more surprised when I got your mother's email. I know she hates me." Gina's eyes went from Faith's dark stare to Sloane's frown. "Your father and I were only married for two and a half years, and he spent most of that time talking about your mother. But that was years ago. We've all moved on. I hoped maybe this was your mother's way of showing me forgiveness for what happened."

Faith tilted her head. "I'm sorry. What did you say about why you are here? I didn't even recognize you until Sloane said your name." Faith hadn't recognized Gina because her hair was much shorter and her clothes fit. In previous years, she wore her dresses so tight, low, and high the brothers of the church nicknamed her Sister Oh-My-Goodness. "I thought May Bell invited you as an elder-advisor." That elder part was petty, but the part about the invite was true. "You haven't crossed my mind since the day I put Preston out, Gina." That was an enormous lie.

Her mental photo album scrolled back to the betrayal that ended her family's fairy tale existence. She could never forget Gina giving her testimony during that Wednesday night service where she bragged to the church about how wonderful Deacon Henry had been to her during his numerous visits to her home.

If Faith's marriage died by a thousand cuts, that performance from Gina was cut nine-hundred ninety-nine. As the pain passed, Faith admitted to herself that by the time her ex-husband became involved with Gina, their life together was a theatrical performance the public expected to see every day.

Still, it was based on a true story.

A story Gina edited in the middle of the final scene. Faith didn't like the revised ending and she didn't like Gina. She extended her hand. "May I see that email?"

Gina's hand went elbow deep into her massive purse. For the first time, Faith wondered about Gina's life. The homewrecker wasn't wearing a wedding ring, but she had on enough necklaces and earrings to open a pop-up shop. A checkered turtleneck hugged her well-endowed breasts like a second skin. A vision of her ex-husband's face buried in that ample cleavage caused a large vein on Faith's neck to throb .

She couldn't make peaks like that using all the underwire at Nordstrom's. Gina looked different, but was she a changed woman? Faith didn't trust her.

Gina unlocked the screen to her phone with her thumb. She pushed her glasses up the bridge of her nose and read, "lawyerfaith_henry@gmail.com."

"That's not her email address!" everyone blurted simultaneously.

"She's had the same address since they invented email," Sloane added. She walked over and grabbed the phone from Gina's hand. She scanned the message and said, "Mom doesn't write emails like that. It's way too short. She goes on and on and on." Sloane looked up, noted her mother's look of exasperation, and stopped going on and on. "Look here," she turned the screen toward DK, the platinum afro sporting lifestyle columnist for the local newspaper and Faith's best friend of the past five years.

DK read the email and nodded in agreement. "Yep, she's right. Three words are misspelled." Everyone chuckled, except Gina who was tight-lipped. "We all know Ms. Grammarly would not overlook one misspelled word, let alone three. A'ight?" She showed the message to Faith before turning back to Gina, "Do you mind if I forward this to myself? I'd like to have one of our journalists trace it, if possible."

Gina quickly closed the three feet between her and DK, snatched the phone, and put it back in her purse. Ignoring DK's question, Gina said, "So you guys weren't expecting me?" Her question was answered before she asked. They watched her squirm. "That's why you had to get another chair, I suppose...." Her voice trailed off. She seemed nervous and uncertain about what to do next.

After a long minute, May Bell broke the silence. "Sister Gina, our steps truly are ordered. The Lord allowed it, so let it be. This is not the night for solving mysteries. Everything happens for a reason. What's not a mystery is Sloane's court record. She needs our help to recover from this rather unfortunate detour in her walk with Christ. Whether or not Sloane accepts our collective wisdom is up to her."

"She has no choice," Faith said, straining to lift her voice beneath the weight of her worries. "It's this or a jail cell. I used every favor I was ever owed to work out this deal. It's this or...." her voice faltered.

The room blurred. Inside, she was beating herself like a drum. Would both of her offspring be swimming against the tide if she'd stayed married and lived unhappily ever after? She couldn't decide if she gave them too much or too little. Either way, she doled out the wrong amount of love based on the results. She was so good at business matters. She'd experienced great success as a city leader, attorney, and, in her second act, a podcaster. But her golden touch failed when it came to her personal life. She clenched her teeth and stared at Sloane like the stranger she had become.

May Bell squeezed Faith's shoulder as she assumed the center of attention. That squeeze was a boost of strength to Faith. It was a small infusion of peace.

May Bell asked Sloane, "Are you going to cooperate or not? If not, you can trot off to jail and we will gladly reclaim our time."

Sloane's shoulders dropped, and she slumped in her chair. Faith could see surrender in her eyes. But her daughter was a fighter. Faith wasn't sure what she was going to say when she opened her mouth again. It took a long minute, but Sloane finally spoke the words Faith prayed she would hear. "Yes, ma'am, Aunty May Bell. I apologize. I'm anxious. This is a lot. I know I am in a situation that could cost me my freedom, my husband, and my son. If I could take everything back, I would."

CHAPTER 2

An hour later, Faith sat at the kitchen table drinking a cup of tea and trying to compose herself after the extremely stressful day. She was sorting through her ; when she heard a car door close and seconds later, Sloane stormed into the room like a warrior on the attack. "What is happening right now? I am a thirty-year-old, college-educated, married mother of one perfect child. I'm the little black girl Martin Luther King dreamed about. People like me don't get arrested!" She plopped into a chair at the table and screamed her pent-up feelings so loudly the neighbors' neighbors could have heard every syllable of her privileged meltdown.

Her daughter balled her fists and folded her arms over her chest: a human shield against the troubles of this world. When she paused to huff, puff, and tap the toe of her right foot, the electronic ankle monitor emitted a familiar beep. Furious, she kicked the table as if it were the nefarious "system" she blamed for her impressive series of poor choices.

Faith yawned and re-folded a teal paper napkin into a smaller square. Their faces were so similar they could be mistaken for a lightly filtered before and after of the same person.

"Daughter, people like you get arrested every day. And people like me bail them out. And people like me represent them in court and on it goes. You are exceptional to me, but not to the legal system." Faith blinked away the mist pooling in her eyes and balled up the napkin. "To that system, you're just black, and good luck with that." She smiled wryly hoping to lighten her daughter's dark mood.

"You have jokes, Mom? I'm glad your sense of humor hasn't been impacted by this tragedy, because I haven't laughed in weeks." She bolted from her chair and paced to the stainless-steel double oven. The tickety tack of her heels pounding the ceramic tile echoed throughout the room. With her fingers laced behind her long, narrow neck, she stared at the round baking pans inside for a moment before turning around. A caravan of tears streamed from her eyes. Her arms plunged to her sides in miserable surrender to the genius chess moves of fate. "Can't you do something? You're the former mayor!"

Faith wondered what would happen if she had a dollar for every time Sloane had used that line to impress someone. She grew wary, recognizing the telltale signs of all hell breaking loose in her dramatic daughter. Her oldest offspring displayed the same reaction to stress now as she did at the age of two: full-blown theatrics, red cheeks, bulging eyes, tight fists, and the fatal inability to think logically. Faith massaged her "former Mayor' temples and took a deep breath. "Honey, I have done everything I can. You're fortunate I still have enough clout to keep you from behind bars. Give me credit for that."

She felt a dark undertow in the lake of love for her oldest child. She shook her head to disperse the nagging doubts about getting Sloane released from jail with a slap on the wrist for punishment. The deferred adjudication included alcohol and curfew compliance monitoring, community service, and psychiatric counseling. Faith orchestrated the sweet deal through back channels, and she called in a lot of favors to do so.

May Bell gave her the idea to suggest group counseling at their church; it had worked in the past, she said. Faith agreed Sloane might be more amenable to that idea than talking to a total stranger. Sloane and Trey grew up in the church thinking of the Reverend Leroy and May Bell Carson as extended family. Plus, May Bell was certified in Christian counseling. It seemed like a good idea when Sloane was sitting in jail waiting for arraignment. If Sloane didn't break any of the conditions of her probation and elevate the charges from a misdemeanor to a felony, the judge would eventually dismiss the case and she wouldn't have a criminal record. Yet, a small part of Faith felt the way her ridiculously beautiful daughter behaved since puberty deserved incarceration.

With a stoically measured pace, she continued, "Heaven knows I desire the best for you, Scott, and my precious grandson. You must know I support you completely. The three of you have been living with me for over two years, and," she bit her tongue to keep from adding the part about them not paying rent even though Scott had a perfectly good job with stock options and benefits, "and, uh, I feel we're closer than ever, but at the same time, the escalating tension between you and your husband is hurting all of us." Sloane started to speak and Faith raised her hand. "Wait a minute. Let me talk. I know you two will work it out, but you must stop taking out your frustration on everyone who crosses your warpath, especially Ever."

As if on cue, they both looked at the refrigerator door. The precocious child's artwork was displayed in that place of honor. He'd drawn the spitting image of Taylor Swift—if she had blue crayon skin—and handcrafted a full-length gown using dry pinto beans and grains of quinoa. There was a red "A+" in the lower left corner of the drawing just opposite his perfectly penned cursive name—Ever Lee. Her grandson seemed to be flourishing, but Faith worried about the long-term psychological side effects of having such a self-centered, volatile mother. She sighed loudly and finished her thought, "Honey, I only suggested a divorce because—"

The D-word made Sloane erupt again, "Because you're a man-eater and you can't stand to see anybody in a stable relationship! You've been waiting all this time for my marriage to crumble like yours." She wagged her finger toward her mother's startled expression. The half dozen designer bracelets on her arm clanged out an angry symphony. "You're the real reason I'm having relationship problems and probably why my little brother is dating that senior citizen. Look at our role models. This is not my fault. The least you can do is support me in my fight to keep my family together. The last thing the world needs is another single black mother."

Faith lowered her eyes to the checkered design on the spotless floor tiles. She struggled to remain calm. Support her? Seriously? The girl's self-absorption disturbed her more than the accusations. She reviewed their recent history.

Before she needed a place to stay, she only called me for money or information. I had to Friend her on social media to see what my grandson was up to. Now, I am literally feeding her family and she questions my role in her life? Jesus, be a fence right now!

She stilled her body and her tongue refusing to bring up the agape generosity of her resources, nor did she point out her daughter was sitting in a kitchen with an island the size of the 6 by 8 foot cell she could be occupying. Faith closed her eyes and inhaled for four seconds, then exhaled for four seconds. Her former therapist, Sahay, told her that's what Navy Seals do when they need to be calm in a crisis. It didn't work. She still wanted to jab her daughter in the throat. Maybe there were additional instructions for the Seals, but she had to go with what she had.

"That's not my experience. My marriage to your dad was a success—overall. We had many happy years together. True, we didn't stand the test of time, but you don't get to judge us." Faith unconsciously lowered the pitch of her voice when she became angry and her vocal cords were in the pure bass range.

Sloane's hazel eyes widened. She plopped onto a barstool. Her lips were tight. Faith dabbed her moist forehead with the origamied napkin and loosened another button on her blouse.

"Put the ceiling fan on high," she said, leaning her head back and fanning herself with her hand. "I don't know what possessed me to bake today, as hot as it is."

Sloane rose from her perch and slowly did as instructed. "You're baking because Ever asked you for cake. You spoil him."

"Like I spoiled you?" Faith ignored the side-eye daggers coming her way. "Besides, you spoil him much more than I do and you know it. The child's room looks like a mini F.A.O. Schwarz. Listen, you were in Austin attending college when things got difficult between your father and me. Funny thing is you've never, ever asked me what happened or how I felt about it."

Faith rose and walked past Sloane to turn on the oven light. She peered at the marble cakes on the middle rack before adjusting the temperature, then turned back to Sloane with exasperation. "Your brother had a million questions, but all you wanted to know was how the divorce impacted your inheritance."

Sloane's face blazed crimson. Faith couldn't be sure if she was angry or embarrassed. Untucking the damp hem of her blouse, Faith added, "I respect your narrative, but as far as I know, you grew up in a happy home with loving parents who denied you almost nothing. Help me understand why you feel I'm responsible for any of the bad decisions you've made."

She pointedly looked at Sloane's ankle monitor as she filled a cup with ice and water from the refrigerator. She moved by the sink on the other side of the island watching her daughter from a safe distance.

That was good, Faith. As much as you wanted to, you did not slap the teeth out of your daughter's mouth and choke her until she had a near-death experience.

Sloane's superpower was the ability to focus completely on herself and persuade others to do the same for long, uninterrupted periods. "What house were you living in while I was in high school?"

Faith arched her right eyebrow as Sloane went on, "Why do you think I chose UT over TCU or SMU?" They faced off over the slab of cold granite between them. Sloane reached below the island and retrieved a bottle of Pinot Noir from the wine rack.

"You cannot drink wine, Sloane. We have been over this numerous times." She cut her eyes at Faith as if she had made the rules of her probation and not the court.

"I wanted to get as far as I could from the stress of you and Dad's charade of a marriage. If you call two parents not talking to each other for weeks at a time, and both of you finding any possible excuse not to come home in the evening a 'happy home,' I guess you need a new thesaurus." Faith flinched expecting the wine bottle to crack when Sloane placed it on the counter with a thud. "I didn't major in history, but I knew a Cold War when I saw one."

Faith pressed her lips together and nodded once, waving a virtual white flag to the epic clap back.

"How will they know if I have a drink?" Sloane demanded. The pitch of her whining hurt Faith's ears. "Are you going to tell them?"

"I won't have to. The electronic bracelet on your ankle tests sweat for your blood alcohol concentration." She was irritated that Sloane was still questioning why she had to do community service and refrain from drinking. Faith took a sip from her cup to steady her nerves. "Your probation officer and I have explained this over and over. Alcoholic drinks make it more likely that you'll sweat. If that equipment detects alcohol in your system, you are going to jail."

Pleading for a truce, she offered, "We'll agree to disagree, because I have many more happy memories than unhappy ones from that period of our lives. Not despite, but *because* of the mistakes I made, I've moved forward and become stronger. Have you? When exactly does personal accountability for your life begin? Take a minute. I'll wait."

It didn't take sixty seconds for Sloane to wiggle out of that corner of their verbal boxing ring. "Mistakes in the past?" She threw up her hands. "Are you kidding me? Let's review, Mom. You left Dad or whatever. You hooked up with your admin, poor on again, off again Raymond, who you toyed with as if he were a human Yo-Yo until he finally realized you're a middle-aged savage psychologically castrating one man after the next." She wagged a finger at her mother's startled face. "Convince me that's not accurate testimony from an eyewitness, Counselor," she challenged. "Take a minute. I'll wait."

Savage? WTF? Faith had no idea what that meant, but it rang true. Perhaps that should be her new screen name on the dating site Snatch.com. She took another sip from her glass while praying Sloane would talk herself to sleep like she did when she was a toddler. Boys are so much easier to raise, she thought for the zillionth time. She swirled the cold water around her mouth before swallowing the bitter thought.

"Should we review the series of unfortunate swipes right? Let's see, there was the Congressman, the civil engineer, the pilot with cataracts, and the bluegrass singer with feathered bangs," Sloane spat.

Faith envisioned acid dripping from her daughter's mouth onto her scattered dirty laundry. *She reminds me of myself arguing in the courtroom on behalf of a client. We may be more alike than I want to admit.*

"I call that your abstract expressionism period of dating," her daughter snapped. "Seriously, I can't even remember all their names. I doubt you can either."

Faith shrugged. True. True. And, *hmmm*, she had recently tried to remember all their names and she couldn't.

"Your like life is busier than the entry door at a Krogers. Someone is always coming or going. You say there are no good men left, but I know the real truth. Mommie Dearest, when it comes to matters of the heart, you are the poster child for emotionally unavailable."

Faith took a deep breath and moved back to her seat at the dinette table. She removed her glasses and kicked off her shoes. With each name from her dating calendar of horrors, she took another sip of tea as if to drown Sloane's words -- or perhaps Sloane herself. She loved her daughter but she didn't like her much at that moment. Faith had been an "A" student in every area but romantic relationships, and the idea that she had become a laughingstock to her own family made her heart hurt at the seams. She stared at the cabinets, vividly recalling the countless sacrifices she'd made so her offspring could have better chances and choices than she. She reflected on the practices, recitals, birthday parties, outdoor festivals, and vacations their family attended together, year after year, building bridges and character—or so she thought.

"Wait one damn minute," Faith said firmly. The waterfall of sweat from her scalp to her shoulder blades prompted her to snatch the lace front wig off her head and throw it at her daughter with MLB accuracy.

Sloane tried to duck below the island but a few strands of the synthetic tresses caught in her hoop earring. Seeming stunned, she slowly stood letting the wig dangle on her shoulder as if nothing out of the ordinary had occurred.

Faith pounded the cool granite with the palms of her hands. "CAN I BE A HO' FOR A MINUTE? Huh? Can I?" She marched around the barrier and got in her daughter's face. "When does the judgment stop? How long will I live down to your expectations?" For someone who wasn't a screamer, Faith was exhibiting professional level skills at it. "Where do these rules for mothers come from, exactly? I have to dress like this and talk like that and listen to the Clark Sisters all day or something is wrong with me. Who decided you get to rank my choices? Nothing is wrong with me when I'm rescuing you from your latest hot mess. I'm perfect then. Right?"

Sloane nodded an affirmation and attempted to scurry away from this madwoman in her mother's body.

Faith grabbed her wrist and spun her around. "Hold up. Answer my question. Can I be a ho', too? You got to be a ho', didn't you? You hooked up with Scott while you were still in college and got pregnant. Since we're remembering things, let's remember that, too." Her words came fast and hot like bullets from a Glock. "Your brother was a corporate ho' before he met that middle-aged woman he's living with. Your father was a damn Deacon ho' when he had an affair with a woman from our church. Or did you conveniently forget that's the 'whatever' that led me to Raymond? Ho', ho', ho'!"

Noting Sloane's deer in the headlights expression, Faith twirled and waved her hands in the air. "Why so serious?" she said, imitating her grandson's favorite D.C. Comics character, who happened to be bat doo doo crazy. "Ho', ho', ho-ing must be fun. Everyone is doing it. So I ask you again: When do I get to be a ho'?" She pointed her lips at her daughter and tilted her head to one side. "Think about it. I'll wait."

Sloane smiled wryly and wrapped her arms around her mother's shoulders. When she buried her face in the crook of Faith's neck, the cease fire commenced.

The fury drained from Faith quickly. She whispered into Sloane's hair, "Daughter, you are responsible for your happiness. If you want a better marriage, I suggest you spend less time appraising me, and more time becoming the perfect mother you didn't have."

Sloane sniffed. "I'm sorry, Mom. We both know I'm a marginal daughter some days."

Faith's familiar laughter broke the tension. The oven timer beeped and Faith kissed her daughter's cheek before breaking out of their huddle. She knew nothing had transpired that a slice of marble cake with chocolate icing couldn't help. It was a comfort that never failed to soothe. She thought they'd made a breakthrough, but --like any good mother -- she had doubts.

CHAPTER 3

An hour later, Sloane was sitting on her king-sized bed, fresh from a shower, applying lotion to her legs when Ever burst through the door. "Mom! We're Ie grabbed her in a baby bear hug and squeezed like he had been gone for days.

Sloane secured the towel wrapped around her body with one arm and hugged him with the other. She smiled at him. "And where have you been little one? I was looking for you to read me a bedtime story."

He giggled. "Mommy, you're silly. We went to see Grandma and Grandpa Henry. Me and Dad helped Grandpa put their new aquarium together. It's so cool. It's bigger than the one we had in our house in Austin." He sat next to her. "Me and Grandpa are gonna pick out tropical fish this weekend. I hope we find a clownfish like Nemo."

Sloane nodded and smiled as he babbled on about his day. When Scott appeared in the door, her smile slipped and his face went from hopeful to wary. He had his camel-colored Wolf and Shepherd Crossover shoes in one hand and his spotless black messenger bag in the other. "Hey darling, how was your day?" he asked as he carefully placed each item in the exact places they belonged in the walk-in closet. He removed his suit jacket and hung it up in the area he reserved for things that needed to be dry cleaned.

Sloane pumped more lotion into one of her palms. "Hey Scott," she replied, without answering his question. She took Ever's smalls hands into her and began rubbing briskly. "If you want to have soft hands like me, you have to keep them moisturized," she advised, taking a moment to smooth his curly eyebrows with her thumb. Ever smiled showing the gaps where his recently shed baby teeth left his smile resembling the skyline of downtown Fort Worth.

Scott sat on the edge of the large armchair next to the closet. "So," he began as he slowly unwound the half Windsor knot of his elegant tie. "I'm guessing you don't want to talk about the meeting tonight." He removed his cuff links and rolled up his sleeves. "My parents send their love. We ate dinner over there. I figured you and Faith would have eaten by now, but my mom sent food for y'all. It's in the refrigerator if you want it."

"Fifi made me a cake," Ever interjected. "She is eating a slice and drinking wine from the bottle, but Daddy said I can't have any because I had a cookie already."

Sloane was surprised by what Ever said about her mother. *Cake at this hour and she's drinking wine from the bottle in front of Ever? I wonder if I should check on her? What a cluster this day has been.*

"Daddy's right, Lil Man. Besides, it's late. You have school tomorrow. Go get ready for bed. I'll come down for my story time in a minute," she teased.

Ever obeyed without hesitation. He kissed his father on the cheek and left the room. Scott remained on the chair as if frozen. Sloane let her towel fall to the bedroom floor. She removed a t-shirt and the largest panties she owned from the dresser. After quickly dressing, she went into the bathroom and started blasting profanity-laced hip hop through the speaker of her phone. She could see Scott undressing in the mirror while she applied a charcoal mask to her face. His body had become as soft as her hands, she thought. Granted, he wore a suit better than any man she knew. That was one of the things she loved when they first got involved. But advancing age, along with spending all day driving to hospitals and clinics had turned her Big Poppa into an XXXL-sized poppa. Her father was the same age and he was about the same size as he'd been since she was a child. She'd asked him to talk to Scott about losing weight for health reasons and their public optics as a couple, but he refused her request, something he rarely did.

Scott walked into the bathroom naked except for his favorite Dallas Stars themed socks. "Would you turn that down, please? My head is hurting a little."

Sloane complied reluctantly, still observing him from the mirror. He raised the toilet seat. As he relieved himself, she rubbed her cheeks with an exfoliating cleanser. "Let me guess. Your mother made greens with pork, beans with pork, and pork chops."

Scott made a sound similar to the word yes, flushed the toilet, and turned on the shower. She dried her frowning face.

"You know pork gives you a headache and it's not good for your enlarged prostate. I swear I feel like I have two children sometimes." Scott removed his socks and yanked the shower curtain to the left before stepping into the tub. "I'm going to tuck in Ever," she said over the sounds of water and Drake's latest rap song.

The squeal of the metal curtain hooks scraping the curved shower rod reverberated through the small bathroom. She footnoted Scott's attempt to partition her out of his personal space.

Downstairs, she peeked into the kitchen. Her mother seemed okay. She was listening to a Christian podcast and washing dishes. Sloane read Ever two bedtime stories and played with the woolly curls of his afro until he began to snore lightly. She heard the shower in her mother's bathroom as she tiptoed back to the stairs. She hoped she'd stalled long enough for Scott to fall asleep. She was running out of excuses for not having sex.

He was sitting in the middle of the bed wide awake. His unclothed body glistened with baby oil like an Afro-American Buddha. He had covered his joystick with a hand towel but the beast beneath the towel was awake, as well. She rolled her eyes and closed the door. His dark pupils twinkled above a hopeful smile. He directed her attention from the towel to the nightstand with his finger. "Surprise, Bae. I have prepared a drink for you and I am going to give you a nice massage to help you relax."

She looked at the drink and the full bottle of massage oil next to it. Avoiding his gaze, she turned to throw her robe on the ottoman. *Jesus, let's just get this over with*, she thought.

"I don't need a massage." She gulped the contents of the glass and passed him the bottle of oil. "Use this. I don't know where the lube is."

He looked like he had questions that he dared not ask. She removed her nightwear as he liberally applied the oil to his semi-erection. She folded her body over the edge of the bed and straddled her legs, assuming his favorite position. He swiftly moved behind her and grabbed her waist. She was surprised when, a short time later, she felt him become soft. He tried to keep going but between the oil and his flaccid state, it was a no-go.

She buried her face in the comforter. *Not again.* She fixed her face into an expression that she hoped looked understanding. "Didn't you take a pill?" she asked, trying not to sound as annoyed as she felt.

Over the past few months, the expression on his face became more horrified each time this happened. When he put his hand over his eyes, her heartfelt a twinge of pity. She put her hands on his chest. His heart was pounding like an African drum. She hid her discontent by recalling the years they'd spent having hot, passionate trysts here, there, and everywhere before his fierce battle with ED commenced. The erection pills had given her hope for better nights to come but damnit, they only worked sometimes. Those times, a life of leisure, and the sparkle of the multi-carat diamond on her left ring finger deterred her from going job hunting or man hunting. For now.

He lowered his hand. "I took two." They both sighed. "My urologist said a lot of men in their fifties, like me and your father, require a little more foreplay."

She reared back, removing her hands from his body. *Hold up. He did not just bring my father into this, did he? Really?*

You know, some encouragement for the big game."
They both looked down. The team needed every cheerleader
in the NFL at that moment. He tried to kiss her. His tongue
met the wall formed by her tight lips.

She hated the pleading look he gave her. If I don't get
this done, he will pout for days, she thought before
dropping to her knees under the crushing obligation of
inspiring his team of one to play ball. She composed a song
in her head to distract her from the sheer boredom of the
task. She matched the melody of the music still playing on
her phone with the lyrics, "I want to sleep and my jaw hurts
so much right now. Right now. Right now."

What felt like an hour later, Scott pulled her to her feet
and flipped her over the bed. He came in under three
minutes. Since he wasn't running track, setting a new record
for speed did not earn him a medal. She pecked his dry lips
and went into the bathroom.

"I love you," he said, yawning as he crawled into bed.

"Uhm hmm. Luv ya, too."

He was sleeping soundly when she emerged. She felt a
jumpy restlessness stirring in her body. It was partly a lack
of fulfillment. But the other part she couldn't yet label.

~ ~ ~

Faith was in her office, wearing her favorite Minnie Mouse pajamas engrossed in a video chat when a shadow fell across her desk. She looked up, surprised to see Sloane standing on the other side of her desk. Her eyes zigzagged between the screen and Sloane a few times before she spoke into the Bluetooth headphones around her neck. "Raymond, my daughter just walked in. I've gotta go, but I really love your idea about asking various celebrities to record an intro for my show. That will attract new listeners" She beckoned Sloane to come closer to her desk.

Sloane backed up. "Don't get off, Mom. I didn't want anything. I saw the light and...."

Faith shook her head and gestured for her to stay. "Right. That's a plan. Good looking out. Get some rest. Talk to you tomorrow."

She turned off the monitor and placed the headphones on her desk. "Can't sleep, Honey?" *Please don't let this be another crisis*, she begged God. *Raymond's call brought me back to my happy place and I'd like to end this day in that vicinity.*

Sloane walked in and stood by the desk across from Faith. "Wow. Nice bouquet." She leaned over to smell the large mixed arrangement. "They smell so good. Are those Peruvian lilies?" The vase sat next to her mother's coveted signed copy of Michelle Obama's memoir, Becoming. The hardbound book was the most organized thing on the desk. Piles of notes, folders and mail covered the remaining surface. That was atypical for a woman who arranged her bras in a drawer by color and style. "Are these from Raymond?"

"No," Faith replied as she shut down her pc. "Those are from a media company that wants me to sign with them and move my podcast to L.A."

"Really? I don't see you in L.A. Besides, you could never leave this amazing house or me, could you? You've spent so much time working on both of us."

"Indeed I have." Faith chuckled. She knew Sloane believed dear ole mom was permanently settled, but since Raymond had left, her thoughts on staying put had become less concrete. Ever was the only thing keeping her tethered and that string was growing thinner. Soon he'd be in middle school, and she knew that signaled the end of Knock Knock jokes and hanging out with Grandma.

Sloane sauntered to the floating shelf on the wall between Faith's degree from law school and a proclamation from the Governor of Texas. She smiled at the row of miniature black angels Faith had collected over the years, as if the sight of them brought a pleasant memory to mind. The smile disappeared and quickly as it arose. She dragged her slippered feet across the room to the full floor to ceiling bookshelf, winding her diamond bracelet around her wrists over and over.

Faith watched and waited.

"Mother, I can't turn my mind off. I have never had so many problems at one time in my life."

"That's understandable. You have a lot going on." Faith turned off her desk lamp. "I heard you reading to Ever a while ago. You must have been pretty funny. He giggled the whole time."

"Yeah, he likes it when I make up voices for the characters."

"And I like it when you show that sweet side of yourself. Have you considered being like that more with uhm," she stopped herself from naming Scott, in particular, "others? You were so popular in school because you're smart and charming." Sloane looked pensive. "Don't lose that part of yourself, Honey."

Sloane was unusually quiet. She removed a book from the bookshelf, thumbed through it, and put it back on a different shelf.

Faith pressed her lips together tightly. She wanted her to file the book properly. She also wanted her to wash the dishes she frequently left in the sink and shop for groceries now and then. She beat those words back into the basement of her mind. "Why don't you take a seat Honey? Let's unpack this box of blues." She was glad Sloane finally understood her life had been rather charmed until recently. She picked up her glass of fresh squeezed orange juice and took a sip. A case of copy paper occupied the high-backed chair in front of her desk. Sloane transferred it to the floor, sat down, and folded her legs onto the cushion. "Do you want anything to drink?" Faith pointed toward the couch. "I got a mini-fridge slash end table last week. Help yourself."

Sloane didn't look. "No, thanks."

"Is this about earlier in the kitchen? We were both a little upset, but I felt like we cleared the air. We should have had that conversation years ago." Faith made it a point not to apologize. She had recently become aware that women apologize more frequently than men and often for things beyond their control. She was tired of being sorry.

"It's not that. I guess I'm maturing. There are a lot of things I see differently now than I did before all this stuff with Ever's teacher happened."

Faith smiled to encourage her to continue.

"Like I realize you really can't rely on other people. I wish people only had two-faces, but they have a dozen. Look how Tabitha turned on me at the Counsel meeting.

That's exactly why I don't have a lot of girlfriends. You can't trust them."

"I'm not sure that's fair to say. I have great female friends whom I trust. Between DK's curious mind, Diamond's hustle, and May Bell's wisdom, I'm covered in the friend zone."

Sloane wagged a finger at her mother. "Bam. You made my point. What happened to all the friends you had before you got divorced?"

Faith searched her wide vocabulary looking for words but she couldn't find a good response.

Sloane loosened the belt of her robe. "Auntie May Bell is a pastor's wife. I think she has to be loyal or she'll go to hell. Diamond worked for you when you were mayor. You gave her a job she wasn't even qualified to do and you stood by her after she went to jail for stealing equipment from the city." Faith leaned back -- away from the truth. "And DK is a new-ish friend. You just met her a few years ago. They are good people but your circle of friends was way larger than that before the split up."

"That's one way to look at it, but I try not to dwell on the could have beens." Faith felt like the day would never end. She wanted a time out from her life and Sloane's life. She walked around her desk and perched on it. "Honey, we don't know why people make the choices they make. If I tried to analyze everything that happened in the past ten years, I would lose my mind." She put her bare feet on the edge of Sloane's seat. "Are you worried about me? I appreciate the thoughts but I'm okay."

"I can see that, but I didn't realize until now how difficult things must have been for you. No one made an announcement, but it's clear some of your friends chose Dad over you. I see the posts of their bae-cays and birthday parties and weddings and shit on Dad's Facebook page and—"

"SLOANE HENRY LEE!"

"Sorry for cursing, but what the heck, Mom? All the stuff you and Dad attended together and they were sooo proud to have 'their dear friend' Mayor Henry present. Please, say a few words, Mayor. Ladies and gentlemen, the mayor is here tonight. Blah, blah, blah. It's been ten years and they still treat you like divorce is, she twisted a lock of her hair searching for the right analogy, "uhm like divorce is some rare cancer with no cure but another marriage." Faith had to smile at the grim but accurate comparison. The sound of water rushing through the pipes above made them both look up. Sloane rolled her eyes. "That's Scott going to the bathroom again. Anyway, I'm saying this patriarchal culture punishes women after a divorce."

Faith crossed her feet at the ankles. "That's an insight that comes with age. Part of me wishes you remained unaware of the disparity but it's a different world for women sometimes. Honestly, I don't think anyone is intentionally being malicious." She stood and stretched. "The suburbs are designed for couples. Everything comes in pairs, including invitations. I admit that aspect of single life caught me off guard, but I adapted."

"But you loved playing dress-up with the other socialites."

Faith laughed softly, "Yes, I did. I was about that life." Faith preferred they talk about Sloane's future rather than her social life from Christmases past. She looked for a space between words to merge and change lanes.

To Faith's disappointment, Sloane removed the furry throw from behind her and spread it over her feet.

Oh, dear, she isn't going to bed anytime soon.

"I know. That's just wrong," she said, looking out the window behind Faith's desk. "And when I see them at the mall or wherever, they always ask about you like you live overseas. Sloane struck a socialite pose and made her voice nasally, "Sloane darling, how is your mother? Give her my best. Kiss. Kiss." Sloane's face became somber. She chewed the cuticle on her thumb as she'd done since becoming a mother herself, with all the worries thereof. "They went on without you, Mom, and you went on without them. I can't do that. I can't start my adult life over."

CHAPTER 4

"Hello and welcome to Never Close Your Heart! I'm your host, Faith Henry. Whether you're a new listener or a friend : next episode, you have my promise of an exciting half-hour for the single, sassy, and almost woke. Take another sip of caffeine, click that 'Subscribe' button, and stay tuned. After this sixty-second ad from our sponsor, Chuck Smith's Steak House, I'll be back to start our journey through the ten--yes, ten--levels of intimacy. Count yourself lucky if you've made it to level eight. That's as good as it gets for most people. Are you curious about what's beyond love as usual? I know you are. Don't touch that screen, mouse, or dial. I'll be right back."

Faith rubbed her hands and grinned. She still found it hard to believe that she walked away from a successful career at a law firm to host a podcast when she only had a thousand subscribers and no revenue. She pushed her headphones above her ears and gave a thumbs up to her audio engineer, Daniel, seated a few feet away. He was a student about to graduate with a bachelor's degree in broadcast production from Ulysses Community College. He was the best intern the school had ever sent her. It was a sweet quid pro quo where he earned college credit toward his degree while she got free help.

In their short time working together, Daniel had found their new home base at a cheaper, much nicer recording studio in Plano. He connected her Facebook, YouTube, and Twitter pages to the podcast for live streams, and he brought two major sponsors on board. His roommate was a developer who created a custom, mobile app for "Never Close Your Heart-The Podcast." If he had done that for free, she could only imagine what he would do when she started paying him. They'd already agreed for him to stay on at least through the end of the year. She was working on the employment agreement for her soon-to-be "Executive Producer" to sign upon graduation,

He grinned at her over the lip of a can of Red Bull. He had the look of love in his eyes. Or maybe that was fatigue. She wasn't wearing her glasses, but occasionally he gave her GILF (grandmother I'd like to freak) energy. He was a cute cub but she wasn't a cougar. She preferred her men with grains of salt in their beards.

"How do you like the headphones, Mayor?" he asked.

She cupped the earpieces of the AKG Q 701s. She wouldn't have bought them because the name is too long, but Daniel had convinced her to give them a try. "They are very comfortable," she said. "I was so accustomed to the cheaper ones I started with that I didn't realize how much better the sound quality is with a premium model. I can't thank you enough for all you've done. And again, call me Faith. I haven't been a mayor in years."

"My folks taught me manners, ma'am. I can't be that familiar with a trailblazing pioneer. Consider it a sign of my respect, Mayor."

Before Faith could object to the title again, he raised ten fingers for the countdown back from commercial.

Faith adjusted her earphones, leaned toward the mic, and went into performance mode. She checked her appearance in a mirror strategically placed outside the view of two mounted cameras recording every movement. If she had her way, her program would be strictly audio but she had to stay current. Those video clips Daniel posted on Instagram TV, YouTube, and Twitter ushered a lot of listeners her way per Google analytics. Those viewers often turned into paid subscribers for her premium content. She had learned to follow the money.

"I'm Faith Henry and you're listening to, Never Close Your Heart. Today, our hot topic is the Ten Levels of

Intimacy. Like Rihanna and Celine, I've loved and I've lost. But I genuinely believe every person who enters our life is there to teach us a lesson. There are soft lessons and there are hard lessons. Our mission is to learn from every course or spend our lives re-taking every test. My story is public record. I was married for many years. Two kids, gym membership, fine dining, and then, Poof!" She slammed her palm against her forehead. "It was over. The relationship died. It melted so slow and simple I didn't realize the extent of the damage until every one of us was burned. I didn't want to love again and risk feeling that excruciating pain in the jigsawed organ beating beneath my ribs. Then, oh but then," she paused dramatically, lowered her chair a few inches, and smiled into the camera, "Against every odd, I met my One. I met the greatest love of my life! And you know what? He took my mind, body, and soul to a place I'd never known. Nor, will I ever forget. I can best describe it as a supernova connection."

She noticed Daniel staring at her as if her next sentence might solve all of life's mysteries.

"Most people never know the ultimate intimacy possible with another human being. Your love for your family is another box. Put that aside. This connection happens between two consenting adults who do not share ancestry. It's intense as flying close to the sun; beautiful yet so dangerous.

"There are ten levels of relationship, from something a little less than empathy to something a bit more than agape. That tenth level y'all? I've been there and it's a black hole of feelings. Once anything falls into a black hole, it doesn't come out. Scientists say you must exceed the speed of light to exit a black hole's darkness. Isn't that ironic? By now, you're wondering where your connection falls on this scale from one to ten. Let's see."

She removed her phone from the stand in front of her. "I made notes on my phone so I don't forget anything." She pinched and zoomed in to enlarge the letters. "I should've printed this out at home. Whew, y'all if this is forty-nine, I'm a little scared of turning fifty." She chuckled. "When I enlarge this, I lose some of my notes." She was very conscious of the fact that, unlike the viewers watching her live broadcast on social media, anyone listening to the podcast later, would encounter a period of silence if she stopped talking so she narrated her movements to avoid dead air. "Folks, be patient with me. Hey Daniel, play that commercial for Snatch.com while I find my reading glasses."

She fumbled in her purse a moment before realizing her reading glasses were hanging from the V of her shirt. When she looked at the phone again, she noticed a text notification from her ex-husband. She hesitated to open it, but curiosity got the better of her and she had about sixty seconds before recording resumed.

(Preston) Leave me out of your podcast, please.

She quickly tapped an answer. I didn't say your name. This isn't about you.

(Preston) Exactly. But you keep talking about our divorce.

Anger coursed through her arteries. She turned her chair to put her back to the cameras. She did not have a poker face. Her eyes talked too much. They could scorch the earth without her uttering a word.

She frowned, then replied. Stop listening like you did when we WERE married.

Was it irony or arrogance that she was doing a podcast on love when she still harbored ill feelings toward her ex. After they divorced, they barely spoke for the first year but they had to interact because of Trey and Sloane. Eventually, it seemed they both got tired of being hostile and eased into a *frenemy* type of relationship. Every time she thought, they'd put the past behind them, he would do or say something to set her off. She was weary of the back and forth.

Bouncing dots appeared on her phone. (Preston) …

She tapped her way back to her note cards before he finished typing his response. She was fuming inside but she smiled for the cameras. *He's such a control freak*, she thought before adjusting her microphone. She looked at Daniel for her signal.

"Woo hoo, I was blind but now I see. Let's do this! It starts at Level One. The Casual Encounter. This happens every day. You smile at a stranger on the elevator or smile at the new co-worker sitting in her cubicle looking awkward. It's a pleasant but unmemorable exchange.

"From there we can go to Level Two. Acquaintance. This is someone you know on a first-name basis and with whom you engage in small talk. Think classmate, someone on your team at the office, the neighbor you chat up in the yard. Levels Two through Five are nonsexual, but there are more points of connection as the relationships deepen."

She glanced at the comments on her Facebook page. "Give me a thumbs up if you're enjoying this friends and let me know where you're listening. I also need you all to click that 'Share' button so your friends can join us. These levels get hotter as they get higher. Hey Jaime in Boca Raton, thanks for listening. We're on Level Three now.

"For Level Three, think Social Network aka Your Tribe. These people are your friends on and off the Gram and Facebook. Y'all attend each other's birthday parties. You exchange texts on holidays. You might introduce them to another professional in your network or reach out if you learn they are ill. Basically, you care, but you wouldn't loan them your new car.

"Level Four requires a little more face time. Let's call it 'Good, Good Friends.' This is where the circle starts to narrow in diameter. These are the people with whom you've built a level of trust. You share similar values and goals. You may vacation with them. You probably know their parents and siblings by sight, if not by name. You return their calls as soon as possible. You would help them move on the hottest day of the year in Scottsdale, Arizona. You would complain like hell the entire time, but you would help. You care about them deeply."

Daniel signaled her to stop for another commercial. She took a sip of water and stood for a quick stretch. When they resumed ninety seconds later, Faith said, "We're back. You're listening to Never Close Your Heart and we're exploring the levels of intimacy. Somewhere between work friend and fi-ah is Level Five. We're talking about your besties. This is a heart-to-heart connection that doesn't fall off because they have a bad day or you say the wrong thing. You always give each other the benefit of the doubt because you have been through a lot together, from births to deaths and every Happy Hour in between. With Level Five-ers, if their name appears on your Caller ID between 8 and 5, you step out of the work meeting to call them back or text 'You okay? Call you in a sec.' They get you. They can explain you to the people who don't get you. They will not let anyone criticize you, but they will certainly tell you the truth about yourself with nothing but love."

She noted the time and ended her segment with "Thank you for listening to this episode. Our time is up, but I'll be back next week to share the final five levels of intimacy. You don't want to miss it. If you have questions or comments, post them and I'll personally reply in a post or on air. Remember to subscribe, like, follow, and share. New subscribers get a free trial of LegalArmor prepaid legal services for three months *plus* one month of free access to our paid subscribers-only content. Click the links below to learn more. Peace y'all!"

When she was sure the cameras and microphone were no longer live, she opened her texts app. She gripped the phone tighter as she began to read Preston's last response.

(Preston) I think you're still projecting. You--

She stopped reading at "you" and deleted the message. *Next time I see him, he's going to find out how savage I can be. Enough is enough.*

~ ~ ~

Faith parked and moved Ever's pink scooter out of her path to pull closer to the garage door. A year ago, he decided pink was his new favorite color, and geez, was he in love! He wanted pink linen, pink socks, pink shirts, and pink cupcakes. She thought of his smile every time she saw the color.

Her smile dropped as she was reminded that she couldn't put her car in the garage anymore. There was barely enough room for the pastel scooter. After ten years of being single, the two-car detached garage remained crowded with things from her former, bigger life. She had downsized houses, but downsizing a decade of white-collar collector's items, like those skis she never used, was taking a bit longer. It didn't help that Sloane and Scott refused to get a storage unit when they moved in with her, promising they would find a house soon. She should have asked them to define the word "soon." She laughed to herself. That was only one of their many "money-saving" tactics that somehow ended up costing her. Scott and cherry-cheeked Ever, her gender non-conforming grandson, could stay forever, they were a joy to be around, but Sloane and the ankle monitor? Not so much.

She decided to call Raymond for a chat before heading inside. She let the front windows down and turned off the engine. She donned her wireless earbuds and called her ex, Raymond Hart, for comfort and the only thing she craved more than chocolate: intellectual stimulation.

When he answered, his image momentarily dissolved into a million pixels as her phone switched to the home Wi-Fi. She turned the phone holder horizontally and watched the screen fill with seven inches of his FHD splendor.

"Hey, gorgeous! How was your day?" His voice filled with concern. "You look stressed. Have you eaten anything today?"

"Not well. I'm ok. I forgot to eat." After years working side by side, followed by more years of phone calls and round trip flights between Faith's home in Dallas and Raymond's home in Santa Fe, where he had moved to run his family's trucking business, they needed fewer and fewer words to communicate. She understood and admired his decision to leave Texas; still, she believed they would still be together if he were closer.

"That's not good. I've suggested you put alarms in your phone, but I suspect you're on another silly diet so I'll leave it alone." He made a funny face to take the sting from his rebuke. "My day was so hectic I missed your podcast."

She smiled to show appreciation for his concern, but she was thinking *I wish Preston would forget to listen to my podcast permanently.*

"You didn't talk about the Counsel meeting did you? If so, do not go into that house alone!" He chuckled, but he knew her daughter's temper was no laughing matter.

He instinctively honed in on the most pressing entry on her worry list. She loved not having to explain herself to him. He just knew. "That subject is off-limits for the show. I do not have a death wish." She smiled ruefully. "My daughter was defiant, as expected. She acted as if we attacked someone instead of the other way around."

He listened with empathy as she went into great detail about the Counsel meeting and her heart to heart with Sloane minus the ho', ho', ho'-ing outburst.

"This grown-up thing is harder than it looks, Raymond. Maybe I'm the problem. I guess I don't act my age. I still have trouble believing I have adult children and a grandchild."

Raymond chuckled. "So do I, but only because you don't look like you have a granddaughter, Fifi."

"Grandson." Her tone changed when she corrected him.

"Right. My bad. Forgive me."

She took a deep breath. She didn't want to project onto him. He was trying to compliment her. She reached to turn on the radio and remembered the ignition was off. "And for the record, I am only Fifi to young master Ever. YOU do not call me Fifi." They laughed easily in the same note for the same amount of time. It was rehearsed yet natural and refreshing, like a Kirk Franklin song on Sunday morning. She heard a thumping sound in the background on his end. The mood sobered abruptly as Raymond's head snapped around. Faith felt a familiar ache in her chest.

"Did I call at a bad time? Is that Eva?" she asked.

"You know her name is Eden." He lowered the phone until the only thing she could see was the image of his strong jawline. He seemed to be frowning, but it was hard to tell from that angle. She assumed he was alone because he took the call. He usually sent her calls to voicemail when his girlfriend was around.

"That wasn't anyone. I think the wind's blowing the screen door. Eden is working late tonight."

He seemed distracted. He held the phone sideways as he walked through the dining room. Faith recognized the Chacasso signed print she bought him for his last birthday on the wall next to black and white framed photos of his parents. They were outside their one-bedroom starter home near Santa Fe, New Mexico, knee-deep in snow and debt during the big blizzard of 1967. It was during that natural disaster that his father got the idea to trade the family's modest life savings for a neighbor's used delivery truck and a snowplow. With the help of his devoted wife, by a decade later Papa Hart had turned that rusty truck into a multi-million dollar company with a fleet of trucks and clients all over the country. "My pops does not accept the word 'No'. He always finds a way," Raymond often bragged about his hero.

He didn't speak again until he made it to his study. She heard the door creak as it opened. She imagined she smelled the odor of the pecans he always kept in a bowl on his desk. He settled his chiseled body on the beat-up leather couch. Faith could take credit for some of the beatings. That thing they used to do over the arm of the chair with her body forming a sexy "Y" or I'ma-need-a-chiropractor-after-this "W" when she planted her heels by his tailbone. Ahh, that was another grain of sand on the beach of her regrets. She tried in vain to think of one path she'd chosen that didn't lead to two fingers of Jack Daniels.

Raymond moved the phone in front of his face and she was blinded by the glow of his smile.

"So how are your parents? What did the doctor say about your father's blood pressure medicine? Are they changing the dose?" Her concern about his father was genuine, but she really wanted to know if she crossed his mind as often as he crossed hers. She also wanted to know if he'd dump big booty and take her back, but she didn't have the right or left to do so.

"They're good. They ask about you all the time," he said. "I do mean ALLL the time."

He smiled again and scratched at his nine o'clock shadow. She recalled the sensation of those short, wiry whiskers on her forehead as she snuggled in his arms. She struggled to remember what they were supposed to be talking about.

"That's sweet. Tell them I said hello."

"I will," he agreed. "The doctor says my dad has to cut back on the salt. He thinks the dosage is fine."

"That's good. I'm sure your mother is all over that." She wondered if every innocent sentence somehow seemed to have sexual undertones for him, as well.

He nodded. "Yes, she is, and I hope I don't get caught in the wake of sea salt and Mrs. Dash. I'm a plain old Morton's guy."

The wake. The sleep. What was she thinking to let this man get away? Why couldn't she surrender to him after all this time?

She changed the subject. "The good thing is you can cook. In fact, for my birthday, Please make me a sweet potato pie and overnight it here. You make the best sweet potato pie on earth."

"You flatter me, my friend," he said. "But it's true. Even my mama says so and it's her recipe."

Laughing with Raymond ranked near the top of her "fun things to do" list. "You could deliver the pie yourself," she offered hopefully. His engagement aside, they were a perfect match. He had to know that, she thought.

"I could do that," he agreed. "I'm due a trip back to Texas. Let me check with Eden and see if she's available around that date. We have a few things lined up and she keeps the social calendar. She's heard a lot about you though, and I know she wants to meet you."

Part of Faith was pissed that he included his girlfriend, whom she had not invited anywhere. The other part was pleased he was seriously considering the trip. He had not been to Texas since announcing his engagement in a misspelled, possibly drunken text at two am on a fateful Thursday morning a few months prior.

After that, she dated every Broken Bobby on snatch.com. If one more man complained to her about what his baby's mama was doing with the child support money, she was going to give an entirely new meaning to the word "snatch." It took creeping around to make her realize how amazing Raymond was in comparison. She didn't know how, but he would be hers again. That was, quite possibly, the only certainty in her life.

"That sounds good. Check with her and let me know. I look forward to meeting her."

He smirked. "No, you don't."

"You're right. I don't," Faith consented with a wry smile. She tucked a two-strand twist behind her ear. "I do want you to be happy, Raymond. If she makes you happy, that's what matters."

"I wish you meant those words," he said softly.

She turned her face away from the bright floodlight on the garage to hide her eyes when she lied. "I do mean them." The long pause that followed made her look at him. He looked far from convinced.

He frowned. With forced calmness, he said, "No, you don't, and I wish you'd stop playing these games. I asked you to marry me multiple times before I left Texas. Remember? You said no every time. You wouldn't even agree to live with me. That's how much you care about how I feel." He started pacing. "I get it. You want your freedom. You're tired of titles. You didn't date much before marrying at a young age. I've heard all your excuses."

C'mon man! She longed to say. She tried to stop his passionate tirade. "Raymond. I--"

He cut her off in untypical fashion. "Hold up. Let me finish." She brought the phone near her face to see him better. "I want marriage and living together and building a future with my partner."

His words were fast. *As if rehearsed for this moment,* she thought as she rested her chin on her fist. *Why the hell did he go and get into a serious relationship soon after they broke up?* It made her think he wanted the title of husband more than he wanted her.

"I want all of married life with someone who is totally committed to me. No questions. No baggage from the past. I don't want friends with benefits and that's all you were offering me." He looked and sounded more resigned than confident.

"Raymond, I wanted that too." She swallowed the lump in her throat. "In time." She hated herself for hurting him, but she was so afraid of marriage. Her previous marriage went from a Disney Princess fairy tale to the twelfth hour of The Purge with no warning. If she still didn't understand why, how could she stop it from recurring?

"In time? We're almost fifty. Time is up. I've moved on." He plopped into a chair and stared at her.

He didn't understand. He never had. When her so-called perfect marriage failed it damn near killed her. What if she blew it again? She couldn't survive another heart quake. She wanted to be optimistic and look on the bright side, but the dark side had her on a short leash. He was fuming everywhere but his eyes. The love she saw there never changed. She marveled at that. How could he get into a relationship with another woman and still look at her that way? Man, if his girl ever saw that lust. *Hmmm, on second thought, he* should *bring her to visit.*

She was about to respond to his moving on comment when she heard a loud crash. Raymond jumped. "What was that?" Faith shouted. "Should I call 911?"

Raymond's eyes darted in the direction of the door. "No, no need. It was the wind. I can hear it rattling the ridge vents. Let me check it out. I'll talk to you later. Okay?" He hung up abruptly.

It wasn't really a question. They talked every day and texted several times a day without fail. Faith opened the Weather Center app on her phone and entered his zip code. The graph projected precipitation at 10%, humidity 34%, and the wind 0 mph. Something caused that unusual sound she heard. And it was not the wind. Why was he lying to her?

CHAPTER 5

The following day, Faith was in downtown Ulysses on her way to a meeting with Sloane's attorney, J.D. Person, the mayor pro tem and a thorn in her side during her entire four-year mayoral term. She rounded the corner of the parking garage and spied her sister-from-another-mother, DK, on the sidewalk a few feet ahead of her. "Hey, girlfriend!" Faith exclaimed. DK spun around to greet her. Faith buried her face in DK's gravity-defying coils as they hugged it out.

"Hey, ya self! Don't you look runway-ready, Superstar," DK sighed appreciatively. She squinted and eyed Faith from head to toe. "Yes, please. I need those when you get done." She pointed to Faith's gray square-toed shoes and made a sound of approval. "Me like. I got dibs on all of this. Dry clean and hand it over."

At 5'10", DK was almost as tall as Faith, who measured six feet without heels. They wore the same size and had the same taste in clothes. They knew how to share: double the wardrobe for half the price. Both were on a budget, but for different reasons.

"What's mine is yours," Faith responded. She checked her iPhone to see how much time she had to chit chat. "So I'm headed to the courthouse to meet with Attorney Person for a quick strategy session on keeping my child out of jail. Some asshole complained the district attorney is giving her special treatment because she's my daughter." Her eyes rolled like dice. "Person's in court all day. I'm trying to get with him during a recess so we can get ahead of this."

DK nodded, "Yes, I heard. There's been a lot of talk about that at the paper, too. I called last night to fill you in, but it went straight to voicemail."

Faith waved at a passerby. "Sorry about that. I was talking to Raymond when you called. I meant to get back with you, but I was so exhausted. Between work and my family drama, my head is spinning." She twirled the ruby ring on her thumb and bit her lip. "What more do they want? Sloane doesn't have a criminal record. An alternative sentence and probation are reasonable in this case. This isn't special treatment. The judge ordered electronic confinement and community service. Plus, she has a child to take care of. There's no reason to lock her up." Faith's volume went up with each item on her list.

DK smiled sympathetically. "I know. I know. Don't get yourself worked up. She's following the court's orders and she's getting counseling." She paused, twisting her mouth to one side. "Correction. We're getting counseling. Sloane showed out at the church. Didn't she? When went in on Tabitha—"

Faith felt like DK subtly changed the subject. "Don't remind me. That meeting was a hot mess. Tabitha said she's done. She's not participating anymore." Faith thought about calling the whole Counsel thing off. If every meeting was going to be like the first one, it was a waste of time.

"Can you blame her?"

Faith groaned. "No, I can't. But, let's not talk about that right now. What brings you to the courthouse this early? Which celebrity's bid'ness is going to be in your column tomorrow? And, for the record, you're the only reason I subscribe to the *Courier*. I don't think I ever told you how dirty they did me when I was mayor, but that's water under the bridge." She was so happy to see her friend. It was a welcome distraction from thinking about all the fires she needed to put out. DK was unusually quiet as Faith babbled on. "Oh, how was that Black Lives Matter protest last night? I saw your videos on Twitter. I was glad to see such a large, diverse crowd." She felt a little envious that her friend had such a seemingly fun life when all she did was work and try to keep Sloane out of jail.

DK waved her off with a small smile. "It went well. It was peaceful and the speakers were great. I've been volunteering to cover other news stories. The celebrity gossip thing is stunting my growth as a journalist." She paused and fiddled with the tassel on her purse.

DK was no nonsense most of the time, not the type to fidget. *Why is she acting weird?* Faith wondered. She locked arms with DK. "Walk with me to the courthouse."

DK pulled her arm free. "I can't. I'm headed across the street to the county admin building." She looked everywhere but at Faith's face. "I got a tip that Raymond is over there roaming the building and chatting up officials. I thought that was worth looking into." She raised one eyebrow. "Did you know he's in town?"

Faith drew her head back in surprise. "My Raymond?" DK nodded. Faith blinked rapidly as she rewound her conversation with Raymond. "I talked to him last nite and he was at home in Santa Fe. He would have told me if he was flying here today. Are you sure it's him?" Faith moved her bag from her shoulder to her hand and swung it like a pendulum.

"I don't know, but he was your right hand for four years. He's pretty well known around here. If it's not him, that's fine. If it is, and you don't know anything about it," she paused dramatically, making Faith more nervous, "then that's suspect. I wanna know what he's up to."

"So do I," Faith mumbled. They moved from the sidewalk to the grass and allowed two police officers on bicycle patrol to pass. Faith waved to them. DK did not.

"What did you two talk about? He didn't give you a clue about his plans?"

"If he's here, it's not because of me," Faith replied with a hint of regret in her voice. Her head snapped up and she gasped. "Wait. The County Clerk's office is in the admin building. Maybe he's here to get a marriage license."

"Not likely. They live in New Mexico."

"But I think his girlfriend is from Dallas or Fort Worth. Maybe that's why he didn't tell me he was coming here. They're having a big Texas wedding and—" Faith felt her heart pounding. The idea of Raymond legally bound to another woman made her dizzy. She wanted him to grow old with her, not Eden.

"Girl, stop. You're letting your imagination run wild. He's the CEO of a national company. Right? It's probably a business trip. That's what I'm thinking. I want to get a scoop on whatever he's doing and write a story that will convince the higher-ups to let me return to investigative reporting."

Faith's watched beeped a notification. She blew a puff of air from her cheeks. "Never a dull moment," she said, more to herself than DK. "I've gotta go. Good luck and please let me know what you find out. I don't want to keep Person waiting."

"He's not waiting," DK informed her, pointing toward the courthouse. "He's headed this way."

Even from a distance, J.D. Person's custom-made cowboy boots and long, confident strides were unmistakable. Faith felt embarrassed that he caught her gossiping with her girlfriend when she was supposed to be meeting him about her daughter. She pasted a professional smile on her face and greeted him. "Counselor, I was about to come inside and I bumped into a friend." She turned to DK. "J.D. Person, please meet my good friend DK Clemson." Faith was the only one attempting to be cordial. The pair stared at each other with open hostility. "Well, uh, if you don't know who he is DK, I have a mnemonic I use to keep his initials straight. It's J.D. like the juris doctorate we earn when we graduate law school. Get it? J.D." Her companions looked at her as if they both thought that was the stupidest thing they'd heard an adult say all day.

"She knows my name and I know her byline," J.D. said curtly. "She loves to put me and my wife in her trashy column. Don't you, DK?"

DK looked like she wanted to spit in his face. Faith wondered what had happened between them. The animosity seemed excessive for a little gossip in a local paper. She knew from experience that he loved any kind of publicity as long as they spelled his name correctly. Faith turned her face so Person couldn't see her expression and gave DK an inquisitive look. DK was unusually intense. Her ability to bring light to any darkness was one of the things Faith loved about their friendship. *What on earth is going on?*

J.D. scoffed. "Hmph. Your good friend? She's the reason I just met with the judge about Sloane's probation. Her front-page story has everyone up in arms about your daughter getting political favors because of her mama. What was it you said exactly?" He removed his glasses and pinched the bridge of his nose. Faith braced herself for what she was about to hear. "If my memory serves me correctly, she referred to you as the 'popular influencer and powerful former mayor of Ulysses.' Was that how it went?"

His face was solemn, but Faith noted the triumphant smile in his eyes. Her narrowed eyes shifted from his face to DK's. "What? Did you write a story about Sloane? Why would you do that?"

"Why *would* you do that?" J.D. repeated. He set his briefcase on the sidewalk like he expected the long version of her explanation.

DK looked at J.D. like she wanted to fracture his skull before pleading with Faith. "I was about to tell you. They were going to assign the story to Peter Knight. The courthouse is his beat and you know how he is. Whatever he wrote would have been inflammatory and speculative. I begged his editor to assign it to me so I could manage it and protect you." She swallowed hard. "Protect Sloane."

Faith's jaw dropped. She backed away from DK, socially distancing her newly fractured heart. She balled her hands into tight fists. *I thought this bitch was my friend. I helped her get a job at the paper. Is there anyone I can trust?*

As if hearing those thoughts, DK pleaded, "Babe, before you go left on me. Read the story in today's paper. It's only the facts. I didn't add anything that's not public record. I would never betray your confidence." She reached to touch Faith's arm but she swatted her hand away. "Please listen to me. You gotta believe me. I'm trying to help."

Faith was on the verge of a meltdown. The last time she had cried in public she was staring at the closed caskets of her mother and father, side by side in life and death. That was shortly after Trey was born, almost 30 years ago. J.D. watched her. If he was looking for a sign of weakness, he would be disappointed. She wouldn't give him the pleasure of seeing her break or seeing two women catfight. He didn't know it, but he had just lost his position as her least favorite person in Ulysses, Texas.

"Let's find somewhere private to talk," she told him, turning her back on DK. "I'm done here."

~ ~ ~

When her meeting with J.D. ended, Faith called Raymond on her way back to the parking garage. He said, "Hey" and she replied, "Why didn't you tell me you're in town?"

There was a perceptible pause. "Ulysses *is* a small town," he joked weakly. "It's a quick business trip. I knew I wouldn't be here long enough for us to get together so I didn't mention it. My bad."

She struggled to keep her tone level. *How could he?* They were six hundred miles apart most days of the year. He thought being in the same city wasn't worth mentioning. She enunciated each word carefully, pronouncing every ending consonant to avoid sounding like the angry black woman she was. "I would make myself available if you only had five minutes free. You must know that."

"I do. I just thought it would be easier to not see each other this time. You know?"

She didn't understand. "No, I don't know," She heard a jackhammer. "Where are you right now?"

"I'm in Grapevine. I have a meeting in a few minutes," he replied.

Grapevine? Something about his voice didn't seem right. She couldn't put a name on it but he was being cagey. "Sure. Uh, so are you available for dinner?" She chided herself for seeming desperate. "I get it that you're here on business. I'm not trying to mess up your money as the millennials say." He laughed at that. The familiar sound brought her some relief from the agony of knowing he was so close, yet she couldn't get a simple hug.

"It's going to be a long day. I have another meeting after this, then a presentation. It's stuff for the company." She noted the vagueness. In the past, he'd been a straight shooter with her. "I'll be tired when this is all done, and I have an early flight."

"I see."

"'Preciate the invite and it's always nice to hear your voice. I'm glad you called." She heard him greet someone, then he said, "Sorry. I need to get in there. I'll give you a call this eve if it's not too late when I get done with all of this."

"It's never too late," she assured him.

"We'll see," was his response. A quiet moment ensued. She thought he might say more but he ended the call with a clipped, "Goodbye, Faith."

She fell asleep at midnight, still waiting for his call.

CHAPTER 6

Junior Henry strolled into ladies' night at his main strip club in Addison, Texas. He was on the verge of celebrating eight profitable years of self-employment and he couldn't be more proud of himself. His mind replayed the impossible journey that led him to the promised land of steady paychecks.

Everyone marveled that Junior Henry, a man without a college degree or trust fund, parlayed an extremely lucky day at Winstar Casino into the largest private chain of gentleman's clubs in the state. They thought it was all a fluke but he knew winning that $75,000 jackpot on the five dollar slot machines was the beginning and end of his luck. At that time, he was still delivering bottled water to small businesses in the DFW area. He'd dreamed of owning a more conventional type of business, like a 7-11 convenience store, but when that soft breeze of opportunity wafted through the window of his ordinary life, he had to act fast. He didn't know much about slushees and lotto tickets, but he knew a lot about the type of entertainment men craved.

What he didn't know, he learned, fast, and in less than a decade, he opened twenty-nine locations across the Lone Star State.

He made his way to the bar and dapped up the lead bartender. "The usual, Boss?"

"Nah. It's been one of those days already. I'ma need the hard stuff." Junior dropped on a barstool and turned to survey his kingdom. "Been busy tonight? The ladies drinking up?" he asked over his shoulder.

"Yessir, it's been nonstop action since the doors opened." He placed a sweaty bottle of Brewmeister Snake Venom near Junior's hand. "Boss, I hope it's okay. I know you said no men are allowed in the club on Ladies' Night but your nephew arrived a half-hour ago. He wants to talk to you. Something important, he said. We put him out of sight in VIP 1. I tried to reach you a few times. Did you see my missed calls?"

Junior peered in the direction of the VIP booths. A distinct odor wafted through the air and his nostrils flared. "I've been busy," he said. His days of explaining himself to anyone but his mama were long behind him. "Tell security to find the table smoking Kush and throw them out. He scratched his head, wondering if stupid was contagious. *Cannabis ain't legal in Texas yet and we ain't getting shut down over that mess. Don't these fools know how to vape? They ain't gone mess up my paper. No sir.* He grabbed his sweaty beer and walked in the direction of the VIP booths.

The twenty-yard winding lane from the bar to the high-roller section gave him a moment to reminisce. He recalled signing the lease for his first location: a small, abandoned building owned by a connection who was desperate for an occupant after three years of vacancy. Junior took two weeks of vacation and spent it remodeling the space into something resembling a lounge. He found used tables, chairs, and a commercial-grade bar on eBay. He enlisted the aid his former sis-in-law and legit true friend, Faith, to get his permits and licenses fast-tracked.

He couldn't afford a legitimate stage, but a buddy who owned a repair shop gave him a four-post auto lift he didn't need anymore. Always resourceful, Junior bolted it to the foundation of his new club, fastened composite decking across the tire rails to form a dance floor and, with minimal investment, created a power stage to lift the "featured dancer" eight-four inches into the air. Beneath her, four other women danced around the corner posts like stripper poles. Over the years, his design team made needed safety enhancements like adding plexiglass to the top level after one of the girls fell off the platform. Luckily, she landed on a customer who was as big and cushiony as Jabba the Hutt. The guy was so wasted he thought she fell from heaven and didn't protest when Junior added $100 to his tab for a lap dance. The car lift stage had become the patented, signature piece of the clubs.

Upon reaching his destination, he noted the huge shit-eating grin on his only nephew's face. Junior usually thought he favored Preston, Junior's big brother, but in the dim light, he looked more like his mother, Faith. He wondered how much that 80-megawatt smile was going to cost him this time. They greeted one another with a vice grip and one-armed hug. "You good, my man?"

Trey nodded, maintaining that thirsty grin. "Yep. Keeping it real. You know." He traced his slender mustache with the tip of his fingers. "Yeah, so I was in the neighborhood. I figured I'd fall through and check-in."

Junior sat next to Trey and loosened his tie. He owned dozens from around the world, but for some reason they all felt like expensive, hand-painted nooses around his neck. He sighed. "I'm glad you came by. I ain't seen you since Mama cooked neck bones last month."

Trey laughed as if his uncle was the featured comedian at the Improv a few miles away. "Yeah, yeah, you right. I'll do better but Grandma Henry put her foot in those neck bones."

"Corns, bunions, and all!" Junior laughed from his diaphragm and loosened another button on his shirt. "Shit, Mama had her ashy ankles up in them bad boys. Let's sit.

You came on a good night. Nothing but titties and apple bottoms as far as the eyes can see. If I wanted to, I could charge these Boss bitches twenty dollars for a cup of tap water. They'd pay it, too, trying so hard to impress their fake friends. I ain't kidding. They be like, eff Obamanomics, it's ladies' night!" The barrel shape of his stomach bounced against his starched shirt. "They used to come here with their men, now they come with their girlfriends and make it rain so hard we bought a money vacuum to clean up!"

"Today's fempreneurs work hard and play hard. My lady is the same way." Trey's phone started ringing. Junior watched him decline the call from his girlfriend. Junior looked at him with an expression of disapproval. Trey cleared his throat. "I'll call her back," he explained. "But, Uncle Junior, you were saying your female patrons have a lot of disposable income. Have you thought about hiring male strippers for ladies' night? I bet the ladies would love a Magic Mike Night!"

"I thought that, too, but crazy as it seems, they prefer seeing women dance. The girls were making three-four times the moola of the male strippers on lady's only nights. I was surprised but I meet my customers' needs, so women for women's night it is. " He looked around the empty VIP section, imagining it filled with well-heeled customers later that evening.

"Already," Trey agreed. The DJ's music coming from the speaker above them became louder and he raised his voice to match. "I have been enjoying the view while I waited. Nothing but bottles popping and booties clapping." He downed the contents of the shot glass. "But, uh, Unk, I need to holla at you about a personal matter. Can we go into your office?"

"Can't nobody hear us," Junior said and took another swig of his beer.

Trey nodded. "I know but we're kind of exposed and the music is loud. I thought it would be easier if we went into your private office. I don't want my dad to…"

Junior's mood changed abruptly. "Why you worried about him?" He looked at Trey as if he was insulted. The emotional land mines leftover from years spent in his older, faster, allegedly smarter brother's shadow were lethal when triggered. "How you gone be worried about what *my* General Manager thinks about *my* guest? Preston don't run shit up in here, unless I tell him how far and how fast. Every dime he loans your broke ass came out of my pocket and don't you ever forget it!" Trey was still and speechless. Junior motioned for a cocktail waitress. Two women practically ran to the table.

"Yessir?" and "Need something, Boss?" they spoke in unison.

Junior pointed at the space between the women. Looking quizzical, they turned and parted. A petite woman with Dallas Cowboy blue hair and a waist the size of Junior's right calf muscle walked between them carrying two shot glasses filled with a clear liquid. She placed them on the table and took the empties.

Trey nodded his gratitude and Junior said to the others, "That's how she earns as much as the dancers without taking her clothes off. Look, study, and learn. Always anticipate the customers' needs, especially if the customer is my nephew. We talked about this in the team meeting last week."

They protested. "We didn't know he was your nephew, Junior."

"You should have known," Junior responded. Noting their expressions matched the worried look on his nephew's face, he chastised himself. *Get a grip. Don't take out frustrations on them.* The chip on his shoulder was growing when it had every reason to shrink. He changed the subject and softened his delivery. "By the way, Fellatia, HR tells me you haven't made your benefit elections. I know they told you the deadlines in the new hire orientation. Handle your business, young lady." He waved them off with a fake smile and turned toward Trey. He stared at him as if he were studying him for an exam.

Trey fidgeted with his shirt buttons and chuckled nervously. "Take no prisoners! Right? I came to listen and learn from the master." He bobbed his head and watched the tassels on a dancer's chest go round and round.

"Right on."

Trey pushed his back into the velvet cushion. They watched the girls dance for a few minutes before he said, "I commend your diversity initiative up in here. I think you have a woman for every fetish: tall, short, thick, dark, redhead, tatted up. Every one of 'em is a dime, too. You are officially the G.O.A.T. when it comes to women. No doubt."

Junior was almost immune to the sparkling, scented flesh. He forced a chuckle. "Greatest of all time? You're playing in the paint, Son. How much is that title gonna cost me?" He stroked his bald head. The dreadlocks of his younger days were long gone. "So, what's up? I got work to do. We both know what this is. You're already in for five hundred. I ain't no ATM." Trey shifted in his seat and bit his lower lip. "I asked you a question, nephew. Do I look dumb to you, son? You keep coming back to my savings for loans with them sad eyes for collateral. That was cute when you were five years old. Now, you're twenty-eight with a college degree and a forty-five-year-old cougar in your bed. You're the G.O.A.T. Not me."

Trey raised his palms in protest. "Nah, unc. You don't look dumb. Fall back. I'm not here for a loan. I wanted to see you and pops. That's all. I haven't seen my Dad in a minute. He hasn't returned my calls or texts. I got a little worried."

Junior seemed surprised. "We had lunch together today and he was yapping like y'all regular bowling buddies. Trey this and Trey that. How he know so much about what you doing then?"

Trey shrugged. "I dunno. Maybe Sloane. You know she's a Daddy's girl. Matter of fact, yesterday we were talking about his new house. I'm glad you told us because he hasn't said a word about it. If he hasn't told his favorite child Sloane about it, it's really hush hush."

Junior nodded his head. "I know. He's preoccupied with that project. I told him he better focus on getting all our locations streaming on Instagram Live. Have you seen what LaBoy is doing with virtual strip clubs? He's killin' the game!"

"For real. That was a genius move to make with the economy the way it is. People aren't going out as much, but everyone is online. My girl told me about it. We watch it together sometimes."

The screen of Junior's phone lit up with a photo of his favorite gal pal. "Hold up, nephew, I gotta take this." He swiped and placed the phone against his ear.

"Hey. Sounds like you're in the club. I can call back later."

"I can talk. Matter of fact, I'm sitting here having a drink with your son. You good?" Trey smiled and waved at the phone. "Trey says hello."

Faith paused at the warning. "Hi, Trey. I'm fine. Am I on speaker?"

"No. You know me better than that. What's going on? How was the Counsel meeting?"

"Everything is fine. It went as expected. You know your niece is special."

"Yep. Like the *Journal of Mental Health* special." They both laughed in politically incorrect agreement. Junior cut his eyes at Trey who was scrolling through memes of large breasted women on his phone despite the dozen large breasted women in living color a few yards away.

"This can wait. Call me later and remind me to tell you about Gina. She came to the church, believe it or not."

Junior's eyebrows went up. "As in Preston's ex-wife? Really? Yeah, I wanna hear how that went down. I was gonna call you anyway, about the art teacher Sloane jacked up. I heard he took a turn for the worse. They had to intubate him. That probably ain't good for niecey, huh?" He was protective of Faith. His brother had failed her, in his opinion, but he would not.

"I don't know. She won't tell me or her attorney the full story. She says it was an accident. He slipped and she was trying to help him. I dunno. She has a way of not being accountable. I want to believe her, but I don't. The girl is two fries short of a Happy Meal." Junior howled. "Did I tell you I had a lock installed on my bedroom door?"

"We both know that's not why you got a lock," Junior responded still laughing. "I'll git at ya later but know this, I always have time for you. You don't just hit me up when you want something, unlike some people." His eyes bore into Trey's. Trey slid his phone into his pants' pocket and looked away. "Hey, don't let that girl twist you up. You're doing the right thing." He ended the call and turned his attention back to his nephew. "Where was we?"

Trey shrugged. "I was saying my sister is probably telling Dad my coordinates. I know she calls him every day. I think she talks to Pops more than her husband." Trey stood up and stretched. "I'm headed back to the crib. My girl is blowin' my phone up." He jumped when someone grabbed him from behind. Instinctively, he elbowed the perpetrator in the ribs.

"Ouch! You trying to kill your old man?"

Trey spun around. "Dad?" His fists were reflexively in a defensive position until he had visual confirmation of who grabbed him, then he relaxed. "Old man, you're 'bout to get hurt coming up on me like that." He pushed his father's shoulder.

Preston playfully slapped Trey's clean-shaven cheeks. "Why not? What you gone do, young blood?" Both crouched and started punching the air the between them, bobbing and weaving as they'd done since Trey was a toddler.

They were laughing until Junior said, "That's enough. Cut the bull. This ain't no playground."

"What? Now, I can't horse around with my son for a minute, Boss?" Preston objected hotly. His eyes shot poisonous darts at his brother. Trey scratched the nape of his neck and looked away.

Junior met Preston's volume and tone. "You can't when you're on my dime. You've been gone all morning and I doubt you remembered to pick up a few cases of 'Tron and Crown like I asked."

Preston adjusted his belt and looked down. "That's the bartender's job."

"And it's your job to make sure the bartender do his job." The customers yelling their support of the dancing machines filled the air around them. Junior barked, "I asked y'all to make sure we never run out of either. Right? Why we got a dozen bottles of Moscato don't nobody want and not one ounce of Crown? This ain't no damn wine bar for colonizers." He wiped the corner of his mouth with his thumb.

Trey felt bad for his father. He hated getting dressed down at work. He felt his dad's pain. His uncle had the right to run his business as he pleased, but sometimes he acted like a jerk.

Junior was on a rant. "We have a state of the industry inventory system but nobody remembers to scan the bottles half the time. It would be nice if my so-called manager gave them better training." Junior pushed against the table to stand up and the table tilted.

Trey was able to grab his arm before he completely lost his balance. "Whoa. Hey, I got you, Uncle Junior." Preston didn't move to help him.

Looking a bit embarrassed, Junior glared at Preston and walked away.

CHAPTER 7

"Let's go in my office," Preston suggested to Trey. He wanted to be as far from his brother as possible. "This music is so loud, it feels like that bassline is coming outta my chest."

Trey followed him to the small room at the rear of the club. An L-shaped desk occupied most of the space. Part of it was covered with samples of fabric, wallpaper, and paint. There was a dust covered computer monitor and keyboard on the other end. The arms on the leather office chair were torn. Everything looked used because it was. Preston removed a rolled-up poster from a low stool in the corner and pushed it toward his son with his foot. "Sit here," he said. The music from the club was dulled by the walls. He hung his jacket on a nail sticking out of the wall and sat behind the desk. Trey remained standing and he couldn't blame him. The room was a mess.

"That's okay. I'm on my way out." Trey folded his arms at the waist and tapped one foot.

Preston couldn't read Trey's expression. Crinkling his nose like that usually meant he was uneasy, but maybe he was disgusted. He was probably recalling his father's pristine real estate office when he was a top agent. Sunshine streamed through the large window of that room, its bright rays illuminating the numerous top agent awards lining the walls. There was enough room for his desk and a conference table in that office. His current workspace was dark and desolate like most things in the A.M., as he referred to the period after his ex was elected mayor. Every good thing in his life happened during the B.M. years, before her mayorhood ruined it all: getting into college on a basketball scholarship, marriage to his college sweetheart, fatherhood, six figure annual earnings, and the home of his dreams. He had the golden touch and then everything changed. Every night he cleaned his plate of regrets and every morning brought another serving of crap for him to consume.

"Listen, Dad, you seem a little down. I know it's hard having the roles flipped with Uncle Junior." Trey paused. "I remember him coming to our old house for dinner. He was always hungry and broke." That got a small smile out of Preston. "Now, he has a pretty big enterprise and you probably think he's feeling himself, but....".

"But what?" Preston wanted to know.

"But I think he acts like that toward you because he's under a lot of stress. He didn't go to college and learn business like us. He's learning on the job." He dragged a finger through the dust on a corner of Preston's desk. "That hard attitude and tough talk is a shield."

Preston glowered at him. "I've had a lot of thoughts about Junior's behavior toward me in the past few years. I must admit, that's not one of them." He had mostly fond memories of his brother until Junior became a business owner. That's when he changed into a tyrant. He didn't care that his brother was good friends with his ex-wife. He did care that he didn't show him respect, especially in front of his son. *He would have failed miserably in this business if I hadn't come on board to run things. That's what my son didn't learn in his pop psychology classes.*

"It's something to consider," Trey said, clearly pleased with himself and his advice. Preston refrained from challenging his logic. He was tired of fighting other people's opinions.

"By the way," Trey started, pausing to lick his chapped lips. Preston watched him expectantly. "Did you look over the spreadsheet I did on the positive impact to y'all's bottom line here if you let the dancers keep sixty percent of their profits instead of the standard fifty?"

Preston's mouth fell open. "Why would I do that? Most of them are banking six figures-- and that's just the part they accurately report to us and the IRS." He'd seen strippers leave at the end of their shift with bags of money under security escort. He hadn't received any complaints about the pay structure. No way was he going to Junior with that idea.

"That might have been true in the past," Trey argued, "but now that most of the customers are using Venmo and CashApp, especially for VIP services and private rooms, it's harder to get away with under-reporting. The ladies will agree if you incentivize them with a higher rate and they'll recruit their friends to work here. Then, in a few months, cut out the free hair and make-up services. A few months later, start charging them one or two hundred dollars for the champagne room. It's all detailed on that spreadsheet. The key is not to make too many changes at once."

Preston nodded, feeling a little more open to the idea. "I get it. I get it. Like when YouTube and Spotify first launched, they were free. After I got hooked on the Old Skool Gospel Station, they started showing more ads. I put up with it 'cause they got bills to pay but the ads got annoyingly frequent after that."

Trey cut in. "Yep, then they offered you a subscription or call to action to stop seeing the ads. By then, you're in too deep to leave. You've got your favorite playlists and curated new releases. It's like a dull woman who cooks your favorite food every day. You ain't leaving."

Preston hollered. "Damn sho' ain't leaving home cooking every day. Hmmm, I'll take a glance at your spreadsheet, Son. It's a good idea. Data driven. I like that. I'm not yet convinced to make that move, but I'm glad that college tuition wasn't wasted. Let me review it and, I promise, I'll take it to your Uncle if it makes sense for us."

"Sure, if you have any questions let me know." Trey seemed to have something on his mind.

"Was there something else?" Preston asked. "If it's about the loan, I can't do that right now." He saw the air leave Trey. All his cash was tied up in the construction. Once the dust settled, he'd be in the clear.

Trey recovered quickly. He almost sounded unfazed by his father's statement when he said, "I could be off on this Dad, but you look sick. You good?"

"I'm fine. I needed to drop a few pounds, anyway." He tapped his flat abdomen.

"You dropped too many, if you ask me. You look like an extra on *The Walking Dead.*" There was no mirth in his voice.

"I'm alright, Son. I've been working nonstop. Between the construction and managing the clubs, I've missed a few meals. Not sleeping. Grinding day and night. You know the deal." Trey seemed satisfied with his explanation. He prayed his son didn't pry more. The phone in his shirt pocket began playing a whimsical melody. "That's your sister. Gimme a sec." He unlocked the phone with his Face ID. "Hey, there's my favorite girl."

"Dad," the loud whine in Sloane's voice could be heard all over the room. "My life is so horrible right now. I wish I could go away to the Hamptons or Tybee Island. All this stress is too much."

"I know, Baby Girl. You don't deserve any of it. I'm still mad at that judge." Trey rolled his eyes. Preston smiled at him. "Your brother is in my office. He says hello."

"Put me on speaker, Daddy."

"Okay. Done."

"'Sup, Sis?"

"It's hard out in the streets," Sloane responded, as if she had ever been on anyone's corner. "I am so busy. Ever has homework and birthday parties galore. Scott needs my support and I must fit community service in with all that going on. Unbelievable."

Preston and Trey's eyes met. "I'm fine, Sloane. Thanks for asking. Enough about me, let's talk about you," Trey answered casually, grinning at his father.

Without missing a beat, Sloane volleyed back, "Great. Bring me a half gallon of Dutch chocolate Blue Bell ice cream on your way home to your geriatric girlfriend. I'm sure she needs a prescription refill or more disposable underwear." Preston laughed so hard spit flew out of his mouth. He looked at Trey's face and said, "Daughter, I'll bring you ice cream when I get off. Go lie down and try to relax. Okay?"

"I will Daddy."

Preston hung up and put his phone on the desk. Trey smacked his lips and dismissed his sister's worries. Preston watched him, feeling like he was looking in a mirror at his younger self. The self who didn't understand a woman needs to feel like you give a shit -- even when you don't. He had so many lessons to share with his son but today was not the forum for life lessons.

"She's like that because of you," Trey accused.

"Probably," Preston admitted. His phone rang again. He answered, saying, "Hey, hang on." He muted his caller. "Son, I need to take this." He waited until the door closed behind Trey. "Thanks for calling me back, Gina. I've been trying to catch up with you. I heard you were at the Counsel meeting…."

CHAPTER 8

Faith sat up in bed, startled and disoriented. The red numbers on her bedside clock glowed with a three and two zeros. She couldn't understand why her eyes were open until a small hand touched her arm.

"Fifi, it's me," Ever said. Faith fumbled for the lamp switch. He was standing next to her wearing his favorite pj's—the too-small Star Trek pants, and a Sponge Bob tee.

Faith stared blankly, thinking *who in the hell is this and why is he in my house?* She had never been a morning person. Then, reality dawned on her and the grandma instincts kicked in. "Ever, what are you doing up at this hour? What's wrong? Are you sick?"

"I feel funny," he said. He swayed side to side as he spoke. His eyes were a little red but it was 3 am.

Faith touched his forehead. No fever. "Does your tummy hurt?" She sat up and pulled him in for a hug and reassuring pat on the back.

"No, ma'am."

"Is it your ears again? Are they ringing?"

"No."

"I hope you didn't fall asleep in that tutu. That thing is too hot."

"Unh, uh. Come flying with me. I'm an astronaut waaayyyy up in space. Will you make me pancakes on Mars? Daddy won't stop snoring and I'm scared to ask Mommy." He yawned and Faith detected the odor of a pastry.

"Have you been eating cake?" Something that looked like chocolate was smeared across his rather large upper, front teeth.

"Eating cake?" he repeated sounding embarrassed. "Don't be mad, Fifi. Don't be mad, okay?"

"Ever, what have you been doing and why are you up at this hour?"

"Only I just...don't tell mommy...cause I wanted some San Pellegrino from the refrigerator...and I know I'm not supposed to get it without asking...but I saw a little dessert on the counter and I ate it. I think it was—"

"BROWNIE!" She went from mild alarm to full panic mode, vividly recalling the brownie she'd removed from the locked mini-fridge in her office after everyone retired to their rooms around 9. She microwaved it and…she tried to recall how much while unlocking her phone to call poison control.

Wait. They weren't that large or potent, she told herself while imagining twenty screaming Sloane clones surrounding her.

Fool, any amount of a pot brownie is too much for a ten-year-old.

She locked in on a mental visual of her leftovers. It was less than a fourth of a brownie. More like a brownie bite. She pulled Ever onto her lap as she mulled over her choices while texting her edible supplier, an elderly neighbor named Blanche.

Blanche, are you awake?

Blanche?

She didn't expect a response at that hour but she frowned in disappointment when Blanche didn't respond to her third, fourth, or fifth text.

"Are you mad at me, Fifi?"

"No, grandson. I'm mad at me." *And thankful I did not lock my bedroom door tonight.* The child was high from eating cannabis-infused edibles she baked to self-treat her mild arthritis and insomnia. And she had her own carelessness to blame.

How could she leave that plate on the counter like that? She remembered getting a glass of water and wandering to the den to watch the news. She went to the bed after that without returning to the kitchen. Her mind spun like a roulette wheel. She leaned Ever against the bed and sprang off the mattress with the swiftness of a woman half her age and weight. She was thankful for two things: school was out and it was a Friday. Her daughter usually slept until 10 or 11 am and Scott worked from home on Fridays. Hopefully, he wouldn't get up with the roosters, as usual. All she had to do was get some food and water in Ever and tuck him back into the daybed in what used to be her home gym before his parents woke up. It wouldn't be her finest hour but, if her plan worked, it wouldn't be her final hour either.

She grabbed his hand and dragged him into the master bathroom and made him sit on the toilet seat while she filled a glass with water. "Drink every drop of this water. I need to get dressed. We're going to McDonald's!"

Ever gave her a lopsided grin and spilled half the water on her memory foam bath mat. He squealed in laughter.

Faith planted her hand over his mouth. "Hush, child. Don't you dare wake up Angelica. I cannot explain this to her or your father."

"Who is Angelica, Fifi? The mean girl from the cartoon-hmmm-from *Rugrats*? Right?"

I need to keep my snideness to myself. His comprehension was pretty good for a kid with THC in his system.

"You're making fun of Mommy? Right? Bwaaahahaha!" He laughed louder than before.

Faith dragged him into her closet and closed the door. His parents' bedroom was directly above hers. She hastily donned her Adidas sweats, thinking of an alibi in the event they had to go to the hospital. With all the legal problems Sloane had, the last thing she needed was a visit with Child Protective Services. The idea of sharing a cell with Sloane made Faith dizzy for a moment. The only bible verse she could readily recall was "Lord, save me." Peter called out to Jesus when he sank while trying to walk on water. She identified with that feeling.

"Ever, I want you to whisper the words Lord, save me. Okay?"

"Yes, Fifi. Lord, save me. Lord save me..."

That kept him occupied for the moment. The first wig she located got to come out of the closet. She slapped it on without looking in the mirror, dragged Ever through the house, and quietly exited. As soon as they were in the car, she called Junior.

He answered on the second ring. "Faith? What's wrong, Sis?"

"Fifi, I think I'm saved," Ever said out of the blue. "I need to tell you something. Mommy said don't—"

"Not now, Ever. I'm talking to Uncle Junior. Code Blue, Junior. Meet me at the McDonald's near my house."

"Code Blue?" he repeated with emphasis. "I'm on my way." The family's two-word emergency action phrase "Code Blue" was reserved for matters needing immediate attention. There was no acceptable answer but some variation of "I'll be right there."

She glanced in the rearview mirror. Ever was giggling and explaining why he preferred playing Roblox over Minecraft to her umbrella. At one point, Ever and the inanimate object seemed to be having a heated disagreement about a character named Skull Trooper. She made a sharp right turn and ran over the curb.

Ever yelled, "Weeeeeee! To infinity and beyond!"

"Please hurry! I'll meet you in the parking lot."

She heard a grunt and the sound of a zipper before he responded, "I'm putting my shoes on. Be careful."

Faith spied a police car and hit her brakes a little too hard. Ever's face lit up as he expressed concern for the umbrella and told it to be "very, very brave." Then he rolled down the window, and unlike a good neighbor, threw Faith's umbrella onto the street.

Faith shrieked, praying the police officer didn't see what Ever did and think they were hastily discarding the evidence of a crime. The last thing she needed was a top-of-the-fold headline reading, "Former Mayor Faith Henry Feeds Cannabis to Innocent Child."

"Fifi?"

"Yes, Ever?"

"Are you mad at me about what I did?" Ever's voice quivered. He'd gone from euphoria to what sounded like despair.

Faith glanced in the rearview mirror but she couldn't see his face. "Honey, no. This is my fault. You naturally did what any child in the world would do if they spied a brownie on a plate and no one was around. That is most definitely on me."

"No. Not about the brownies, Fifi. I mean, are you mad because I changed my name?"

Mad? Hell no. He'd insisted on being called Ever since the age of three. With that kind of assertiveness and his brilliant, creative mind, she only had to hold out a few more years and she'd be living rent-free in the grandmother suite of his mansion. The therapist said he was healthy and happy. His was the brightest future in the family at this point.

She examined her words and carefully selected the ones to utter. She was tired with so much on her mind, and Sloane's condemnation of her parenting still torturing her. Heaven forbid she scar another child for life. "Ever, I love you and I will always love you, no matter what. I admit I was honored when your mother and father included Faith as part of your name and legally, it's still part of your name, but it's not a big deal if you use it or not. What's important to me is that you *have* faith, joy, and peace in your life." He was very quiet, so she asked, "I'm not sure where you heard that name initially, but I'm guessing you picked it out of a song. You've always loved music. We sure don't know anyone by the name. But when you said to call you Ever, I looked up the origin of the name. Do you know what it means in Hebrew?"

"No, I only liked the sound of it, I think."

"Ever means 'beyond,' Honey. I couldn't imagine a better name for you. You're amazing and I suspect you are going to be very well-known someday." She glanced in the mirror for signs of flashing lights. "Let's pray today is not that day."

Her second call was to DK. After their encounter with J.D., Faith read the article and regretted her haste to judgment. By the third ring, she feared DK might not answer.

She picked up sounding hoarse and groggy. "What's wrong?" DK asked as if the incident with J.D. had never occurred.

"I need your help."

Without pause, DK responded. "Where are you?"

Faith explained the situation and hung up. Her tires squealed from another quick turn into the brightly lit parking lot.

Fifteen minutes later, Faith, Junior, and DK were having a heated debate beside the trunk of Faith's car. Ever had fallen asleep. He was in the backseat drooling on the armrest.

"He doesn't need more water. I already gave him a bottle of alkaline water." Faith was beside herself. "You heard him talking gibberish before he fell asleep. We can't be gone too long. Scott gets up a hundred times a night to go to the bathroom because of his prostate issues. He's sure to notice the child is missing."

Junior took his wallet out of his front pocket. There were wet spots under the arms and around the collar of his gold silk shirt. "I'll buy him a large fry. My girls at the club say fatty foods help you come down off the high faster. Do you think he'd eat a burger, too?"

Faith shook her head. "He's vegan-ish. Picky, like his mama. Get the fries and another bottle of water, please." She was reaching into her purse for money when the police cruiser she had seen earlier crept by. "Y'all act natural. There's a police officer behind you. He's staring. I'm sure he thinks this is a drug deal. Here we are exchanging money in the middle of a parking lot at 4 am This is great, just great."

DK objected hotly. She stretched the sides of her black tee. "This says Black Lives Matter for that reason. Standing in the parking lot while black is not a crime, Faith. That thought should never cross our minds but this is America so it does. But I wish he would roll up on us." The loud buzzing sound coming from the golden arches above them made Faith's head hurt worse. DK continued her rant. "*He* would be the headline tomorrow, not us. Trust me. You're not the only one with *politricks*, Faith."

Junior patted DK's shoulder. "Calm down. You can write all about the revolution later. Right now, we gotta take care of this boy." DK poked her cheek with her tongue and rolled her eyes. Junior opened a palm toward the road. "See, the cop kept it moving. Stay here with Faith. I'll be right back." Faith tried to give him a twenty dollar bill, but he pushed her hand away.

When Junior was out of sound range, Faith said, "I owe you a big apology. I read the story. It was well written. You were fair and impartial. Peter Knight would have crucified Sloane." She clasped her hands together as if in prayer. She threw pride aside and pleaded with her sister from another mother. "Please forgive me. Our friendship is so important. That you came tonight means the world. You're always there for me. I should never have doubted you."

DK opened her mouth and closed it. She moved to embrace Faith in a tight hug. Faith felt hope bubble up inside her for the first time since that day at the courthouse. When they parted, both had tears on their face.

"I forgive you, and I apologize for not trying harder to reach you before it was published. I should've made sure you knew what I was doing and why."

Faith shook her head, more in agreement than condemnation.

"We're good," DK said. They both looked toward the fast-food restaurant. "What's taking him so long?"

Faith perceived the sudden irritation in her voice. She also noticed DK had not directly addressed Junior since she arrived at the scene of the aiding and abetting. "Are you still upset with him because he wouldn't let you be an undercover stripper?"

DK's chest heaved up and down like it was tight. That answered Faith's question.

"That's not personal, DK. He's looking out for his business. I guarantee there is illegal activity going on, whether he knows about it or not."

DK nodded as if she heartily agreed.

"Trey and Sloane go by there often but I stay away. God only knows who frequents that establishment or what they do in that back corridor. The bouncers look like armed sumo wrestlers for a reason. I don't set foot in the place."

DK pulled her lower lip between her teeth like she was biting back words.

Faith tilted her head to the side. "Is there something I should know?"

"Nope." DK combed her fingers through her short hair. She had on more rings than Junior and a bracelet on each ankle. "I'm worried about Ever and you right now. Oh, I meant to tell you. I Googled marijuana intoxication. If Blanche's brownies are microdosed as you said, and he ate a bite of a small brownie, it's unlikely he will have any long-term effects."

Faith took her first deep breath in an hour after hearing that newsflash. "But why is he so sleepy?"

DK bugged her eyes. "Hell, I'm sleepy and I didn't eat a brownie. Do you know what time it is?" She patted Faith's shoulder to soften the blow of her words. "No one has ever died from a brownie overdose. Their professional words, not mine." Her eyes drifted to Faith's hair and she started laughing. She pointed the phone in her hand toward Faith. "Be still. I gotta get a picture of this."

The flash temporarily blinded Faith. "Are you serious right now? This is no time for pictures. We don't need any documentation from this night."

"This is for me," DK replied. "Every time I have a bad day, I'm going to look at this photo of you with your wig on backward and laugh my ass off!" She doubled over, snorting and howling in merriment.

Faith looked at her image in one of the car windows. She looked like a chocolate Ringo Starr circa 1962. Quickly, she jerked her wig around 180 degrees.

DK was laughing and trying to capture another shot. She couldn't catch her breath. "Hold on. Bwahahahaha! I have something—I can't breathe. I can't breathe! Woo lawd. Bwahahahaha!" She exhaled puffs of air until her shoulders stopped bouncing. "Okay. Okay. Faith quit looking at me like that. I didn't do anything. I'm just the messenger, girlfriend. Let me fix it. It's still crooked."

She reached for Faith's wig and Faith slapped at her hand. DK started laughing again. After about a minute, she was able to finish her thought. "Seriously, I have something in my car that might help. I don't do it anymore, but you know I used to smoke weed."

"Of course, I know. That's why I called you. You act like you're high now, heifer."

DK rolled her eyes. "Don't judge me with little Snoop Dogg in your backseat. Do you even know what a heifer is, city girl?" She waved her hands in Faith's face. "Stop interrupting. I'm trying to tell you I switched to CBD oil. I get the effect I want without the smoke and loss of ambition. A few drops under the tongue helps with my anxiety."

Faith felt doubtful. DK persisted, "It reduces the psychoactive effects of the THC in weed. It's a natural cure-all. I don't know if it will work for this situation, but it won't hurt him. Besides, what have we got to lose except your 'Grandmother Card?'"

When Faith shrugged in agreement, DK leaned into the car and foraged through her glove compartment. "Not to change the subject," she mumbled, "but my friend at the county clerk's office said Raymond did not get a marriage license."

Faith stiffened, but tried not to react.

DK removed her car manual and put it on the seat. "Where is that bottle? I just had it yesterday." She tossed four pairs of sunglasses next to the manual. "And my guy at American said he has a return flight to Santa Fe on Friday. You talk and text with him every day. He hasn't admitted he's in the area?"

"No, not a word, which is so out of character for him." Her mouth drooped.

DK closed the glove box and stood upright just as Junior exited the restaurant. "Here you go!" She and Junior uttered the same words as they presented their respective remedies to Faith. They exchanged a knowing glance that set off Faith's sixth sense. Hmmm. She mentally photographed that moment and stored it in the virtual cloud of her mind. *I'll come back to that and the intel about Raymond*, she thought.

Junior looked at his phone. "I gotta go. The alarm went off at the club. The cops are on the way. I might as well meet them since I'm out. I hope those meth heads hanging out by the dumpster didn't break another window." He hugged Faith and started to hug DK before he stopped abruptly upon seeing Faith watching him. His extended arms, frozen in midair reminded Faith of the walking dead. Comically, he grabbed his wrist and pulled his right arm across his chest until his shoulder popped. "Yeah, that feels better. A'ight. I'm out."

Faith was grateful for his help, but disappointed by his departure. She had planned to ask him to follow her home. Ever had eaten his carbs and promptly fallen asleep . He was much too heavy for her to pick up and carry to his bedroom.

After DK drove off, she tried to reach Trey, but he didn't answer. "Come to think of it, I should drive over there and bang on his door," she said to her comatose passenger. "He should be helping. The edible brownies were his idea, anyway." Reluctantly, she called the only other person she could think of who had the strength and discretion required for the circumstances.

~ ~ ~

Dawn was stretching its iridescent arms across the horizon as Faith and Ever arrived home. She felt a swell of relief upon seeing Preston's car idling in the driveway.

As she parked behind him, he jumped out and ran to Faith's car. Her hand went to the door handle but froze at the unexpected sight of his cheekbones protruding from his sallow face. Preston had been adamant about his workouts and diet, forever trying to maintain his "playing weight." The sight of his undersized body in ill-fitting sweats made the new term "praying weight" pop into her head.

Though they exchanged texts periodically—mostly legal advice about Junior's business—she had not seen him in over two months. His demeanor suggested he was anxious until he spied his only grandchild sleeping soundly on the back seat. He stopped and looked him over before opening Faith's door.

"What the hell happened?" That tone. As if she'd done something wrong. She recognized the anxiety in his voice, and she had made an error in grandparenting, but she didn't appreciate his rush to judge. Some tigers never changed their stripes.

No sense in engaging the prosecutor prematurely, she had learned. "Later for that. Right now we have to get him inside and put him in the day bed, quietly and quickly. Sloane doesn't need anything else to worry about." The urgency in her voice and reference to his favorite child were enough to draft him back onto her team. Ten years of divorce could not erase the million nautical miles they had navigated together as spouses and parents. He didn't try to awaken Ever. And the limpness of their grandchild's body, deep in sleep, indicated that effort would be wasted.

"I'll get the door," she said, leading him and the bundle of joy along the path to the rear entry. A hissing sound made them stop and stiffen, turning their ears toward the sound. When the neighbors' cat emerged from the shadows, they snickered. Continuing their stealthy mission, they passed through the dark kitchen and treaded lightly down the hall to Ever's room. "Don't worry about the linen," she suggested. "Just lay him on the bed. He doesn't keep the sheet on him anyway." Preston grunted in acquiescence.

Faith turned sideways to let him through the door. He was so close to her that the flow of his labored breathing parted her sparse bangs. He paused, their eyes locked. She realized they had not been that physically or emotionally on one accord in light-years. His eyes fixed on her tight t-shirt for a moment too long before he smiled and stepped into the makeshift bedroom. Faith felt the toe of Ever's feet drag across her ribcage where bold gold letters proclaimed, "Somewhere Between Proverbs 31 & Cardi B. There's me."

Faith observed from the hall while Preston tucked his grandson into bed. Despite her suggestion, he insisted on removing his bunny slippers and tucking him in. She had a feeling Ever wouldn't remember much of what had occurred. If he did recall any details, she would assure him and his parents it was all a dream.

Preston came out of the room and said, "I gotta use the restroom and then we're going to chat before I leave." Nevermind asking or giving her a say in the matter. A reminder of why they had parted ways and remained parted.

Faith looked past him at the wall over his shoulder. She hated having "talks." On her long list of things she did not want to do, that activity ranked below reading law journals and popping pimples on her nose.

She rubbed her temples and told him, "Sure. I'll be in the den."

CHAPTER 9

Faith sat on the couch and removed her shoes. She was exhausted. She turned the television on to keep her awake. Preston had ten minutes to chastise her and he was outta there. She closed her eyes and leaned back against a soft twenty-four-inch pillow pretending it was Raymond's chest.

"So what happened?" Preston asked.

Faith's eyes flew open. Preston was standing over her with his hands in his pockets. She stopped herself from gasping. In the full light, he appeared to be fifteen to twenty pounds down from his usual weight. "Are you sick?" she blurted.

"Don't worry about me." He lowered his voice and sat next to her. "Tell me how Ever got a hold of an edible brownie. That is so irresponsible."

Crossing her legs and repeatedly kicking the coffee table took some of the sting from his words. It also annoyed him, she was certain. "I left a few crumbs from an edible brownie on a plate in the kitchen and he ate it." Before he got wound up, she added, "Spare me the lecture. I made a mistake but he's going to be fine". *I'm not playing the submissive wife role tonight*, she told herself while waiting for the sarcastic response that greeted her confessions to him in years past.

He tugged his upper lip through his teeth. She held her breath. "Why are they here?" he finally said. He removed his hands from his pockets and sat next to her.

"Why is who here? What are you talking about?" She was too tired for word games.

He chuckled without merriment. "You're too smart to play dumb. You know who." He pointed at the ceiling. "Why are they still living here? This wouldn't have happened if they had their own place."

She couldn't believe it. He didn't start ranting and raving about her carelessness? *Who is this skinny man looking like my ex-husband*, she marveled.

"You wouldn't let them live with you, as I recall. So they asked me."

"Hmph. No, I wouldn't and I won't because—"

"You are still mad at your best friend for getting your daughter pregnant ten years ago."

He looked across the room and tapped his foot on the carpet. She watched his stare bounce from one object to the next. He seemed to be looking for some sign of his existence from their previous life, but she couldn't be sure. "You're wrong," he finally said. "I'm over that." He stood and walked to the fireplace. He picked up a framed photo of Faith and Idris Elba. He peered at it a moment and put it back without comment. "Scott is a healthy man with a good job pimping doctors to write prescriptions for overpriced drugs. He told me himself that they sold their house in Austin at a premium. They ain't broke. Put 'em out."

Faith was stumped. She didn't want to agree with him, though he was right. But she was charging them rent. They hadn't paid it for quite some time -- but technically she was their landlord.

"I have a big house. There's plenty of space and I like having my grandson around. I like hearing sounds I didn't make. Honestly, I need them more than they need me." She rubbed her eyes and yawned. "Besides, you know it's a seller's market. Real estate is tight around here."

"Not one thing you just said matters. If you're lonely in your big 'ole house, downsize. They need to go," he said firmly.

She was beginning to remember things she'd worked hard to forget about him. She wanted to tell him she liked his brother better for that very reason. Instead, she tried to change the subject. "The alarm went off at the club. Junior headed over there from McDonald's."

"I got a notification on my phone right before you called," he replied. "Don't change the subject. Why don't you put them out?"

To her, the answer was as clear as the Waterford crystal frame around her and Idris Elba. *Because we're divorced, Raymond is linked to another woman, Trey is leaving and cleaving, and my parents are dead. I can't risk losing access to my daughter and grandson, too.* Loneliness was an irrational fear, but it scared her nonetheless. Silence hung between them like a heavy curtain until she finally responded. "I dunno."

He sat down again, rubbing his hand on the cushion in the space between them. Faith leaned forward resting her arms on her thighs. Her eyes went to his empty ring finger. There was a faint scar above the knuckle. Her mind flew to the day he dislocated it while playing basketball for their alma mater. They were college sweethearts then, so when the doctor yanked the bones into place, it hurt her almost as much as it hurt him. They were so in love. How had they gotten here from there?

She made herself recall the myriad of good things about him. Like how he made sure the yard and home repairs were taken care of and how he spent quality time with the kids, especially when they were young. He seemed relaxed. She wondered if he ever thought about their mutual history.

She scooted back on the seat and tried to look beyond his faults. "Why do you think we snap at each other? Why is there so much tension between us, Preston?"

His face registered surprise. "Honestly, I don't know. I was mad at you for a long time for leaving me." He rolled up his sleeves.

"I was mad at you, too. We've talked about what happened and why before. I—"

He stopped her. "May Bell told me something profound. She said hurt people - hurt people. And she's right. I get it now. Let's leave all that in the past."

"Agreed but I need to say you're an important part of my life, of our lives, and you always will be. I didn't think about it at the time, but I guess that's partly why I called you tonight."

"It's good to be needed," he responded with that impish grin that always made her laugh.

He put his hand over hers on the cushion and squeezed gently. "It's water under the bridge. Let's forgive and forget."

"*Really* forgive," she said, emphasizing the word "really."

"Really forget." She raised her fist and he bumped it.

With those simple but sincere words, the air around them became lighter, easier to breathe.

He picked up the remote and changed the channel as if he were at home. "Seems like you've made sure everyone gets what they want but you? Was that your plan?" He put his arm around her shoulder without scooting over leaving a small gap between them. It was odd but somehow fitting. "That's not the Faith I know," he added thoughtfully.

She remembered that tone, as well. *And that's the Preston I used to know.* She leaned her head back against his arm and closed her eyes. *Boundaries work both ways, Faith. Don't be the girl who can't say yes.*

~ ~ ~

Faith's eyes fluttered, then closed again.

She dreamed someone was smothering her with a wet towel in the hottest sauna on earth. She drew her head back. The TV was on. She heard the words "breaking news" as her eyelids reluctantly parted. The distinct Donaver blue accent pillow she had ordered online was an inch from her nose. That hot weight pinning her turned out to be a third arm.

"Holy shit!" she exclaimed in a loud whisper as she pulled herself free. "Get up! It's 8 o'clock." She jabbed her motionless companion with her elbow until he stopped snoring. He cleared his throat and turned on his back. The sectional creaked beneath them. "Preston, get up and leave before everyone wakes up," she hissed. Her heart pounded in her ears.

"Wha'? It's eight? Day-um!" He leaped to his feet with the muscle memory of a former athlete. His undershirt was pasted to his body with sweat. He picked up his pullover from the floor and punched his arms through the sleeves.

Faith got up and searched the room looking for more evidence of their impromptu sleepover. Seeing nothing, she had the strangest thought that this was the perfect moment for a cigarette. She had never smoked, but, at that moment, she was beyond reason and wanted either nicotine or caffeine badly. While he slipped on his shoes, she pretended to check messages while trying to determine if her wig was on straight.

At the same time, they reached for his key fob on the end table. She snatched her hand away. His lips shifted into a pout as if he were hurt by her actions.

His phone made an impatient sound from the back pocket of his jeans. He let it go unanswered. "We have nothing to apologize for," he offered. "We're friends. Right? I know you don't want me here when they wake up, but we haven't committed any cardinal sins. Leroy couldn't write a decent sermon about what happened last night."

They had not been together in so long she had forgotten how easily he once made her laugh. The humor lessened her anxiety about someone waking up and seeing him there, but not completely.

"I'm outta here. And don't worry. I won't say a word to anyone, especially my brother."

"Exactly. There is nothing to tell," she said, looking in the direction she wanted him to walk. He seemed unable to move as if he had more to say. To hasten his departure, she offered a tepid hug. His strong arms pulled her to his rippled chest and, against her will, the gesture filled the blanks between them with ancient history. The soft kiss he placed on her forehead felt like a promise. The rumble of an engine outside broke the trance and she stepped back.

Turning to leave the way he arrived, he stopped abruptly and removed a wad of cash from his pocket. He pressed it into Faith's hands.

"*Now,* we're friends again," she teased. She always preferred paper over CashApp and BitCoins. She and Benjamin Franklin shared the same Faith.

In God we trust.

When she heard a floorboard creak, she shoved the money into her purse and went into the kitchen. She was filling a glass with water when Preston returned through the back door carrying a bouquet of yellow rosebuds. Her eyes grew wide. "Where did those come from?"

"I don't know," he said. "They were on the hood of my car."

Faith was puzzled and a little worried. Red roses were for love. Yellow roses expressed infidelity. Was that the message someone was sending? If so, who? And why?

~ ~ ~

Later that morning, Faith woke again. The sun was battling her blinds for entry to her bedroom. She was comfortably stretched out on her adjustable mattress, thrilled she had no pressing engagements. She briefly thought about the evening with Preston. It was good to clear the air. It wasn't good to fall asleep in his arms but she refused to beat herself up about it. The battle with tired and lonely was ongoing. Sometimes she fought them off and sometimes they took her prisoner. Neither a white flag or territory was the end goal. She was trying to survive being single in a double bed.

She made her way to the bathroom but felt so weak she sat on the lid of the toilet, her eyes filling to the rim with tears. She was angry with Raymond for dodging her, but it was his arms she wanted around her. She loved him to the edge of her emotional waterfall. That had been enough for her, but not him. Accepting the friend label meant having him in her life as a trampoline she could bounce things off. That was better than not having him at all. Or was it?

She recalled the year-old video call that took them from "someday we'll be together" to "we're just friends" for the zillionth time. She could recite it in her mind word for word.

His voice was somehow both cold and hot when he said, "Faith, tell me the truth."

The whole truth hadn't been told from her lips in decades. Yes, she knew the truth. She checked on the truth at least once a day and twice on Sundays, but truth, like her daughter, didn't pay the bills. The people who did pay the bills did not want to hear the truth. Not her business partners. Not her clients. Nun'ya. They wanted to hear that she was fine and everything would be all right. That's what helped them survive the day and sleep through the night. So she lied to them -- and to him, truthfully.

She recalled the moment those eyes scorched her skin, activating the sprinklers in her secret garden. The two of them were alone in her office at City Hall during her re-election campaign. They were both simply doing their jobs, but when he touched her hand, something clicked between them that became the catalyst for a 180-degree change in the course of her life.

She snapped out of her reverie with a current and pressing thought. *Did Raymond leave those yellow roses on Preston's car?*

CHAPTER 10

Around 10 pm, Sloane returned from her self-prescribed retail therapy and found Scott in their bedroom. She dropped her purse and jacket onto an and collapsed on the bed. "Get me a drink?" The lilt in her tone implied a request, but Scott would know it was an order.

Her husband moved into action from his poised and waiting position nearby. He opened the bottle of Ardbeg single malt scotch on the dresser. With practiced hands, he produced a neat pour with a single drop of distilled water to open the flavor, just as she preferred.

He's a damn good bartender but I would love some alone time. The massage, mani-pedi, and eyelash extensions satisfied my craving for guilt-free pampering, but er'body was chatty. Between their blah, blah, blah, and the screaming in my mind, today has been an endless choir of noise. But I can't ask him to leave the room, can I? Deep in thought, she removed her heavy earrings and dropped them on the nightstand. *Bae did work all day and he looks tired as hell. Play nice, girl. Aaargh, since that mess with Ever's teacher, every-single-thing annoys me. Maybe I need something for anxiety.*

"By the way, how was your, uhm, meeting with the Counsel?" he asked, tentatively. "You didn't want to talk about it before."

She glared at him, sat on the edge of the bed and took the tumbler, swallowing the contents with ease. In the same manner she once swallowed him, she thought wryly.

"You said I don't show interest in your activities. See, I'm showing interest."

Sloane huffed. "The fact that your dumb ass is telling me you are showing interest because I complained makes it not count, Scott. You are hopeless." She held the drink out for a refill. "You're right. And I haven't brought that subject up because I didn't want to talk about it." He grimaced in the same manner as Ever when she scolded him.

She softened her tone. "The meeting was awful. All those women lecturing me like they're beyond holy, practically in Heaven's waiting room. But—I was perfectly calm and reasonable. You should have seen them going ape shit up in there." She closed her eyes and rubbed the smooth skin between her eyebrows. "I still can't believe Gina was there."

"I didn't know she was part of it. Who invited her?" He moved to the foot of the bed, leaning against the dresser.

She appreciated that he didn't play devil's advocate to help her see their side. They didn't believe her so she didn't give a flea's eyelash about their side. She sat her glass on the nightstand. "Hellifiknow." She filled him in and he listened attentively, as always. He did have some good qualities when he wasn't being annoying.

When her glass was empty, he tried to refresh her drink. A few drops of the caramel liquid dribbled onto her hand. She stood up abruptly, startling him. He almost dropped the bottle.

"Can you do nothing right? How hard is it to poor scotch from a bottle into a big ass cocktail glass?" Her mocking gaze went to his annoying, trembling hand. "Are you cold? Seriously, what the hell is wrong with you lately?" He ignored her question and went into the bathroom for a towel.

Stop it, you idiot. Stop being mean to him. What is wrong with me? I should tell him what I'm feeling. I would but he'll go overboard with the empathy and I'll start crying. Heaven knows if I start crying, I may not stop for days. I gotta keep it together.

He returned and gently dried her hand. "Ever finished his homework, and he's in bed. He wanted to wait up for you, but I insisted he go to bed. I made sure he removed his afghan. I tried to take the fake pipe, but he started whining so I relented." He paused. She looked at his puppy dog expression as if he were awaiting her approval of his good parenting.

She blinked slowly and turned her face toward the fireplace. He was working her second to last nerve.

"Do you want dinner or a hot bath? What can I do to help?"

She scooted across the bed and propped herself against the leather headboard, pouting and wishing he'd stop acting like she was mentally fragile. He wouldn't do anything she requested without asking a zillion questions since she got arrested. "Nothing. There's nothing you can do for me, but keep all those words in your head. So many words." She paused and pointed at him. "Wait! Did you repot those marigolds on the patio for Mom? If she asks me about them one more time, I swear, I will smother her in her sleep. Tell me you took care of it today."

There was a long, long, long silence before Scott replied, "Darling, I tried. I mean I started to. Uh, did you get my Marco Polo? I sent you a video. I had a question."

She felt her scalp boiling. If the top of her head exploded, it would his fault. "What in God's name did you need from me to repot plants, Scott? How hard is that?"

"I wasn't sure if you wanted me to put the plant in the pot and then the soil or vice versa. I know you like things done a certain way. I wanted to be sure."

"Has that cholesterol medicine lowered your IQ, too? That is the stupidest question on earth! Why do you think I care how you repot plants that don't even belong to me?" She put one of the king sized pillows behind her and leaned back with a huff. "You had one simple task today and from what I'm hearing, you didn't get it done and now you're trying to somehow make that my fault."

She looked through him and removed the elastic from her ponytail. Her hair plummeted to her shoulders in sandy waves. She didn't have to look at him. She felt the fear swirling in his chest: the eyewall of a *her-ricane.* Whenever she got upset, he thought she was going to leave him. She knew because he'd made the tactical error of telling her so numerous times. The smooth scotch began to tranquilize her emotions. Scott rubbed his hands together. *Here it comes,* she thought. *What will he offer me this time?*

He drummed his fingers against the arm of the chair. "I'll take care of those plants first thing tomorrow. But speaking of doing things around the house, we've been here two years. "Upon hearing his mother-in-law ascending the stairs humming "Take Me To the King," he paused and called out through the open door, "Faith do you need something?"

Faith appeared in the doorway carrying two air filters. "I didn't realize you two were still up. I'm going to install these before it slips my mind again."

"Be careful," Sloane advised while taking advantage of the lull to pour more scotch into her glass.

Scott took the filters from Faith's hand. "Not happening. As long I'm around, you will not go into that attic for anything." Faith started to respond but he stopped her. "That's not a question. I got this. I'll do it in a sec and I'll put the old ones out with the trash in the morning. Go get some sleep."

Faith hugged him and waved at her daughter. "Night you two." She closed their door and hummed her way back downstairs.

When she was out of earshot, Scott put the filters on the floor and cleared his throat. "Darling, my point is perhaps, I mean....Don't you think it's time we move out of here? Decorating always makes you happy. Let's start house hunting."

"My mother needs help. You just said she shouldn't be climbing into the attic at her age. We can't leave her here alone. She wants us here and we're all saving money by living together."

Scott looked at the photo of Faith and Ever on the dresser like he wanted to make sure they were talking about the same person. "Faith is pretty independent, and I make more than enough to pay a mortgage and support our lifestyle. Plus, we have plenty of savings."

"I'm too tired to talk about this right now." She removed her blouse and unhooked her bra. "There's a lot you don't know about my mother," she added cryptically.

"Maybe," he responded, removing his phone from his pants and unlocking it, "but I'm fairly certain she doesn't need money from us to pay her bills." He stared intently at something on the screen. "Truth be told, there's a lot I don't know about you," he charged, looking her squarely in the eyes, "like why it took you all day to get a manicure and massage. I don't see one shopping purchase on our account." He put his phone on the dresser, picked up the filters, and opened the door. "Next time, remember to buy something before you come home."

Surprised, Sloane reached for him. "Big Daddy, I—" He snarled and stomped away.

~ ~ ~

Faith adjusted her microphone and said, "Hello y'all! Happy Saturday and welcome to Never Close Your Heart. I'm your host, Faith Henry, and today we continue our series on the Ten Levels of Intimacy. I admit I am excited by the record-breaking number of downloads we had with Part One. This subject is resonating with you and I'm looking forward to your comments and feedback after you hear levels Six through Ten. This is the good stuff, fam, the gold coast of love. But I don't think you're ready.... Are they ready, Daniel?"

Daniel responded with a short clip of a song he'd queued up. "It seems like you're ready...Girl, are you ready???"

"Wait! Stop!"

Daniel hit pause and sat up straight. He looked confused. Then, his mouth fell agape. "Too soon?"

"Are you seriously playing R. Kelly while I'm talking about levels of intimacy between consenting adults? Dude. Really?"

Daniel blushed. Faith cupped her ear, the signal that he could speak on-air. His fingers flew over his keyboard as he said, "My mistake, Mayor. Is this throwback better?" The O'Jays rendition of *Stairway to Heaven*, "Here we go walking the road of ecstasyyy," brought a smile to Faith's face and a screen full of hearts from the viewers online.

"Okay. I'll forgive you. That's a much better intro to this tender subject matter, my friend. Thank you, Daniel, and a special shout out to our paid subscribers. As always, there will be additional content later for your ears only. If you haven't joined this exclusive group, click the link in my bio, and get access to premium content for subscribers only."

She adjusted the angle of her tablet and said, "For those of you just joining, I'm Faith Henry and whether you're a new listener, or a friend returning for the next episode, you have my promise of an exciting half-hour for the single, sassy, and almost woke. Take another sip of caffeine or whatever you're drinking, click that 'Subscribe' button, and stay tuned. After this 60-second ad from our platinum sponsor All You Need Event Planning, I'll be right back. Do not touch that screen, mouse, or dial or I promise you'll regret it." She fake laughed until the commercial began.

A minute later, she pretended to strap on a seat belt and said, "Alright, let's blast off. Come ride with me to Level Six of the ten levels of intimacy. She explained the addictive endorphins of Level Six and the hazards of mistaking Level Seven for real love.

"Alrighty then! The blessed and favored advance to Level Eight. *This* is a good place. It's a perfect day on the perfect beach with your soul mate. This zone is where most long term couples spend their days. It's 70 percent physical because while you're in each other's heads and hearts, there are one or two rooms in your mind that your S.O. is not allowed to enter. They never know, because you never admit that you're 'all of me' is not quite all of you. At the same time, the space you share is so sacred, your Level Eight lover would take a bullet for you. There's a lot of trust and shared interests. The sex is good because you know each other's bodies like the fading letters on your keyboard. Most long-term relationships reach this Xenith around a decade in. It's a wonderful place: comfortable, reliable, predictable, and good more than bad. We spend years slipping back and forth from Eight to Seven, Eight to Five, and sadly, for fifty percent of us, we slip like Jack and Jill and tumble into the frenemy zone. That's the equivalent of Level Zero.

"So don't go there. Elevate yourselves to Level Nine. Hmph. Level Nine is *that* couple. They don't have to do public displays of affection for you to know they are of one accord. Watch the way they move around one another -- as if they have their solar system. See their nonverbal expressions of a language no one else speaks. A light touch between them is electric. No matter how you appraise them, it is clear they see each other as close enough to perfect. Expressing love through service in and out of bed is the hallmark of Level Nine. Let's put it this way. If my first cup of coffee every morning had arms to hold me, it would be my Level Nine.   You have to know how much I love that java juice to understand the magnitude of that statement.

"Finally, there is Level Ten. This is the Mauna Kea of love, the tallest mountain a couple can climb. It's commonly said that Mt. Everest is the tallest mountain in the world but it is only the tallest above sea level. The highest peak from base to summit is Mauna Kea in Hawaii. Like Level Ten of intimacy, most people don't know Mauna Kea exists. Reaching the summit of this level introduces the relationship to the natural beauty that is equally physical and mental. There is harmony in your thoughts, your dreams, and the rhythm of your hearts. Two effortlessly become one. When you are alone together, place, time, and temperature do not exist. You are literally in a black hole of passion where nothing else matters. Every caress, every kiss, every word from your lover fuels your non-opioid addiction, keeping you perpetually high. These feelings linger as if they were carved directly into your nerves. This is rare, supernatural, unforgettable -- and *dangerous*.

"Why is it dangerous? Most people never experience level Ten. They live happily at level Eight with an occasional peek at level Nine. It is better that way. Once you experience Ten, nothing else will satisfy you. Imagine the strongest addiction possible, with no known cure. Anyone can caress your body, but only someone made from the same handspun silk as your spirit penetrates the hidden recesses of your soul.

"If this relationship lasts, it's the best type of love. Epic. If it ends--and that's possible--you become walking dead. You'll live, you'll work, you'll smile and emit a sound like laughter, but you will never be..." Faith paused and sighed before she finished, "*never* be fully satisfied again."

She found herself unable to speak. Those feelings she'd attempted to describe attacked her all at once. She signaled for her producer to cut to commercial without her usual sign off.

Daniel killed Faith's mic and made his mic live. "Don't forget to click subscribe, share with your network, and download this amazing episode of Never Close Your Heart! Sign up now for a premier subscription and get exclusive content plus access to Faith Henry's live broadcasts from the historic Essence Festival in New Orleans this summer!"

Even with his ad-lib, the show was a few minutes ahead of schedule, so he quickly queued up a commercial for their top advertiser, hoping they'd notice the freebie. By the time the outro music played signaling the conclusion of the program, Daniel was by her side with a bottle of water. She hadn't moved or spoken a word, since telling the world she could get no satisfaction. She took the bottle and thanked him with a nod.

He perched near her and rubbed the toe of his shoe across the carpet. "Uhmm, so you good, Mayor?"

She took a sip of water. "I'm as good as I'll be." He nodded as if he understood. She knew he didn't know what he didn't know. Changing the subject, she inquired, "How was I? Did I lose the audience? I think I got too deep."

He shook his head. "No, ma'am. It was perfect. I guarantee we'll have a record-breaking number of downloads for Part One and Part Two. You killed it! You got me looking at my girl a little sideways now."

Faith chuckled.

"Seriously," he insisted, "she's maybe a good six, but I'm now convinced I need to keep looking. I mos def want that solid eight."

"Not a ten?"

"Can I be honest?" he said, leaning forward into her personal space.

"You can."

"No disrespect, but whatever happened to you that's got you in your feelings and walking dead--your words, not mine--isn't a risk I want to take." He smiled. "But Ms.-Almost-a-Dime at Level Eight sounds like a woman who will make me happy, accept me as I am, and not expect too much. That's all I want. Is that bad?"

"Not if that's what you want." She smiled and raised one eyebrow. "It's unfortunate that your current girlfriend doesn't fulfill those needs."

"It's mutual," Daniel inserted. "I've known for a while we were going through the motions. It's comfortable but boring. If I'm being honest, one of the trillion reasons I wanted to intern for you is I've always liked powerful women. You're brilliant and you have this aura about you. I can't even describe it."

Faith blushed. "Stop. You already got the job. C'mon."

He smiled. "They don't make 'em like you anymore. These women are all about buying things. I want to build things. You know what I'm saying? Yeah, me and my girl are wasting time. We're not bringing out the best in each other. Most nights eating dinner with her is like watching a towel dry."

Faith doubled over laughing. "Hush!"

"I'll hush if you tell me one thing."

His tone changed in a way that made her raise a questioning brow. "Yes."

"Rumor has it Grapefruit Satellite Radio is looking to acquire your podcast. That would be," he spread his arms as wide as possible, "*huge*. We're talking major syndication nationwide. Any truth to that?"

Faith stopped smiling. "Where did you hear that?"

"There's chatter in the podcast world. They're saying all the top talent lives on the West Coast and broadcasts from the main studio. Would you move to L.A? I hope not."

"Well, there you go. The Internet has spoken. I'm cancelled before I start." He didn't press but he looked a little nervous. *He's more worried about his job than mine,* she thought. She shooed him away. "Get out of here. We've talked enough shop. Go."

As he walked away, she hoped her expression gave nothing away, but her heart was pounding. Her communication with Grapefruit Satellite Radio was not a topic she'd discussed with anyone. She was flattered by their attention, but they were clear that they wanted the communication to remain confidential. They would not participate in a bidding war with Sirius XM, Radio One, or Cumulus Media. She didn't think there was a remote possibility of that happening, but she wasn't about to put the chance of a lifetime in jeopardy.

She went to the car and opened the trunk. She removed her heels and exchanged them for her favorite flip flops. Her toes unfurled and squealed with joy. She had a lighthearted memory of recording her very first podcast in the closet of her master bedroom. The clothes were a cheap substitute for acoustic paneling, and she was able to wear her comfortable, raggedly pajamas. *My, my, we've come a long way from there,* she told herself.

She closed the trunk, got in the car, and started the engine. The time on the large digital instrument panel was off by an hour. That bugged her. It happened every few months for no reason anyone at the dealership could explain. She used her phone to search for "Genesis and how do you set the clock." Sweat beaded her forehead as she followed the YouTube video instructions. She paused it to adjust the AC. Some vague sense of unease made her glance in the rearview mirror. A man wearing a Cowboy hat and dark glasses seemed to be staring in her direction. He was several rows away, somewhat hidden between two pickup trucks. She couldn't identify him, but he was definitely holding an object in front of his chest, pointing her way. She looked in front of her and saw nothing of interest. She checked the side mirror but that only made his image smaller. Heart racing, she hurriedly located her prescription sunglasses and turned to look through the back window. He saw her and ran in the opposite direction. Things like that happened often when she was in office, but now, not so much. Her doors locked automatically, but she checked them to be sure. She thought about calling the police and changed her mind. Nothing bad actually happened. Had it?

CHAPTER 11

Pastor Carson rose from his throne-like chair on the pulpit. His shadow looked like a fingertip on the giant screen behind him, where the sermon's video transitioned from a large, wooden cross on Calvary to a Madonna-like scene of a church mother and her child. Sloane felt a little bit of bile in her throat.

How long is this gawd awful Mother's Day program going to be?

She couldn't recall the specifics, but she knew God did a bunch of stuff in one day. He was efficient. He had made clouds, animals, fish, and ski lodges on a Tuesday morning and Reverend Carson was going into a second hour of talking about nothing. She used selfie mode on her phone to apply lipstick. Then, she liked a few posts on Twitter and played a game of Candy Crush. She glared at her husband sitting on her left, beaming as if he were somebody's mama. She closed her eyes, bowed her head, and audibly repeated her standard prayer, "Why God, why? In the name of Jesus,

Timothy, Phineas, and ten other white men. Why?" Her fervent but ineffectual prayer was interrupted by a light tap on her right shoulder.

"You okay, Mama?" Ever scooted over until their thighs were touching. He moved his small hand from her shoulder to her forearm.

She opened her eyes and turned to her son. He seemed worried. He was perpetually anxious since she got arrested. When she was home, he was forever lurking nearby. She reminded herself to be more patient. Feeling guilty, Sloane took his hand and squeezed it in a gesture of reassurance. "I'm fine darling. Thank you for asking."

"I'm going to pray that you don't go to jail," he whispered and bowed his head.

A spotlight circling the room shone on his angelic face. As usual, Sloane was pleasantly surprised by how well he turned out in the looks department. He was seventy-five percent a replica of her with the appropriate masculine touches. The remainder of his appearance stemmed from his relatively unattractive father; a man who looked like he had a boxing match with the wind and lost every round. What possessed her to marry her father's friend, she mused—and not for the first time. She could have had any guy at her college, but she went for the mature guy with a mid-six-figures salary and stock shares: the sure thing with established credit. Sloane often fantasized about what her life would have been like, if only she'd gotten that Lasix surgery earlier in life. She sure wouldn't have married Scott's ugly ass, money or not. It wasn't love that made her blind, it was early-onset cataracts.

The slideshow stopped and the Pastor droned on about motherhood, Mary, and a woman's highest calling. Two rows of the pastor's family: his wife, his children, and their spouses were seated on the stage. She found it unbelievable that every one of them had been called by the Lord God almighty to preach and receive a salary. It was her opinion that if the Almighty wrote ten commandments for Moses, he could post those job openings instead of silently calling all the Carsons into executive management.

"Mom, can I play games on your phone?" Ever whispered.

"No, pay attention," Scott said before Sloane could reply.

Ignoring him, Sloane opened her Tik Top app and put her phone on her lap where Ever could see it. Ever giggled.

At that moment, Pastor Carson told the congregation, "Ladies, the easiest way to sustain a Christlike demeanor for motherhood is having a strong, Christ-loving head of household to cover and guide you."

Sloane was mentally disagreeing with the reverend when Scott grabbed the phone. *What in hell?* Her mouth was agape as she watched him put her most loved possession in his suit pocket.

Oh, now, you wanna be assertive? She decided to let that go for now. She crossed her legs. In that moment, she didn't care that her ankle monitor was exposed beneath the hem of her pants. She swung her leg kicking the pew in front with the toe of her shoe. She wished she was sitting with her father. She leaned to one side and spied him on the front row with the army of deacons dressed in their Sunday best.

She leaned the other way, trying to get a clear view around the ridiculously big hat on the church member in front of her. It didn't take long to locate her mother sitting near the front of the church on her favorite pew, with First Lady May Bell, Uncle Junior, Grandma, and Grandpa Henry, and some man that resembled her baby brother. That couldn't be him, though.

She moved right and left for a clearer view, but couldn't see enough of the guy to be sure. Trey hadn't attended church since he started working as an accounting specialist at Baxter and Faust six years earlier. Thinking about her brother made her tap her restless foot faster. Trey should have accepted the offer from Uncle Junior to do the books for his clubs two years ago. *Dummy.* Wasting a degree in accounting and working 70 hours a week doing data entry when he could join a family business. *Who does that?* His dumb job was his excuse for everything he should be doing -- but wasn't. If she had her phone, she would text him.

She was pondering the mystery visitor when she noticed her husband grip the pew in front of them and stand. She reached for her purse on the floor assuming it was time for the benediction.

Ever whispered, "He's standing for prayer. Pastor Carson said anyone fighting against principalities and strongholds in their home should stand up."

Sloane's hair whipped like Taylor Swift spying Kanye West backstage during an awards show. *Wait? What?*

"Sisters and brothers of the church, if someone near you is standing, that means they have a burden we must help them bear. I want two or three of you to go to that member of the family of Christ and pray for them. We have the power to cast out demons if only two or three can agree!"

To Sloane's horror, a dozen cross wearers began to move toward Scott with outstretched hands; a zombie apocalypse. *Didn't the man say two or three? Really? Er'body needs to pray for my husband?* At that moment, a sister pushed her way past Ever's knees to get closer to Scott. She looked at Sloane as if she expected her to stand and pray for

Scott, also. Sloane waved her program like she was having a hot flash—because she was.

He is determined to embarrass me, she thought. *Now, the entire dang church knows we are having marriage problems and they assume I'm the reason.*

One of the brothers touching Scott started praying loudly and the woman who was practically in Ever's lap said, "Sister Lee, do you need prayer also? You don't have to stand up. I understand. I'll pray for you." She put her hand on Sloane's head and said, "Holy Father—"

Sloane swatted her hand away and stood. She intentionally bumped into Scott. The loud praying paused, then resumed even louder. Sloane dug her nails into Scott's forearm at the seam of his tailored suit. What man in a thousand dollar suit needs prayer? Why was he taking prayers away from poor people with real problems? *Oooh.* She hated him so much right now.

"Please Baby Lord Jesus, please help my daddy," Ever cried out.

Sloane rolled her eyes. Everyone in the church had their head bowed in prayer, except her and that man sitting between her mother and Uncle Junior. At that very second, the slightly familiar figure turned to look at her and flash a lopsided grin. *Trey at the 8 am service?* Sloane had one thought. *He must be broke.*

When church was dismissed, Sloane grabbed Ever's hand, got her phone back, and walked toward the exit. Ever pulled back. "Are we going to brunch with FiFi and Great-Grandma Henry today? We should all go to brunch." He bounced up and down gleefully. "Oh, I hope Uncle Junior sings for Fifi. Remember last year when he stood up in the middle of Eddie V's and sang *The Impossible Dream* and everybody started cheering and clapping? It was so cool. Right? We absolutely gotta go to brunch!"

Scott stopped rubbing his bruised arm to say, "I think that's a good idea, son. Let me see if they have plans." He strode away before Sloane could object.

Sloane and Ever waited in the foyer until Scott returned. "They will meet us at Mimi's," he said, smiling "Your father and uncle are coming, too. We may have to wait a while on a table, but it will be nice to visit with everyone. It's such a beautiful day, isn't it?"

Sloane ignored him and walked in the direction of the car. Scott and Ever followed silently. Scott clutched the seat as the car zoomed down the interstate at 90 mph. "Dare I ask what's wrong now?" Scott raised his visor and decreased the volume of the radio.

"Now? Is something always wrong with me?" Sloane yelled. "Is that why you stood up for prayer?"

"Sloane, everything is not about you."

"And that's the problem. Everything is not about me. For example, it's Mother's Day and you didn't get me a gift. Now, you want me to eat at godforsaken Cracker Barrel where they don't take reservations and every grandmother from the hootnanny trailer park will be waiting in a rocking chair, playing checkers."

"Mommy, we're going to Mimi's. Remember?" Ever offered plaintively. "We know you don't like Cracker Barrel."

"There's a difference?" Sloane asked.

"Sloane, stop. Don't be condescending." Scott's voice was deep and troubled.

"But Mommy, I do have a card for you. I was saving it until we get home. I made it at school."

Sloane looked at her smiling son in the rearview mirror. He was so innocent and stupid. Her eyes softened with a drop of maternal instinct. "Thank you, Ever. I'm sure I will love it better than any card ever made in the entire world."

Scott folded his arms. "You're not my mother, even though you like to pretend you are." He leaned onto his armrest closer to the driver's seat. "The pastor gave me a much needed reminder today. Being head of household is a position that comes with both responsibility and accountability."

Sloane felt something like respect for Scott, but it passed. "Your mother is seventy-five. Trust me." She sped up more, lightly glanced in the mirror and started changing lanes without using the signal. Scott put his hand on the dash and looked over his shoulder for oncoming traffic. "Sloane, what the heck?"

Though she was driving, Sloane crossed her legs to cast further doubt on her sanity. She smiled to herself when Scott double checked the buckle of his seatbelt. "I've never pretended to be a septogonian and the last thing I want in life is to be *your* mother." She looked toward Ever and smiled to let him know she was delighted to be his mother, however.

"Septuagenarian," he said, correcting her through the spaces between his gritted teeth.

"Whateva. You know what I meant. I ain't old like you and your mother, Boo."

He squeezed his thighs with his hands like he had to pee and there wasn't a restroom available for a hundred miles. He exhaled a stormy breath and growled under his breath, "You are going to stop disrespecting me in front of my son."

"Really? Today of all days," her ankle monitor beeped and she pounded her hand on the horn in frustration, "you wanna give me a hard time? Like I don't have enough going on with all this mess?" She pointed at her ankles, but he didn't look. She moved her hand next to his cheek and flapped it like a sock puppet. "One more time or what?"

He grabbed her wrist. She swerved again, almost hitting a motorcycle in the lane next to them.

Ever shrieked, "*Daddy!?*"

The anger in his eyes waned at the sound of his son's plaintive question. "Daddy?" Ever repeated. He released her small wrist. Red marks outlined the print of his fingers on her arm when she jerked her hand back to the steering wheel.

Looking like thunder personified, he spat three words. "Don't try me."

She glanced at him quickly and slowed down.

CHAPTER 12

"Fifi, I learned a new joke from my teacher," Ever said, turning to look at the paper where it was written. He'd recently loss the last of his baby molars. To Faith, the remaining teeth, in various stages of growth, slightly resembled the skyline of Dallas.

"Let's hear it. I need a laugh." She checked to ensure her mic was off. She'd been at the studio recording for hours, but this FaceTime conversation was for her ears only.

He read the first line with the solemnity of an attorney appearing before the Supreme Court. "Knock, knock."

"You sound very serious for someone telling a joke," she said, expecting the twinkle in his eyes to come bubbling through his lips at any moment.

"You're supposed to say, 'Who's there?' You're not doing it right."

She stopped herself from laughing and arranged her expression to match his. "Who's there, may I ask, kind and handsome good man?"

"Fifi!" he said, protesting her edits to his prepared script.

"Sorry. Sorry." The little girl inside her who just wanted to play and have fun did not want to be serious -- even though that little girl noticed all the lights were on in Ever's bedroom at 4 pm Central Standard Time on a sunny day. That explained some of the ridiculous five hundred dollar electric bill in her inbox. She needed to have a sit down in the near future with his parents to discuss utilities and cost sharing.

Reorganizing her train of thought, she responded, "Who's there?"

"Cow says." He giggled and pressed the lined paper to his chest.

"Cow says?" she paused a sec and restated her answer correctly, "Cow says who?"

"Nope, a cow says *moo!*" He threw the paper in the air and did his patented version of the chicken dance as if he'd just won the U.S. Open. Faith got out of her chair and started dancing with him. She stopped flapping her arms and frowned in mild disappointment when her cell phone rang. The incoming call notification displayed the name "Diamond" across Ever's image.

He noticed. "What happened? You don't like my joke, FiFi?" He appeared to be shocked by this revelation. Faith always hyped him up by laughing at his jokes, no matter how bad they were. His expression grew pensive as though he could not imagine a world where his grandmother didn't love everything about him.

"Yes, Honey, I enjoyed your joke, but someone is calling, and then I have to get back to work. I'll call you on my next break. Okay?" She blew him a kiss." Be sure to give your mother back her phone."

"But if I do she might not answer when you call," he protested.

"I'm sure she will," Faith lied. She wasn't sure about anything with her daughter. Why Sloane refused to allow Faith to get the child a phone and put him on her family plan was anybody's guess. Trey was still on it at the ripe age of thirty. Might as well use all the lines.

Ever persisted. "What time will you call me?"

"Honey, I have to disconnect. Goodbye." She ended the call with Ever. "Hello. What's wrong?"

"Why something gotta be wrong 'cause I called?" Faith rolled her eyes.

"Don't be rolling your eyes at me," Diamond declared with speed and accuracy.

"How do you know I rolled my eyes, Diamond?" Hidden body language was the entire point of voice calls and why they would never be replaced by video calls in her opinion. No one wants to see everyone they talk to, anyway. Faith rolled back far enough to put her feet on the desk. The skin on her ankles felt smooth and tight which signaled they were swelling again. She reminded herself to drink more water with her Jack Daniels.

"I've seen you do it a milliontimes. You think I worked with you as your receptionist all those years and I don't know you like drawers in my kitchen?"

Faith chuckled. "I'll concede you know some things about me the average citizen of Ulysses does not -- and should not -- be aware of." She recalled all the times Diamond ensured she had both lunch and dinner on the most grueling days at City Hall. Sometimes the meetings with the Council and concerned citizens were nonstop. The stress of her position, crumbling marriage, and long hours filled with toxic people had made Faith feel like a trapped animal at times. Diamond was rough around the edges then, but she was loyal. She became more than Faith's receptionist. She became her touchstone and confidant. Their friendship had outlasted every trial they encountered.

Diamond knew where Faith figuratively buried the bodies during that four-year power struggle. "What have you been up to?"

"I'm at the new Ulysses Tarry Inn and Conference Center. We're still installing flat screens in the guest rooms. One of the electricians had his head up his butt and got shocked." She made a clucking sound. "We have all these safety protocols in place to prevent electrical shocks, but they wanna take shortcuts. That's what happens."

"Is he okay?" Faith removed her feet from the desk. She was genuinely concerned about the stranger. She got a pen preparing to request his name so he could be added to her prayer list when Diamond retorted.

"He won't be if he damaged that flat screen." Her voice did not have a trace of sympathy. Faith knew the chill on that cold heart came from the hefty investment of funds Diamond had made to purchase the electronics for the largest job she'd ever procured.

Faith put the pen down and smoothly switched to a different topic. "What are the rooms like? Is it nice?"

Diamond whistled. "Is it ever. It will be the best hotel in town. They have put all the bells and whistles in this -ish. Hold on a sec." Faith overheard her respond to someone. "Is he right or left-handed?" There was a man's voice speaking calmly, followed by Diamond yelling, "If he's right-handed and he burned his left hand, give him some gauze and send his ass back to work. Ain't nobody got medical insurance for subcontractors!" The attorney in Faith cringed. Diamond resumed their conversation. "Not only is it dope, but the rates are much cheaper than that place you use for your Netflix and chills."

"Ma'am, kindly mind your business and explain the purpose of this call."

"Fine. I'm tryna help you save money on your booty calls, but anyway, I had to run to Lowe's for a part. When I got back here, girl, you know they opened last week even though the hotel isn't finished and there are crews everywhere—"

"I have a job, too." Faith jumped in. "Is there a point to this story?"

"I'm trying to tell you that when I walked through the lobby, I saw this guy walking to the elevator and he is the spitting image of your ex. I mean Raymond, not Preston."

"I know who you mean. That was Raymond. I talked to him yesterday. He called to wish me Happy Mother's Day."

"Oh reallyyyyy?" She held the "y" on her tongue so long it was ringing in Faith's ears. "Is he here to see you?"

"He claims it's a business trip and he doesn't have a second to spare. He was supposed to leave Friday, but he extended his visit. I think he's flying out tonight."

"From the sound of your voice, it's my turn to change the subject," Diamond answered, wisely.

"No worries. He's busy. You're busy. I'm busy. Everyone is busy." She shuffled the papers in front of her until she found the one with the information she wanted to include in her next newsletter. She attached a yellow post it to it and scribbled "News" on it. If she didn't do that, she'd forget before they hung up. "When I finish recording today, I have to look over some contracts Preston sent over. I need to start charging him and Junior for the legal work they ask me to do."

Diamond laughed. "You are going to live a long time. I bumped into Preston at the food truck in the parking lot earlier. He looks like he has stage three of something bad. Do you have any idea what's going on with him?"

"I do not." She removed her heavy earrings and thought back on their recent entanglement. She still didn't know how that happened, but it must never happen again. She should have awakened Scott to help with Ever instead of calling Preston. She made bad decisions when she was fatigued.

"Come over here and confront him. That's what I'd do if I were you. I can get his room number for you."

"Not gonna happen. For all I know, his lady friend has someone following him or maybe she came with him and he hasn't told me."

Diamond playfully intoned, "If she got somebody following that jigga, he ain't her man. He's probably hoping you'll come through."

Faith was hoping that very same thing about him. Her make up person appeared in the door and pointed at her Apple watch. She nodded. Livestreaming the podcast recordings was a pain. Before the live cameras were added, she could pause her recording software and take breaks as long and often as wanted. *Oh, for the days when she didn't have to put on shimmering foundation only to talk into a mic.*

With her nerves now frayed, she couldn't help but ask, "Are you sure he's alone?"

"Big Booty is in Santa Fe. She was out with her friends last night. She tagged him." Faith opened her Facebook app to look for the post. Diamond added, "I keep forgetting to unfriend him. He never posted anything until he met her. Now, he's all up in my newsfeed every weekend with bootonia clinging to him like a piece of lint."

Faith's voice skirted close to hysteria range, "Don't unfriend him! How will I keep up with him if I can't use your account?" She hated herself for overreacting. Diamond would mimic that moment some day, no doubt.

Diamond giggled, clearly entertained. "You need to log out of my account and stop trolling that man with your swollen ankles. You're too old for that, Faith."

"Do you have a camera in my office?"

"No, I get notified every time you log in, which is way too often. Just kidding, babe." Faith was addictively scrolling through every photo on Raymond's page. "Go do ya thing *blackademic*."

"Yes. Bye," Faith replied absentmindedly. She flipped her phone over and wrote, "Tarry Inn" on a sticky. She passed close to it on her way home. Maybe she should listen to Diamond's advice. What did she have to lose?

CHAPTER 13

A few miles away, on the rooftop bar of H.G. Sply restaurant in Dallas, Sloane brushed her lavender + ginseng + hibiscus rinsed tresses behind her ears. The large, red umbrella overhead allowed enough of the sunbeams through to kiss her sleeveless arms, sending ripples of Vitamin De-light through her limbs. She dismissed the ghost of her probation officer warning her about travel restrictions and alcohol intake. She was only thirty minutes away from boring Ulysses, TX, the capitol of cul de sacs, having much-needed fun with people she liked being around. The sweetness of her Double Under, a beet infused tequila drink, and the crunch of the best street-corn avocado toast north of the Trinity River, brought her as close to an orgasm as she'd been all year. The avocado was so fresh the smell of it made her stomach growl when they brought it to the table. If hanging out with two of her favorite men in the world was wrong...well, it wasn't wrong, she decided. Besides, it was only 75 degrees Fahrenheit outside, the chances of her sweating alcohol through as her mother kept warning was minimal, she reasoned.

In the most pitiful voice imaginable, Sloane whispered, "Daddy, Uncle Junior, I want you both to know that I'm so sorry the family has been impacted by this. I never could have imagined this happening from a simple visit to my son's school." She patted her dry eyes with a napkin. "I am weary from being punished so harshly for an accident."

Preston reached across the picnic table and patted her hand. "It's okay," he said. "Most women would break under the kind of stress you're enduring. They're turning you into a martyr and it's not fair. You are strong enough to endure this injustice. Right, Junior?" he uttered in a way that implied there was only one answer to that question.

"*Sorry* ain't an option," Junior shot back. "You've got come correct or dead wrong. What's it gone be, Sloane?"

"Sir?"

"Don't sir me. I don't agree with your father. It's not okay. You heard Reverend Leroy yesterday. The men in the family have a responsibility: the women. And I don't mean buying you everything you want."

He shot a look of accusation at his brother. She felt the light reassuring squeeze from her father's hands before he drew back.

Junior was exasperated. "You're driving me and your blue-black husband crazy with all this Liza Minelli 'tude." He scrunched his face into a wrinkled map of trials and errors. "Er'body is trying to help you. The Word says, 'sufficient to the day is its own trouble.' Why you always borrowing trouble, little girl?"

Sloane sat up and put her arms on the table. "I dunno." She absentmindedly picked the seeds from a slice of lemon. "Who is Liza Minelli?"

Preston balled up the napkin in his lap and tossed it on the table. "Here we go," he muttered to the sky. His lips trembled with a forceful exhalation air aimed at his brother.

"You don't know Liza Minelli, the goddess of Cabaret, little girl?"

Too late, Sloane realized her mistake. Junior pushed their shared bench seat back and rose to his feet. He took a deep breath and belted out, "Come on babe, why don't we paint the town, and all that Jazzz!"

The diners around them stared or hastened to open their camera apps, mesmerized by the sight and incredible sound of this massive, silk pants wearing black man singing a very Anglo show tune at the top of his lungs. Junior sauntered along the aisle separating the crowded tables of amused diners, arms akimbo as the ceiling fans blew fine mist above his head. He kicked up his red-bottomed loafers in perfect timing with the melody; "I'm gonna rouge my knees and roll my stockin's down! And all that jazz."

Mortified that she might be captured in the background of someone's video breaking her probation in real time, Sloane ran behind him and pulled his shirt. "Stop it, Uncle Junior. Nobody wants to hear you sing."

He kept moving, pulling her behind him. Sloane looked back to her father motioning for his assistance. He was laughing harder than he did while watching his favorite Tyler Perry movie.

The cheers from the waitstaff and diners egged Junior on. He sang louder. When he stopped to serenade an adorable toddler who seemed to be trying to sing along, she leapt on her uncle's back, wrapped her right arm around his huge neck and clamped her small, left hand over his mouth. It didn't phase him. He seemed intent on singing this Minelli woman's entire catalog of greatest hits.

Preston was laughing as he said, "Y'all get back over here before they call security."

Junior tried to stand, but he started laughing so hard that Sloane lost her grip on his silk shirt. She fell on her rear end. Upon hearing her plaintive yelp, Junior looked around. His face filled with concern, followed by amusement at the sight of the toddler offering Sloane her baby bottle.

Sloane growled at the child, tried to stand up, but her sandal slipped on the smooth concrete and she plopped onto her butt again. Junior reached to help her. She kicked at him with the leg bearing her ankle monitor.

Junior howled. "Girl, you did not bejewel that thing," he exclaimed, pointing at her leg. She moved her pants leg to cover the pink crystals her manicurist had added to the electronic tracker to match Sloane's fingernails. It seemed like a fun idea to lift her spirits at the time. No one outside their house was supposed to see it, especially not a dining area full of white folks. That racial disparity somehow magnified her embarrassment.

She accepted her Uncle's helping hand. They made the short walk back to their table with at least twenty mobile phones pointed in their direction. Junior curtsied, basking in the limelight. Sloane hurried to her chair and pushed her empty cocktail glass toward the opposite end of the rectangular table.

Things quieted down when the server brought them a tray of desserts compliments of the manager. Preston declined the offer and said "Be right back, y'all. I see an old buddy of mine."

Watching him walk away momentarily prompted Sloane out of self-absorption. She loved her Daddy to pieces and something seemed off. She whispered to Junior, "I'm worried about Dad. I don't think he's eating or sleeping. Look at him. That snakeskin belt is the only thing keeping his pants up. Do you know what's going on with him?"

Junior looked at Preston's empty plate. "His appetite is healthy today. I'd say he's working too hard, but it ain't 'cause of me. He's building a house."

"That's not it," Sloane responded. "He's mentioned the construction a few times, but Dad has always been a time stacker. I don't remember a time when he or mom wasn't involved in a million projects at the same time." She looked to see if her father was coming back yet. "Do you think he's sick?"

"He ain't sick. I've seen him sick enough to know when he's not well. You think I'd keep pushing him to do his job if I thought he was sick?"

Sloane shook her head. She remembered Trey calling her in Austin every day for months after her parents' divorce. Uncle Junior helped their father through that difficult time. She didn't know who her mother had leaned on -- and as her mother recently reminded her, she never asked. Forgetting she was supposed to be in a conversation, she checked her phone and started responding to a comment on one of her social media posts. Junior was looking toward the skyline of downtown Dallas a few miles away when he absentmindedly volunteered, "I think Pee's seeing someone, 'cause he's on his phone texting more than you lately. And that's a lot of texting."

Guilty as charged. She stopped texting Trey and put her phone down. Her face brightened. "You think he's dating? He hasn't been serious about anyone since Gina that I'm aware of."

"That's my best guest if history is any indicator. He's always been secretive but it gets worse when he's in a relationship." He ate a spoonful of cherry-chocolate chip cookie and ice cream. "This is good. Reminds me of mama's bread pudding a little bit. You should try it."

Sloane was too busy taking a photo of herself. Uncle Junior had said her dad was fine so she decided to post a selfie and tag the restaurant before they left. She'd put a strategic spin on what happened with her Uncle before someone else posted video of her sprawled on the ground with a baby bottle in her face. "I'm in controoollll," she hummed Janet Jackson's anthem to herself.

Preston rejoined them. "I hadn't seen that guy in years. I sold him a house in Southlake when nobody was thinking about moving out there. I bet it's worth three times what he paid."

"That's great Daddy," Sloane beamed with pride.

Preston looked at Junior. He shrugged as if to say, "What have you done for me, lately?"

Sloane wanted everyone to lighten up and stay lit. All the back and forth with the microagressions was depressing.

Junior took a swig from his sweaty water glass and returned to lecture mode. "I got one more thing to get off my chest, Sloane. If I hear one more report about you clowning at the Counsel meetings, I'ma put down my religion, pull off my Gucci belt, and whup your designer jeans all up and down Belt Line! I don't care how grown you think you is."

Sloane pressed her lips together. That wasn't an empty threat. He had done it before. Right in the middle of campus during her third year of college. She couldn't recall which transgression earned that tough love lesson, but she would never outlive the incident. Her sorority line sisters still jokingly referred to her as "Soror Got That Beat Down" whenever they had virtual Happy Hour. She couldn't look at her father, thinking that was probably the first time he'd heard that unfortunate story.

Before the questions in her father's expression reached his mouth, she said. "Ease up, Uncle Junior. I'm a different person now. Goodbye to bygones, already."

She sighed and stared at the building across the street, hoping the photo she posted went viral. She had looked incredible after she applied that Juno filter and erased the blemish on her chin. If she became an influencer, she wouldn't have to listen to everyone's sage advice. Her father was the only one who appreciated her great mind. He seldom fussed at her.

Junior grunted. "Unh huh. I'd love a nap but I stay woke."

"Uncle Junior, please. Can we enjoy this beautiful day and our drinky drinks?"

She had accepted his invitation for lunch because he was dope and she wanted to be around someone who still knew how to have fun. When her father called for his daily check-in, she invited him to join, thinking they'd both slather her with compliments like the old days. She was first child, first grandchild, and first niece in the family. Everybody loved her back then.

Being a grown-up sucked. She looked around for women her age. They were breast-baring, hair tossing, and smiling as if they didn't have a total of two problems. And she had at least ninety-nine.

Her father smiled indulgently. "You're right, Baby Girl. It's a beautiful day. We're with family and, no matter what, family always has your back."

"I'll toast to that," Junior added, bobbing his head to the sound of music coming from the street two stories below them.

With that, her bygones were as forgotten as a pimple on Beyonce's cheek during Coachella. They sidestepped into an easy, familiar banter born of love that overcomes all things.

An hour later, their combined laughter filled the air. "OMG, you two are hilarious! It's refreshing to hear what your takes on other men. I don't get that kind of transparency from Scott."

Junior sounded as carefree as he looked at that moment. "Most men are stressed out. Trying to please y'all and work a full-time job ain't easy. That's why these brand new brothas have no problem being house pets. They don't care if the woman pays the bills and they raise the kids. It's a paradigm switch."

"That's why I got an old, traditional brother," she joked.

"Too old and too traditional," Preston said, but he was smiling.

Sloane was relieved he was still able to joke around. She hadn't seen the lighthearted side of her father in a while. She pointed to a 40-something guy wearing basketball shorts and matching kicks. "But back to the subject. What about him? How could I tell if he's a good man or not from looking at him?"

Junior took a moment to assess the subject. "Oh, he's easy. He one of those jokas that come to the club and order water. He sits by the bar so no one wonders why he ain't making it rain." He held up two thick fingers. "Two words. No goals." He added a ring finger. "Three words. Low self-esteem." He displayed all the gold rings on his right hand." Four words. Allowance from his parents."

"Dad?" she asked, not wanting her father to feel left out.

Preston made a "p" with his finger and thumb. "Poser. He wants to fit in but his paper is short."

Sloane bent over laughing because it seemed strangely accurate. "First, I need you to stop talking like Trey, old man. But I do want to know how you came to that conclusion so quickly."

"Tell her, Junior," he said. "Let your uncle tell you. He's got a gift for reading people. He spots the trouble makers at the clubs as soon as they walk in the door."

He and Junior said together, "Security!" and they laughed hard at their inside joke. Sloane smiled, wondering what the story was behind their amusement. If they were getting along, she was in her happy place.

Junior patted her hand on the table and shook his head from side to side. "Look for the clues, niecey. I've been telling you this since your mama made us do scavenger hunts to find our Christmas presents. Peep it. He has a dirty backpack and he's old enough to be the father of two. We're in the Lower Greenville. Grown men in this area have cars that they leave their stuff in while they shop or grab a bite. Men who ride the bus have a backpack and if they ride the bus a whole lot, they have a dirty backpack."

Sloane declined the waiter's offer of another round and said, "He could be in school."

"And he could be broke with all his worldly possessions in that backpack as I suspect. The line on his edge up looks like Ever drew it. He took a trimmer and shaved his head with a small guard. Brothers with money get a haircut every week even if they're on the road." He pointed to his flawless fade as an example. "To your point, he could be one of the Waltons or Amon G. Carters -- but I doubt it."

"You're awful," Sloane commented, "but probably right. What else?" The specimen in question appeared to have completed his dining experience. He placed his payment on the table and walked away.

"No swag. That dude walks like he just grew legs."

Sloane almost choked on her food.

Junior patted her back. "Sweetheart, you want a man who moves with confidence; he should have machismo. If he's real hood, he'll be like me with a ton of Zulu nation rooty tooty in his booty. You seen me Twerk. Right? I'll show you."

Sloane pressed down on his shoulder before he could demonstrate. "What is wrong with you?" Sloane said, shaking her head. Abruptly, she froze.

Junior looked toward the street to see what had so captured her attention. "What's wrong?"

"Huh?" She squinted and pointed toward the pizza shop across the street. "Isn't that Raymond Hart?"

Junior reached for his prescription sunglasses lying on the picnic table by his unused fork. Preston shaded his eyes with his hands. The man in question was getting into the backseat of a long, black Lincoln Town Car. Oddly, he paused and looked up in their direction. They ducked liked children playing hide and seek.

"That's him," Junior said, peeking over the table to see if he was still looking in their direction. They sat up and watched Raymond get into a car. "I'd know that redbone anywhere," he said."

"Your mother and I would still be married if it wasn't for his home wrecking ass," Preston observed. "What is he doing here? Did your mother mention anything about him visiting?"

They watched the car drive away and Sloane picked up her phone. "No, not a word," she answered as her thumbs flew across the keypad.

"Who are you texting? Your mother?" Preston asked.

Annoyed by the question, she shook her head and said, hastily, "No, I'm texting Scott. I asked mother to pick up Ever from that birthday party this afternoon. When Raymond is around," she stopped herself from saying, *she loses her mind.* "I mean IF Raymond is around there's probably a big meeting or conference going on. Mother is covering it and she may forget about Ever." That sounded as ridiculous to her ears as it probably did to theirs, but it was the best she could do.

Junior started breathing hard. "I assumed you were available to hang out today because Scott and Ever were somewhere father-son bonding. Where is Scott then, and why didn't you go to the party with Ever?"

"Scott had a doctor's appointment and I hate kiddie birthday parties. They don't serve alcohol and the children are hellishly loud. Ooooh look at the present! Ooooh I want ice cream! All that screaming like everyone in the room is hearing impaired." She stopped typing and placed her phone on the table face down. Junior was staring at her. She bugged her eyes. "What? What did I do? We're having fun. Right? Everyone is having fun."

"Scott is at the doctor. Is he sick? What kind of wife are you?" Junior asked. He was looking at her like she was an exhibit at the museum.

"The kind with a life," Sloane said flippantly. "I don't know what's wrong and he's always at some doctor's office. I think he has standing appointments. He is eternally complaining about something bothering him. Last year it was his flat arches. He needed custom made orthotics. Then, he tore his rotator cuff golfing. Like, how frail do you have to be to get an injury golfing? It's not like he's on the PGA tour." She rolled her eyes. "Last month, he tried to dye the gray hair on his arms and had an allergic reaction." She puckered her full lips. "And don't get me started on all the ED drugs he's tried." Her eyes rolled. "If only I could turn back the hands of time. I had no idea what I was getting myself into."

Preston put his head on the table.

"Daddy are you sick?" Sloane asked. He shook his head. "Who knows what it is this time? I keep telling my friends that being married to an older man is grueling." Junior looked at Sloane over the rim of his glasses as if she'd grown a third nostril. Her verbal barrage continued. "And I swear he spends more time in the bathroom shaving than any woman I know. Like you know, when we first got married, I did ask him to do some minor maintenance so I wouldn't get my cornea scratched trying to fulfill my wifely duties. That fool lost his mind with the manscaping. I'm just saying my son should not have more body hair than his father." She waved her hands in the area of her pelvis. "It's creepy."

Preston called for the check.

Junior removed his glasses and rubbed his eyes with his fists. Sounding exasperated, he answered. "No, I don't know, and I don't think it's right to discuss your husband's junk with your uncle and your father. I golf with that man. Now, when he goes behind a tree to take a piss, I'ma be worried about him getting sunburned."

Sloane laughed at that image.

"Nah, let me stop. Jokes aside, you should be more loyal to your husband. He's a good man. And Lord knows any man who can put up with you for this long deserves some understanding. Everything you described sounds like a man trying to impress his woman. Ain't nothing wrong with that. He got a job and he put a ring on it. Stop complaining. You gone end up like—"

"Like who? My mother?"

Preston gave the waiter his credit card without looking at the check. He seemed anxious to end the too-intimate conversation.

Junior gave him a sympathetic look, and said to his niece, "Keep your day job, Swami Westlake. You can't read minds for shit. Before you interrupted, I was 'bout to say, you gone end up like me. A middle-aged man who can't get a woman I adore to take me seriously because she thinks I'm self-centered and incapable of change."

Sloane swallowed hard, a bit taken aback. She thought her uncle lived an idyllic life of sex, rhythm, and blues. It never occurred to her he wasn't beyond thrilled with his lifestyle. Then, she wondered why he didn't compliment her for making a huge personal sacrifice. *Uncle Junior is self-centered. I'm giving up part of my Happy Hour to ensure my son gets picked up on time like a good wife and mother. They never give me credit for trying.*

"Yes, Uncle Junior. I receive that wisdom. I'll do better," she said for the millionth time. She'd told him that so many times she wasn't sure if she spoke the words, or if they came out on their own. She checked her phone for messages. "Scott hasn't texted back. I'm off to Legoland."

Their heads turned to the sound of an expletive coming from one of the wait staff. "He scammed me! This hundred-dollar bill is blank on the back," she screamed. "The guy with the dirty backpack, did anyone see which way he went?"

Junior tapped the table in front of Sloane, "Listen up. This is the last thing I'ma say and I'm done with it. Unlike that thief who just left here, Scott is reliable and respectful, and he'll do anything for you."

She looked down but she felt their eyes on her. "If it makes any difference for me to say it aloud, I have no intention of leaving Scott. I know what I have. Right now, I'm more worried about this court situation." She ran her fingers through her hair. "Honestly, that's pretty much all I think about. If that teacher dies, I won't only lose Scott. I'll lose Ever. I'll lose everything."

CHAPTER 14

A few weeks later, Diamond, Faith, and DK arrived early for the fourth Counsel session. Their cars were side by side, engines running, windows up, A/C on m. It was Texas sizzling summertime hot. Diamond rolled down her windows and invited them to join her in her Navigator.

"Let me move this stuff out of the backseat," she said as DK and Faith climbed into the front.

When they were comfortable and out of chit chat about family and the weather, Diamond asked Faith, "Didn't you have a date with that dude from Snatch Saturday night? I meant to call you Sunday, but I had my grandkids all day and they wore me the hell out!"

DK leaned forward and put her head between the seats. "Yes, she did. I'm guessing it didn't go well since you answered every question in my text but that one yesterday."

"Dang, y'all know me too well," Faith laughed. "Yes, I did have a date and it is not something I should recount on church grounds."

Diamond manipulated the gearshift and drove to the carwash next door and Faith and DK reached for their seatbelts. Diamond parked by the vacuums. "Talk, God can't hear you from over here," she quipped.

Faith hesitated. DK poked her shoulder. "We ain't taking you back until you tell us about it. If we're late May Bell is gonna put all of us in a corner, so spit it out."

"Fine." Faith started laughing at the memory. "Give me a moment to come up with the CliffsNotes version." She paused to replay the night in her mind in real time. She'd spent the past two days trying to forget it happened.

"Silky Soul Stirrer" had caught her attention on Snatch.com. Several intellectually stimulating video chats earned him a meet up for coffee, followed by a few fun dates to Dallas hotspots. At the usual point in these matters, he made it clear he would like some conjugation with the conversation. She knew she had options and she chose to physically compensate him for the weeks of words hoping it would ease the restlessness she'd felt since learning Raymond was in Ulysses for reasons that didn't involve her. This guy was an inadequate filling for the hole in her chest, but he would slow the bleeding love.

"So I met this guy on Snatch. He was nice looking. We exchanged a few messages, went on a few dates, and, like always, he started hinting that it was time to move things along. I suggested we meet at the Hyatt DFW Saturday night."

"Yeah, that point usually comes sooner than later," Diamond said. "Then, what happened?"

She surprised him twice that night. First, with the booty call summoning him to her favorite hotel and secondly, with her state of undress when she opened the hotel door. He smiled from his back teeth thinking the bath towel around her birthday suit was for him but she did it to save time and money. In her experience, at the first hook up, her playdates ripped off her lingerie like it was on fire. That wasn't worth the time it took her to drive to the mall. He remained hesitant after she kissed him. He was probably in shock. No one expected the former mayor to be a freak. She increased the volume of the trap music coming from a blue tooth speaker by the bed. When the towel fell to the ground, he sprung into action.

Faith felt like she was in court in front of a very attentive jury. Her companions were hanging on to her every word. "Okay, y'all really. Aren't we too old for this?"

"No!" They replied at the same time.

"Fine. I greeted him in a towel and made the first move." They squealed in delight.

"Atta girl," DK said. Faith was in her mind racing ahead of the story.

Once he recovered from the shock of having to raise his expectations, he became a Sherpa from Nepal, setting out on a quest to skillfully guide her on a low altitude adventure to paradise. He asked her to lie on her stomach. When she complied, he sat on her thighs and massaged the knots in her shoulders and hips until her muscles melted, leaving her sprawled across the bed as helpless as roadkill. She was ass up, face down, while he carefully pulled her to the foot of the bed. She heard the carpet fold when he knelt to worship the art form that is woman. She started to roll over, but he gripped her calves and stopped her. She buried her face in a pillow, praying he didn't try to rim her butthole. If he did that on the first physical encounter without any discussion, she was outta there because that meant he licked anuses on the regular.

His tongue felt viper-like, almost as long as her pointer finger. She turned her head for visual confirmation. He was doing things with that tongue she'd only seen at the circus. She reached for her phone on the nightstand, thinking she could put it in selfie mode and preserve the performance. He'd never know, but who would she show such a video? She wouldn't go to the mailbox without a bra on. She locked herself in her bathroom to watch porn via a VPN and incognito mode before Sloane's family moved in. And she hadn't let anyone take a nude photo of her since, well, before camera phones. She nixed the idea of recording and rested her head on the pillow. At some point, her eyeballs rolled into her skull and she started Bachata dancing with the mattress.

"Talk woman," Diamond prodded her, "it's almost seven."

Faith bit her bottom lip. "He was good with his, uh, foreplay. Very good. Like I almost videotaped him for future reference."

"That's a good idea," Diamond said, sounding serious. "Online porn gets expensive."

DK was leaning on the console between the two of them. She stared at Diamond over the rim of her sunglasses. "We're coming back to that statement. Faith, go on."

Faith felt the wrong kind of heat stirring in her body. She adjusted the air vents on the passenger side to hit her full force in the face as she relived the next moments of her date.

Between his groans and her moans, she began to feel weightless. The primitive parts of her body responded to his craftsmanship. He was down under so long, Faith felt certain he was a devout vagitarian. Her sauna grew comfortably warm but could never reach the right temperature for liftoff. Despite his good start, he couldn't control his attention deficit tongue. Settle down and focus man, *she longed to say.* You're undoing your work. *She almost cried over the wasted pussability. Why did it never register that when she said, "Ooh, that's my spot," that's exactly what the hell she meant? She reminded herself to book a sexpert for the show. She bemoaned the poor curriculum at Porn University, where they failed to teach men that women have a very small "x" marking the big O. Raymond was her favorite teammate in sexual gymnastics. When he heard those words, he would not move from that precise location until her spine arched into a triple-twisting double backflip and she landed on the mattress with her hands in the air.*

She tried guiding the enormous bald head of Raymond's stand-in to the specific location of her desire with her hands but when she finally positioned him at the correct latitude, he went all Australian motorboat on her. She locked his head between her spin class toned thighs and spun around, forcing him to turn with her. He was on the floor with his back against the mattress. She moved to straddle him and set the tempo but he grabbed her waist, bent his knees, and bucked like a rodeo bull. She hung onto his shoulders and prayed the ordeal would end soon. She might be able to catch the last segment of the Rachel Maddow Show.

"I was responsive to his touch as it had been a while."

DK clucked her tongue, "No, it hadn't. You have sex more than the two of us combined."

"She does." Diamond agreed. They all laughed.

"Hurry up. We're almost out of time!" DK urged.

"Why is this necessary right now?" Faith asked. "We need to be over there." She pointed to the church parking lot. "I see everyone's car but Sloane's."

Diamond put the car in drive and kept her foot on the brake. "Sloane is always late. We'll beat her inside. We need this because Counsel sucks the life of everyone. I know it's for a good cause but it's heavy so we need to laugh."

Faith felt responsible for bringing them into her family drama. Maybe she did owe them a good laugh. She went into storyteller mode.

She made her voice deeper when she quoted him. "You like that don't you, gal? You loving this D. Right?"

She could barely stop laughing and they were doubled over. "I'm thinking, *'If you have to ask, the answer is no'*. I told him, 'Yeah, sure,' but that's when I gave up on the idea of having an orgasm with him in the room. I desperately wanted to tell him please be quiet and slow down before you aggravate my pinched L4. I don't have time to go to the chiropractor this week."

DK was happy crying and Diamond banged the steering wheel.

Faith giggled, feeling the weight of things to come ease its heavy weight off back a bit. "Wait, it gets worse," she explained. "Ole boy had the nerve to say, 'I'm the best you ever had. Right?' I was staring at the wall, thinking, *I hate men with low self-esteem.* You're in the sixtieth percentile, not even close to the best in this decade or the last."

"I know you didn't say *that*," Diamond said. "They would have been calling in a homicide at the Hyatt."

"Girl, nah, I didn't say that to him. I said what we're taught to say in the women's magazines. I lied and told him, '*You're the man.*' I moved my hands to his thick neck and seriously tried to choke him out. I saw that in a *Fifty Shades* movie."

DK looked doubtful, "I have seen all of those movies. The chick took most of the abuse. I don't remember her choking him."

"Did I ask you to fact-check me?" Faith said, smiling. "I'm doing my best to limit oxygen to his brain and he says, 'Oh, you wanna dominate me? I like aggressive women.' And I would've liked for him to stop talking and leave me to my imagination. I was trying to imagine he was someone else."

"Raymond," they supplied.

"Shut up," she told them. "Let me finish this story. It's 6:55. So at this point, his face is so red and contorted, I worried he might have a heart attack. His entire body was drenched. I let go of his neck and in an impressive show of strength, he stood with me on his lap and landed us both on the bed. That's when the joker shouted, '*Call me the Tiger King!*'"

"What?" Diamond gasped. "He did not."

"That was my reaction, too," Faith said. "I'm like, '*Did he just say call him Tiger King?*' The mullet-wearing, middle-aged cowboy who went to jail for hiring someone to murder a woman? Hell to the naw naw naw. That's a role I won't be playing. The Tiger King started feeling himself after that. He put a hand under one of my thighs and pressed upward." Faith made her voice gruffer, '*Gal, put your feet on my shoulders so I can go deeper!*'" Faith tried to finish the story, but she was laughing so it was hard to catch her breath. "I, I, I'm the forty-nine-year-old. Remember? '*If you want acrobatics, Cirque du Soleil is in town,*' I said. He looked at me kinda crazy, so I added, '*But you can put your feet on my shoulders.*'" She spied May Bell's car pulling into the parking lot. "That's it. We finished. He left. The end."

Still howling, Diamond started driving toward the church. DK sat back and blew her nose. "That was worth getting in trouble," DK said. "I haven't laughed like that in a long time. Faith, if podcasting doesn't work out, consider being a stand-up comedian."

Faith smiled, lost in thought and she recalled the part she didn't share.

She glanced at the alarm clock and calculated that roughly the last six minutes of her life had been wasted with this dude and she would never get them back. Determined to finish what she started, she decided to say whatever it took for him to get off her.

"Oooh yeah! Go, Tiger Riger, you're the best. Boom shakalaka! I'm clicking my heels 'cause I wish I was home! Ay, Papi! Git in there, big fella. Dumbo got an ankle bracelet. Free Sade! Make me come, Raymond*!*"

He froze mid-stroke. In what felt like slow motion, Faith slid onto his lap and they were eye to eye as she painfully recalled that his name was Trevor.

DK and Diamond might have found that funny, but she realized it wasn't a laughing matter. Pining over Raymond was consuming her and pushing her further into depression. And that was a problem the Counsel couldn't fix.

~ ~ ~

"It's time to get started, ladies." May Bell moved toward the center of the circle of chairs. Her hot pink bell bottoms rippled as she shimmied across the floor. When she raised her arms, the ruffles on her sleeves billowed. Faith watched smiling to herself. "Thank you all for arranging your schedules to meet earlier than usual. My husband and I are headed to a pastor's conference in Nashville and we have a flight at 8 pm."

"Must be nice to get away," Diamond said, her eyes dancing with merriment. "I haven't gone anywhere since Christmas, and it's late June, but we've almost wrapped up the hotel project. We only have the meeting rooms left to do and as soon as I get the last of my money, I'm on the first plane to Cancun!" The sister circle laughed and all volunteered to accompany her.

"It is nice to take a break," May Bell said. Her smile was bright with anticipation. "But for this point in time, I hope everyone did their homework. The assignment was to read several chapters on managing stress in the book *Anger Management for Dummies.*" Everyone nodded except Sloane. "To recap, after the first meeting, I realized the curriculum I normally use for these sessions was not suitable for this group. I worked with Rev. and social workers from our counseling ministry to develop a course based on this book and *The Five Love Languages* by Gary Chapman."

As she was talking, she walked over to Sloane who was nodding off and gave her shoulder a soft squeeze. Sloane's eyes flew open. May Bell kept walking and talking. Sloane looked at Faith sheepishly and scooted back in her seat.

"At the second meeting, we took a quiz to determine our love languages, and we learned why it is important to communicate with others in their love language: words of affirmation, physical touch, gifts, quality time, or acts of service. We followed that with a well-done lesson from Faith on empathic listening during which we role played different scenarios. I hope you enjoyed that as much as I did."

Faith beamed, needing the unsolicited praise. Words of affirmation were her primary love language. May Bell moved to the center of the circle. "Is anyone willing to share something they remember the last meeting? No pressure, but DK, you look like you have something to share."

DK put the book in her lap on the floor and stood up. They had agreed to start standing whenever they spoke at third meeting, mainly to keep Sloane from going to sleep. "Faith talked about listening to understand and not just waiting for your turn to jump in with your opinion. I realized that's become habitual for me and it's not good as a reporter or a friend to listen half heartedly."

Faith was sitting next to DK. She leaned over and whispered to her friend, "You owe me for telling you May

Bell might do that. She does it all the time in Women's Sunday School."

"Sshhh, some of us are trying to listen," Sloane said, from across the circle. DK rubbed her nose with her middle finger when May Bell wasn't looking, but Faith was.

"What is wrong with you?" Faith said out of the side of her mouth, but she wanted to laugh so badly.

"One more before we move into tonight's lesson," May Bell said, looking at Sloane.

Sloane unfastened her watch and tightened the band. She sighed loudly and folded her long legs. Faith wanted to slap her back into childhood and forbid her father from indulging her every whim. Gina started to speak, but May Bell held up a finger to stop her.

In a war of wills, Sloane was no match for May Bell. They sat there five minutes in complete silence. Sloane blinked first. She stood up, speaking in a strong, clear voice. "I learned there are many different types of listening: critical, comprehensive, appreciative, and empathetic. We choose different types of listening depending on our goals for the content."

The room burst into spontaneous applause. Sloane smiled when May Bell gave her a high five. She looked at her mother for signs of Faith's approval. That was something she hadn't done in a long time, either.

May Bell got a bowl filled with scraps of paper from beneath her folding chair. "Anger and depression are closely related," she said, moving her purse from her seat to the floor. "I believe if we learn to handle daily challenges in a constructive manner, we will internalize less negative thoughts and have less depression."

She passed the bowl to Faith. "Please take a piece of paper from the bowl and pass it around. Don't unfold the paper until I ask you to." They passed the bowl from person to person as she continued talking. "This exercise is designed to help us learn basic skills for anger management. On each scrap of paper, I've written a coping strategy taken from the reading assignment. On your turn, read the strategy and tell us how it helps you counter the stress that often leads to anger."

Diamond stood and tugged up the waist of her leopard print skinny jeans. "I'll go first." She unfolded the square of paper and read it. "Adequate rest." Her eyes went to the left side as she thought. "Healthy sleep means you're getting enough rest and the quality of your rest is good. You should wake up feeling refreshed, not tired like you didn't get any sleep at all. This chapter helped me a lot because I realized my mattress is trash and I need to quit working out right before I go to bed. The end." She threw her paper in the air and bowed at the waist.

Gina jumped up before the applause died. "My turn. My paper says 'maintain social ties' and I'm glad it does."

Faith noticed the paper was shaking. She hoped Gina wasn't still nervous because of her. She'd been as pleasant as she could to the woman. She didn't talk to her directly after saying hello, but she didn't purposefully exclude her from the chit chat before the meetings. DK passed her a note like they were in the fifth grade. Faith tried to read it without May Bell noticing.

She did. "Is there something you want to share with the group, Faith and DK?" They nodded mutely. "Gina, go on." Gina looked like she wanted to cry. May Bell went and put her arm around Gina's waist.

"I pray I can maintain social ties with some of you after we end the Counsel." She blinked back tears. "I know what the brothers in the church still call me -- Sister Oh My Goodness." She looked at Faith.

Faith's eyes bounced to from Gina to the floor to Sloane, who was unusually attentive to the conversation. "And I know the women of the church call me homewrecker, even though I feel I was the one used. But that stops today. I have learned that a big part of friendship is trust. I want you all to trust me, so I have a confession. First Lady, you may want to sit down."

"Uh, okay." May Bell sat in Gina's empty chair.

"My confession is not about me, not really. But I figured out who invited me to these meetings." She looked at Faith. "It was Preston." Faith's mouth dropped open. She turned to DK who had a similar what-the-hell expression.

"What?" Sloane cried out. "Daddy wouldn't do that. Are you saying he has you spying on me?"

"He hasn't said it directly, but he calls me after every meeting nonchalantly asking what we talked about. After I figured out what he was up to, I started telling him to ask you, Sloane."

"So why are you here?" Sloane demanded. "You know I never wanted you here. None of us did."

"I'm here because, despite your suspicions and our history, you've been kind like real Christians should be. And," she turned to May Bell seated behind her, "I believe you were right about things happening for a reason. I needed these lessons more than Sloane. I don't think someone could have befriended me if they wanted to, because I had put up so many walls."

"Being vulnerable is necessary for being loved," May Bell explained. "Thank you, Gina."

Faith removed the legal pad from her lap and put it in her purse. "Unbelievable," she muttered. She was preparing to leave.

May Bell said, "And that right there is your problem, my friend. Unforgiveness."

In thirty years, Faith had not been angry with May Bell -- until she said that. "Excuse me."

"Did I stutter?" May Bell said. "Do you really think this counseling is only about Sloane? This is *family* counseling. Preston didn't make her like this by himself. You had a hand in it, too."

Faith was fuming. *Is she calling me on the carpet in front of er'body in behind this Gina woman? Oh, I am so leaving this church. I should've left after the divorce.*

"Faith, all of you, listen to me. When two become one, they multiply. Everything that occurs after that, addition, subtraction, or division goes back to the source." She walked over to Faith. "Yes ma'am, I am calling you out, because you are a big girl and I know you can handle pressure. What I don't know is whether you realize you haven't forgiven Gina for what Preston did. You've heard Rev. Leroy preach about F-F-M numerous times. What does that stand for?"

As much as she longed to, Faith couldn't ignore May Bell. "Forgive, forget, move on."

"What we usually do is move on without forgiving, and most certainly without forgetting. I would not be doing my duty as your friend or First Lady if I ignored the bad example you are setting for Sloane."

Faith looked around, expecting judgment from the Counsel. What she saw were looks of recognition and understanding. Even Sloane seemed to be listening empathetically. *This heifer done made me part of the lesson*, it dawned on Faith. *Oh my, she's good and she's right. I've been carrying this resentment against her for a decade. I forgave Preston, but not the other woman.*

Faith stood up and May Bell stepped back. Faith saw the love in May Bell's eyes before she turned to sit down. "Y'all aren't going to believe this, but my paper says forgiveness." She passed it to DK to confirm that was the word written down.

"I need to re-read that chapter a few times I guess," she chuckled nervously. She didn't recognize the sound coming out of her mouth at first. She was never nervous about public speaking, but she always had her armor up and May Bell had stripped her of it. "What I recall is that carrying around old anger makes you constantly relive the past, and makes you unable to forgive yourself. I am guilty of that. And it impacts your future relationships."

She stopped there. Something inside her started to crumble. Something she didn't need any longer. She knew it would take time to clear the debris and be completely free but the thought that she could, made her feel light from the inside out. She didn't realize she was crying until DK patted her cheeks with a tissue. That act of kindness led to the best group hug of Faith's life -- and, she hoped, the end of a toxic cycle.

CHAPTER 15

The two weeks preceding the annual Essence Festival the week of July 4th were a blur of fruitful business meetings and four fruitless sessions of the Counsel. Faith was thrilled when July brought the opportunity to escape her busy schedule in Ulysses for a more pleasurable working environment in New Orleans. She jokingly described NOLA as the offspring of Atlanta and Disney World. There were more African-Americans on her outbound flight than she had seen on any of the hundreds of flights she'd taken during her travels across the globe.

At takeoff, a guy with Mardi Gras beads stapled to a Dallas Cowboys baseball cap yelled, "Next stop NOLA. Essence Fest, here we come!"

The plane erupted in cheers. Faith expertly opened her camera app and snapped several photos for her first podcast episode in a series on the historic and iconic festival that celebrated the best in African-American film, art, and music.

Faith was in and out of Louis Armstrong International Airport quickly. A road warrior, she'd learned to avoid checking luggage or wearing anything that might trigger further TSA scrutiny. A Lincoln Town Car with dark tinted windows idled curbside, awaiting her command. Half an hour later, she unlocked the door of her residence for the next four days, a designer decorated Airbnb studio with business-class wifi. Its small balcony overlooked a central courtyard and the full-sized refrigerator was stocked with deli meat, three bottles of her favorite wine, and a half-gallon of chocolate ice cream.

Life is good.

Faith set up her makeshift studio: laptop, wireless mouse, microphone, mic isolation shield, and ring light. She'd do short, live broadcasts at the convention center, but most of her content would be recorded on her pc and uploaded to a shared drive. Daniel would edit it and check for copyright transgressions before posting them to her podcast host for distribution.

She grabbed her phone to review her schedule. As she scrolled through the next day's entries it rang. The distinctive ring tone associated with her favorite pastime (talking to Raymond) made her mouth water.

"Sup?" she answered. She tried not to sound overly excited by his unexpected call, but failed miserably.

"Hey! What cha doing? When do you leave for N'awlins?"

"I'm here. I made it about an hour ago. My room is unbelievable. It looks exactly like the photos online."

"I'd love to see it," he said.

She wanted to ask what he meant by that. She felt a knot in her stomach. She wanted nothing more than for him to be with her. "Yeah, so how are things in Santa Fe?"

"Things are things. But I thought about you last night, because something funny happened."

Faith liked the idea of him thinking about her. "Really? What?"

"I was watching a movie and one of the characters said, 'Sometimes being a ho' is all a woman has to hold onto' and that made me think about you." They laughed together.

"How funny! That was Dolores Claiborne. That's one of my favorite movies." She didn't tell him Vera Donovan said, "being a bitch," not "being a ho'." She sobered at the thought he was probably watching that chick flick with his chick.

"I was wondering if maybe--"

Her phone alarm went off, reminding her she had thirty minutes to get to the convention center. She cut him off. "I gotta grab my press credentials. Can I call you back?" Faith was dying to hear what he was wondering, but she had a job to do.

"Uh, yes. No problem, but I need to tell you--"

She interrupted him again, "Hold that thought. I have to get going. " *Why the hell would he wait until now to be wondering something? Aaargh.*

Faith loaded her backpack and made her way to the Convention Center. She couldn't believe there was such a long line to get into the place. Eventually, she made her way inside and obtained her media credentials. She downloaded the festival's app and used it to navigate the crowded aisles. The room looked like downtown Vegas with huge, dazzling displays everywhere. On one stage, the cast of the STARZ hit series "Weakness" waxed poetically about the upcoming season. In another area, Walmart had seemingly struck gold with their free reusable shopping bags bearing images of regal women on both sides, along with a blinged-out plastic tiara inside. The line to obtain one of the free bags snaked for fifty yards. Video screens large enough to rival those in any professional sports arena proclaimed that it was time the world recognized the Black queen and her "Reign." Faith's smile widened at the thought of a Black queen on the throne again, like Nefertiti in 1330 B.C. or Aretha Franklin in the 1960s.

She stole a few minutes from her schedule to make a music video in BET's interactive display. She was headed to her interview with David and Tamela Mann when she spied a familiar looking face.

Is that Bobby Brown?

She walked closer to the main stage. Yes. He had aged well, but the pain of losing Whitney and his daughter was etched in the lines on his face. Faith listened to him reminiscing. A few people in the packed crowd standing around her became misty-eyed. When Bobby's pain became too palpable, Faith walked away. It was her prerogative. She could do sad by herself.

She was walking and looking at her phone when she felt a force so strong it stopped her in her tracks. The skin on her back tightened, pulling her shoulders up and back. Her eyes darted from face to face, seeking the source of her sudden discomfort but she found nothing out of the ordinary.

She heard her grandmother's voice from long ago and far away explaining what was occurring. "That's the feeling of someone walking on your grave, baby," she'd say. "Walk lightly. Trouble is comin' with friends." She didn't want trouble. They'd spent enough time together in the past. As soon as she zeroed in on trouble, she planned to walk in the opposite direction.

A hand landed on her shoulder. Instinctively, she knew that hand, oh, so well. Her tongue recalled the length and width of each digit. Her breasts knew the calluses by name. Her hips recalled the strength that once lifted her waist high and ever so gently pinned her to the smooth tiles of a steamy shower in France during the best trip of her life. If she'd known that would be her last trip with that hand, she would have limited her sightseeing to their hotel room.

"Hello, Faith."

She spun and took a step back before looking in those eyes. Those sexy, milk chocolate eyes.

"Hello, Raymond." They hugged briefly. She hid her trembling hands behind her back as they stood there staring. She experienced the hyperlapse of memories an unexpected encounter with your endless love invariably triggers.

"This is a surprise," Faith said. She looked at his chin. She couldn't risk any direct eye contact. God only knew what she might do right then and there if she accepted the invitation in his silence.

"I was trying to tell you when we spoke on the phone earlier. I wanted to warn you." He stopped seemingly in midsentence.

"Warn me?" she asked, hopeful but wary about his motives. She watched his Adam's apple bob like a yoyo.

"No. Yes. What I mean is, I would have told you that we're here."

Her smile slipped downward. "We?"

"Eden and me. She's attended every year since they started the festival twenty-five years ago. Her best friend usually comes with her, but she had to work, so I came instead. She's right over there." He pointed in a direction behind Faith. "Come meet her. She knows you're here. I told her all about you."

He said "all about you," Faith noted. She clasped her hand in front of her, white knuckled but steady. She couldn't turn. If she met the woman, her enemy became real. She might be nice or kind or friendly. Faith preferred to battle the arrogant, hateful woman she'd created in her mind. That nemesis deserved to lose her man.

Raymond clasped her hand. "Come on."

He pulled. She resisted. He smiled. She frowned. She was trying to walk with him, but her feet wouldn't move. Her mind raced. *His girl is a music lover, too? Of course, she is. He already told me she cooks every day. Who does that every day when you can have hot food delivered by kind strangers in 30 minutes? She probably does carpentry and electrical, too,* Faith thought. *Aaarrrgh.*

His hand was warm. She was tempted to lace her fingers through his and pull him into the nearest family bathroom for a secular praise and worship service. When she was done reminding him what he walked away from, they would both be on their knees begging for more.

Reluctantly, she released his hand. "I can't," was all she said.

His reddish brows knitted together in a manner she'd always found endearing. He was usually working on payroll when he wore that expression.

He released her hand. "You don't have time, or you don't want to meet her? What are you saying?"

Her smartwatch chirped a notification. Relieved, she glanced at it and said, "Of course I want to meet her, but I have an interview in fifteen minutes on the other side of the convention center so I've gotta run."

His eyes went into new puppy dog mode. He knew she couldn't resist that pleading expression. She threw him a bone of hope. "Let me see how the day goes. Maybe we can meet up later."

He still looked disappointed and a little suspicious about her excuse. He tapped his foot once. She knew what that meant. Overcome by curiosity, she added, "I have dinner reservations at a nice spot in the quarter. Why don't you two join me? I'll text you the place and time."

He grinned and threw his arms around her in a delicious bear hug. "That's my girl. We will be there and dinner is on me."

She walked away with extra swing in the pendulum of her hips in case he was watching. "Your damned straight dinner is on you," she grumbled. She didn't want to meet the other woman. She didn't want her to be humanized, a real person with real feelings. It was easier to dislike someone she didn't know anything about. Her mind would allow a little room for that callousness, but if she ended up liking Raymond's new flame....

That would make her hard life even harder.

~ ~ ~

That night, Faith arrived for the threesome twenty minutes early. Despite her fervent attempts and good connects, she couldn't get a dinner reservation at Bourbon House, Brennan's, or Arnaud's. Slightly deterred, she went to the opposite end of the fine dining spectrum and chose a small bistro near St. Louis Cathedral. She had the Uber driver drop her by the entrance of the historic landmark. The wrought iron gates were locked at that time of night. She grasped two metal rods and peered through them, like a prisoner of her own making. The sight of the rooftop spires piercing the night sky always brought her a measure of comfort she could not explain. She mouthed a prayer in the hope it might slip through the clouds, skate past the stars, and knock on heaven's door in time to bring her the miracle she needed.

She walked the few yards to Toulouse Street, turned left and followed the foot traffic to the Shops at Jax Brewery. This area would normally be more crowded, but most of the festival attendees were attending the Mary J Blige concert tonight. Faith's freelance journalist press credentials granted entry into most VIP areas, but didn't allow all access, so she passed on the free seat in the rafters she had been offered.

Instead, she had planned to spend the evening writing scripts for the fall episodes, but the only time she could say no to Raymond was when he asked for her hand in marriage.

She slipped the hostess a twenty in exchange for a good table on the patio. She sat in an ornate metal chair facing the street. She wanted to observe the body language between Raymond and this woman. Everyone looks in love on filtered snapshots. Cameras can't capture chemistry. If they were really in love, she would see it. And she'd govern herself accordingly. She wasn't sure what accordingly looked like, but she'd figure it out.

She spied Raymond's leg dangling from the rear passenger door of a Tesla across the street. She'd know that leg anywhere from the baseball-sized indentation at the base of his hip to the 110-degree bend of his knee. She noticed he was wearing the Kobe's she got him three years ago. After a few minutes, he emerged from the car and extended a hand to the person inside.

The laws of gravity would not allow that big booty to rise form the low-slung car without assistance from him and Sarah Blakely's best Spanx, Faith thought.

Wow! That's all Faith could think as they walked toward her. Her brain told her face to smile, but nary a muscle moved. Big Booty grinned brighter than the yellow brick road to the Emerald City. And why wouldn't she? That wrap-around dress spray painted across every carved curve of her body was a work of art. Her hair and nails matched the zebra striped thigh-high boot shoes. Faith rose and greeted BB first, following the unwritten female code about such things. As they hugged it out, Faith noted BB's flowing tresses were as soft and natural as a cotton puff.

"Apologies for our tardiness, Faith," Raymond said, rubbing his hand across Faith's waist in a bit too familiar embrace. BB couldn't see his hands and Faith couldn't forget them.

He might have been dressed nicely, as well, but all she could see was the shoes she paid for planted next to the other woman. With great effort, she formed a complete sentence. "No problem. I haven't been here long. I have been people watching."

"Making up stories about them?" Raymond read her mind.

They laughed and both said, "Paris!"

BB laughed also. "Raymond shared some of the beautiful photos he took during your European tour a few years ago. He brings it up often. I could be wrong, but I'm pretty sure that is his favorite to date. I hope he and I can visit Paris and Milan someday soon."

There was not a hint of jealousy in her voice, Faith observed.

"Faith, allow me to introduce you to Eden Sugarberry," Raymond said.

The ladies shook hands as Raymond said more pain inflicting words like "we thought" and "we did" which Faith's mind balked at processing. In her ears, "Eden Sugarberry" was on auto replay. *With a name like that, she had to be good,* Faith found herself thinking. I hope I don't accidentally call her BB.

Raymond gallantly pulled out a chair for his betrothed. He also took her huge Birkin ostrich purse and placed it on the seat next to Faith. Then, he got Faith's permission to move her purse to that space, as well. He was supposed to sit on the other side of the table with Faith between him and BB. That's why she put her purse in the seat across from her in the first place. Now, she had a direct view of his face and those eyes. *Day-um those eyes.* His chivalry while releasing the slender threads remaining between them reminded Faith of the many things she missed about being his first choice.

BB giggled and said, "Let's order, then you can tell me your memories of that wonderful adventure, Faith." She smiled at Faith with her doe-like eyes before turning her attention to the menu.

Faith glanced at Raymond. He looked askance, which she took as confirmation he withheld some key details of that "adventure" from Ms. Thang like the fact they were buck naked for seventy percent of that trip.

"Before we talk about silly old trips, I'd like to know more about you, Eden. Like where are you from. Exactly."

"Before I moved to Arizona, I lived in Louisiana." Faith exhaled with relief. "But I was there because I stayed after graduating from LSU with a degree in economics. I was born and raised in Fort Worth, if that's what you mean."

"Oh, you're a native Texan. How nice." Faith saw the skin of Raymond's forehead move up and away from his downturned eyes as he suppressed his amusement. They knew each other too well.

Are you effen kidding me? She's not only from Texas but she's also from Fort Worth, a 50-minute drive from where I effen live. Ah, hell nah. I am NOT going to their wedding. He better not invite me. She didn't hear another word BB said about her background. She'd never been so happy to have a waiter arrive in her life. Faith predicted Raymond would order jambalaya before he looked at the menu. He loved jambalaya and--in an unrelated memory--he very much enjoyed licking sweet potato pie from the creases between her hips and thighs. *Focus Faith. Look at the pretty pictures on the menu. Focus.*

BB and Faith ordered gumbo and doubles of Sazeracs, the rye whiskey-based official cocktail of the Big Easy. Faith expected stilted conversation that was slow and lumbering, but the small talk between the trio was easy and sweet, more lite syrup than raw honey.

That ended when BB touched Faith's arm and said, "I confess I'm a superfan of yours. I've read your Wikipedia page and at least a dozen articles about you. And I'm a paid subscriber to your podcast so we can skip your background check."

Faith laughed nervously wondering where this was going.

BB said, "Tell me all about that trip, girl," sending a current of trepidation through Faith's spine.

Why is she staring at me with those big eyes with her lips slightly parted? Is that matte lipstick or a lip crayon? This would be the perfect time for aliens to abduct me. Faith shook her head to erase the word cloud in her overactive imagination. She rushed a spoon full of gumbo into her mouth, stalling for time.

Raymond evidently recognized that body language and moment of hesitation from years of working by Faith's side, studying every gesture. He cleared his throat. "Let Faith eat her food, Babe," he said. He blew the heat from the food on his fork. "Mmmm, there is nothing like N'awlins jambalaya." He licked his lips and Faith almost passed out from an overdose of lust.

She swallowed hard and took a deep breath. "We're good. I don't mind talking about our business trip to Europe. It was a great opportunity and we learned so much about their use of their mass transit and universal health care system."

"Really?" BB said, turning to Raymond. "I thought you said you two spent most of the time in the hotel having mind-blowing sex. She has a different memory of the trip than you, Bae."

Raymond spit chicken and shrimp all over the table. Faith laughed harder than she'd laughed in months. BB casually sipped her drink as if she hadn't just dropped a huge nuclear bomb on the table.

Faith looked from BB's endless cleavage to Raymond's reddened cheeks and declared, "I like this one." She realized she'd been holding a knife in her left hand since she unrolled it from the napkin. She placed it between her bowl and lemon peel at the bottom of her empty glass. "As you know, I talk for a living, so I don't want to go on and on. And I'm not exactly sure what Raymond told you about our time spent outside of the hotel." She emphasized the word "outside" to make it clear she would not be discussing their time between the sheets. "Would you prefer the play by play or do you want to hear the highlights of the exquisite sites we visited? I'm happy to do either."

BB squeezed Raymond's hand. "She's more discreet than you, my Big Kahuna."

Raymond coughed as if he were choking. "Bae, you okay?" BB implored. She patted his back until he seemed to breathe easy.

Faith watched them. BB was comfortable with Raymond as if she'd known him for years. Faith felt they had known each other longer than Raymond said. She had a gnawing feeling he was seeing BB before he broke it off with her. Maybe that was why BB wasn't threatened by her friendship with Raymond.

"Faith, tell me everything about Europe like I'm a voyeur." Faith and Raymond burst out in laughter. BB looked at Raymond curiously.

"We're not laughing at you, Bae. We're laughing at your word choice. Voyeur is more commonly used to describe a person watching others be intimate."

BB's eyes clouded over like she might be angry with them. Faith stopped laughing immediately. She never wanted to be cruel. Trying to get Raymond back didn't seem cruel. He was hers in the first place. But mocking someone, even accidentally, felt cruel.

"Eden, I'm sorry," Faith said. "Raymond is right. It's an interesting word choice. That's all. Actually, it's a term used in legal circles with a slightly different meaning so, I mean, what do we know?"

Eden turned to Faith and burst out laughing. Faith exhaled in relief and joined her. "Got cha!" Eden proclaimed. "I know exactly what that word means and I purposefully chose it. I'm messing with y'all."

Faith was delighted (against her will) that Eden had such a wicked sense of humor. She had to add a "pros" column to the long mental checklist of "cons" she had, perhaps unfairly, compiled about Eden based on her online posts.

Eden picked up where the conversation had taken a detour. "On the real, it's been my lifelong dream to cross the Atlantic. Maybe we'll go to Paris for our honeymoon," she said wistfully. She glanced at Raymond. "We're not in a rush, are we?"

Raymond removed his hand from the back of BB's chair and tugged on his earlobe. "Nope, I guess not," he said in a sentence that sounded a bit like a question. He and Faith locked eyes. Two weeks of bliss that could not be recounted in a million words passed forth and back between them.

"Well?" BB said sounding excited.

"Right," Faith began. She motioned for the waiter to bring her another drink. Her companions' cups were, ironically, half full.

Raymond winked at Faith over the rim of his water glass. They were re-experiencing the sensual foreplay of his piano playing fingers between her inner thighs while the cabin lights were out. Between the pleasurable caresses and the vibration of the plane's engines, Faith came within a few feet of the Mile-High Club.

"Did you fly into London or Paris?" BB asked, letting Faith know she had done her homework online or read a travel guide in preparation for their honeymoon.

"We landed in Heathrow. Customs is fast and easy. The Brits do that much better than U.S. Customs, in my opinion. It was 74 degrees on the sunniest British day I've seen. We took a shuttle to the Metropole Hilton."

BB blurted, "They have Hilton Hotels in London?"

"They do, and this one is nice. Plus, I collect triple Hilton Honors points." The waiter interrupted the conversation to refill Raymond's water glass. Faith tried not to look his way, but found herself imagining the joy that glass was experiencing. "London is clean. I asked the driver of our hackney carriage -- aka cool looking taxicab -- for a mini-tour of the city since we only had one day before traveling to Paris. He took us past the 2012 Olympic Village. Uhh, we saw the London Eye, that giant ferris wheel thing. It's quite extraordinary. As I recall, it's the tallest hmmm—"

Raymond supplied the missing words. "The tallest cantilevered observation wheel in the world." BB beamed at him as if he'd just cured the world of poverty.

Faith's intestines hardened into jealous knots. For the first time in her life, she wished she could not see any objects within six feet of her. She had spent her years as a public servant faking enthusiasm, but it was hard to do it under these circumstances. She tried. "Right. What he said. What else? We drove along the Thames River. There are always people walking about everywhere. Lots of selfie-taking tourists and pub after pub of friendly Brits. They drink beer like Parisians drink wine."

Faith had a flashback to her swollen ankles. Eleven hours in a plane without her compression socks wreaked havoc on her extremities, but she wasn't about to share that middle-aged woe with this pretty young thing. "Big Ben, the iconic clock tower, and the Houses of Parliament live up to their appearance on every British program you've ever seen." She let out a big sigh of satisfaction as she bit her lower lip. "It's all quite wonderful. I'm glad you saw the pictures because I can't describe it all: double-decker buses, Westminster Abbey, and the Queens' guards at Buckingham Palace..." she lost her way in the memories.

Eden found her. "Do you have a favorite among all those places? Your entire body language has changed. I can tell you had a great time."

"I can't do it justice. You simply must go, Eden. " *Preferably alone or with someone who doesn't belong with me.*

"Get a local guide the first time you go. They bring the steep history to life with colorful stories you'll never read in a history book. What's going on with Meghan and Harry is nothing compared to what has happened in that royal family over the last 1200 years!"

BB laughed and Faith found herself laughing along genuinely. At that moment, Faith realized she was trying to plow the ocean. Raymond gave her ten years of devotion and she blew it. He'd found a beautiful woman who was confident and smart. The two of them were truly in love. Of course, Raymond would choose a nice woman to make his wife. He deserved that. Part of her was happy for him. But the idea of being replaced by another woman—again--made her want to cry like Niagara Falls.

BB touched Raymond's arm. "Speaking of the royals, Bae, I know you've stayed up half the night to watch every royal wedding in the past thirty years. I say you should tell me about Westminster Abbey while Faith eats. She's barely touched her food and we've cleaned our plates."

Faith looked at Raymond and raised her eyebrows. *Royal wedding watcher?* That was news to her. She thought she knew everything about him but, then again, he went years without telling her his wealthy family founded the largest Black-owned trucking company in the country. It was one of the largest in existence. What other secrets had he kept?

He avoided her curious glance by checking his watch. "Sure," he said. "I'll pick up where she left off. After checking in, the first place we went to was Westminster Abbey. It is bigger than a million bread baskets in height and width. The only somewhat comparable places I've visited are Notre Dame in Paris and St. Peter's in the Vatican City. St. Peter's is larger, but Westminster Abbey is nobler I would say. Don't you agree, Faith?"

Faith had a mouth full of food. She couldn't distinguish the roux in the gumbo from the salty tears in her throat. She nodded agreement when BB looked for her confirmation.

Raymond continued, "Every side of the building is a wonder of statues, arches, spires, and so much incredible craftsmanship. Seriously, a virtual tour doesn't do it justice. Some of the building's character is experienced through your senses of taste, smell, and feel."

The spoon in Faith's hand fell to the ground, landing cobblestone with a loud clang. "Sorry, my spoon is wetty," she stammered. "I mean sweaty. My fingers." She was flustered. She reached for her spoon, but BB stopped her and gave her Raymond's spoon. "Thank you, Eden. Ignore me, Raymond. Finish the story." Faith was no longer able to look into his eyes as the struggle inside her intensified.

Raymond motioned for the waiter to bring another round of drinks. " I was pretty much done. Westminster has three doors at the main entrance like most cathedrals in Europe. That represents the Trinity we were told: the Father, Son, and Holy Ghost. Inside is all dark paneling, but it's not gloomy because there are stained glass windows all around the top. Each one tells a story. We didn't stay long, but we'll definitely take the guided tour, next time."

Who exactly is "we"? Faith found herself holding her breath, waiting for him to continue. She was engrossed in his recounting as if she had not been by his side witnessing the same event. Her primary hope was that somehow his "next time" included her, not Eden.

"Sounds like a plan," BB said to Raymond while looking directly at Faith.

Faith received the full message. She resumed the storytelling with forced animation ending with, "It was quite a day. Thanks to Raymond's logistics, we saw every historical landmark and tourist trap imaginable. By the time we got back to the hotel, I was exhausted." And THAT was the only night of the entire trip that they didn't do anything but spoon and sleep, she recalled.

The waiter appeared and apologized. "I'm sorry, but the restaurant is closing. May I bring the check?"

Faith looked at her phone to see her reflection. She stress of the evening was showing, despite her fake smile. She could see the lines on her forehead and crows feet around her eyes. She relaxed her facial muscles. She didn't want Raymond to see the wrong contrasts between her and his newer, younger model.

She pressed the key to light up the phone and she was surprised at the time. "It's 2 am? I had no idea. Y'all, I have to call it a night." The regret in her voice was genuine. She'd enjoyed spending time with them. "I'm on a prayer breakfast panel at 7 am, then I have a webcast, followed by an interview with Cora Jakes Coleman and—" she stopped talking.

Raymond was texting, seemingly ignoring her litany of excuses. BB was half listening and pouting because she couldn't get dessert. Faith thought about offering her one of the beignets in her purse, but they were already sharing a man -- that was enough. She took her wallet from her bag with no intention of unzipping it.

"I got it," Raymond said. He pointed to a black Highlander pulling up. "That's your Uber." Faith felt that familiar tug of her heartstrings whenever he took initiative to make her life easier. He had a way of being thoughtful about her needs that no one in her life had ever displayed. He added with bass in his voice, "Text me when you're inside your room with the deadbolt turned counterclockwise."

God only knew how much she loved this man. She recalled a line from the *Color Purple,* "You better not never tell nobody but God." Mister was wrong about that. She should have told Raymond, too.

She rode back to her room, thinking something she never expected to think. *I like her. I don't like her with Raymond, but I do like her—a lot. Dammit.*

CHAPTER 16

The next day Faith dragged her fatigued body through a blur of sound bites and selfies. She used her Canon EOS for video and her phone for still shots to save battery and gigabytes. At lunchtime, she took the St. Charles Streetcar back to her room.

The scheduled phone conference with Daniel almost rendered her unconscious. He went into way more techie detail than needed about thumbnails and lower thirds for the video she'd captured that morning. It was a surprise -- but not surprised -- to hear New Orleans style jazz playing in the background of his place. He mentioned Jay Z more than jazz until he learned about her Essence Fest plans. He begged her to tag along, but she didn't budget for companion travel when she planned the trip months in advance. "Okay, I have to go now," meant nothing to him. When he finally said goodbye, a nap was in order. She could not handle the afternoon lecture on the New Jim Crow without resting her mind first. Several hours later, the musical sound of a brass band awakened her. Her curtains were open, but the room was dark.

Unfazed, she made her way toward the melody. The patio door was slightly open. That was a little scary. She hadn't ventured onto the patio since her arrival. In the courtyard, a group of men and women wearing matching attire played an assortment of instruments in what appeared to be a Second Line. Dancing to the jazz music along with the band members released the carefree girl inside her. Dipping and swirling in her bare feet was the most fun she'd had in ages. The band leader wore a bright blue hat and had a smile almost as wide as the blue and gold sash across his chest.

"I'm supposed to be working," she reminded herself. She retrieved her camera, hit record, and zoomed in. The idea of doing a podcast on the longstanding tradition of parades organized by the Social Aid and Pleasure Clubs excited her. They performed for funerals, weddings, and other occasions. She knew it had African influences, but not much more. The block party moved on, leaving her smiling and craving more NOLA culture.

Her previous plans for the evening had been to find a live music venue, but she could check that box as completed. She opened her Facebook app and searched "Nearby Events." A spoken word event at a place called

Café Istanbul wouldn't normally ring her bell, but she was still logged in to Diamond's account and there was Raymond's profile picture next to "is going." She had planned to avoid the lovey doveys for the remainder of the trip, but some force greater than her will compelled her to find her way to the café.

Years later, she might sit in a rocking chair on her porch and tell someone about that night. How she got in for free because the guy at the door loved her drawl. How the drinks were overpriced. How it was too dark and too cold and too crowded. How she stood by the bar because there were no empty seats. How she didn't see Raymond anywhere until she went to the restroom and returned to find him on stage.

Raymond. In the spotlight. With a microphone.

How he looked toward her as he spoke. How she shrank into the dark, but his gaze never wavered.

"I enjoy writing poetry, but I don't perform it in public. So don't judge me." He paused and adjusted the height of the microphone stand. "Yes, so I wrote this for someone special."

He cleared his throat, "The title of the poem is Two Fingers."

As she'd rocked in her chair decades from now, she'd mention how she thought he was going to describe her obsession with the perfect pour of Jack Daniels: two fingers tall. How she didn't know if he could see her because of the spotlight and the crowd. How she sucked in her stomach, waiting for the punch of his words, hoping she was the reason for his rhyme. How he took a deep breath and spoke the intimate words that unbroke her.

Unaccustomed am I to flights of fantasy

Preferring to travel by plane, train, or automobile.

Tonight, I find myself dreaming in color.

I slowly swirl two fingers of magnificent beauty in a hollow crystal.

Thoughts slip and slide through the mirrors of my mind

A lovely kaleidoscope

Held gently by warm, careful hands.

Every shape that forms beneath the twist and turns of my wrist is divine.

Wispy clouds move in and out, up and down,

Arching,

Falling,

Seeming to spin in the slowest motion against the smooth shadow of an earth-toned backdrop.

Magical.

Mysterious.

The music of the thunderstorm, free of frightening thunder.

And I wonder. If lighting strikes no one;

Hurts no one;

If it merely electrifies the insatiable sky, is it a crime?

Or is it something indescribable,

A rainbow saronged around my body after a downpour?

The ice is melting in my palm.

Because it can.

Without commitment,

Without questions.

Free to flow across my lips, beyond the tip of my tongue

To the smile inside my heart.

I console myself with private knowledge

Beneath the regal exterior of the complex cubes flows the currents of a thousand rivers.

How magnificent—

Something so inherently simple,

So unequivocally sensual as the condensation painting my fingerprints

Sits glistening at the delta of creation

Aching for my touch.

I can only imagine.

My muse.

How the room was silent with pregnant expectation. How she shuddered through the eargasm as one inextricably ...connected...convicted...condemned.

How she walked to the door and looked back at him, hoping he might follow.

CHAPTER 17

Trey was pleased with the results of his efforts. Guys night out was long overdue. He wasn't sure he could pull it off as there was standing tension among the squad. Reverend Leroy was annoyed that Deacon Preston Henry had not been to church in a month, claiming he did real estate business on Sundays, his only day off from the clubs. Their long history of regular calls and texts had ceased. Preston and Junior were always at odds in what looked like the world's worst sibling rivalry movie on loop. And Scott had been unusually quiet and sullen at recent family gatherings.

They all loved Trey, though, and the idea that he was finally showing an interest in their favorite past time tipped the scales in favor of a get-together.

Trey's original idea was to meet up at Top Golf, but when he bounced it off Junior, his uncle suggested they start the evening at an upscale cigar bar. Along with the best hand-rolled cigars their money could buy, they ordered small plates of bison meatballs, Wagyu beef pot stickers, lobster deviled eggs, and parmesan fries to share.

"Nice shirt," his uncle Junior commented. "I like the cuffs. Looks like something I would wear."

Trey smiled and popped the collar of his purple dress shirt. He adjusted the contrasting striped cuffs for full effect. "Thanks. Mom, got it for me at Essence Fest I'm glad she didn't get another t-shirt. I have about a hundred from her worldwide travels."

Junior patted his round stomach. "I need to give you the ones she's brought me over the years. I'm too old to wear tight tees."

"You're not too old, you're too big," Reverend Leroy joked.

Preston laughed but he kept laughing beyond the margins of the remark. He snorted and sputtered sloshing the velvet liquid in his snifter.

Everyone looked at him. "What's funny?" Junior said, leaning toward his brother inquisitively. Reverend Leroy peered at Preston over the straw in his glass of Sprite.

"Yeah, Pops. Let us in on the joke," Trey pleaded. He was glad the mood took a turn for the better. No one had said more than hello since they sat down. Trey's ultimate motive was to get some face time with his father, who had been dodging him for weeks.

Preston looked at Reverend Leroy. "Man, every time I think about you doing that funeral service for LaQuinesha's pot-bellied pig, I lose it!" Everyone but the Lord's undershepherd grinned wide. They'd heard the story a million times, but it never ceased to be funny as hell.

The man of God twirled a long Cohiba cigar between his thumb and fingers and tried to look offended. "All God's creatures deserve a homegoing celebration," he quipped.

"Man, I was in the first grade and I still remember that day," Junior spoke, easing his words around the Cherry Bomb Petite clenched between his teeth.

Scott stuffed four large fries in his mouth and mumbled. "I don't think I've heard this one. What happened?" He sucked the parmesan flakes off his fingers as if he hadn't been allowed to eat fries before.

Trey side-eyed Scott. He had never seen Scott display anything less than impeccable manners. Come to think of it, he had not seen him drink Cognac before either. Unlike his wife, Mr. Self-Control typically selected Miller Lite or a Cosmo -- girly drinks in Trey's mind. He relit his cigar and remained silent, mulling the personality change in his brother in law.

Preston blew a puff of smoke toward the ceiling. "We don't know exactly what happened to the pig but there were rumors."

"Naw, those stories were true," Junior quipped, helping his brother tell the story. "LaQuinesha's grandmama ran over it with her wheelchair! She was gone make hammocks for dinner."

Scott was so tickled he fell onto the arm of his chair laughing. "Man, quit lying! That didn't happen, did it?"

"It did," Junior said. "I heard there were tire marks across his pig's feet. It was tragic. The SPCA came out and—"

"Can I tell my own story, Boss?" Preston interrupted sarcastically. Junior's smile vanished. A dark shadow crossed his face.

Reverend Leroy intervened gently. "No one could prove LaQuinesha's grandma harmed the pig, but when the family came home unexpectedly, she had a bloody cleaver in her hand and the dead piglet was in a washtub on the back porch."

To their collective relief, Junior laughed at the image and migrated his cigar from one corner of his mouth to the other. "Go on, Preston. I interrupted your story, man."

"Nah, I'm done," Preston said, without the attitude. He pointed to his oldest friend, "Thanks to you Reverend, there really are pigs in heaven." Preston looked at Trey and they both lit up like sparklers on the Fourth of July.

"That's one of my mom's favorite books," Trey explained in response to the quizzical expressions of their companions. "She kept a copy of it on her nightstand for years. She would read chapters of it randomly and laugh like a crazy woman." Preston nodded agreement. "It was that one and another one. Hmmm...what was it Dad? She had Scotch tape on the spine holding it together."

"*Clan of the Cave Bear.* I couldn't forget if I wanted to. She called me Broud for years. After we got divorced, I read the book and realized that character was a bad guy. One of the many yellow flags I missed, I guess." Preston tapped his cigar against the Arturo Fuente ashtray. He opened his mouth to say more but didn't.

"You never told me that," Junior said. "That was one of my book club's first reads. Broud was a prehistoric ass. Yo, but he did become King eventually. So there's that."

Preston twisted his face to one side as if he smelled something bad. "A show tunes singin' ass negro who's in a strippers' book club? Who are you and what have you done with my little brother?"

Junior made a sound like a giggle, but he managed to turn it into a masculine cough. "I can't with them girls. For the record, they read urban fiction that would make Sister Souljah blush. When I read that book, I was in Faith's book club. For real, I miss those nights and the delicious ham and cheese pinwheels Diamond used to bring. What can I say? I am that singin' ass jigga and Faith is my ride or die. She has the most omnivorous mind I've ever encountered. Man, I still don't know how you messed that up."

Their heads swiveled to Preston waiting for him to disagree or correct Junior's grammar. Preston scratched his eyelid, then looked at his watch. "I've had Diamond's pinwheels. They are good," he observed, changing the subject.

Trey noticed his father's small smile didn't fit with the disappointed expression in his eyes. Preston pulled on the loose skin covering his Adam's apple as if any other words he wanted to speak might be logjammed in that area.

Junior intercepted the awkward silence that slipped into the spaces between them. "Who knows a good joke? I need to laugh."

Reverend Leroy rested his cigar across the rim of his third soda and started, "I have one. St. Peter, the archangel Gabriel, and Bob Marley were sitting—"

"No!" the others said in chorus.

Scott apologized for the group. "Sorry Pastor, but you are the worst joke teller in gospel history. I've been wanting to tell you that for two years. You are blessed and highly favored, but that is not one of your gifts." The good reverend accepted the truth in that assessment, laughed, and waved his cocktail napkin in mock surrender.

Trey announced, "I don't know any jokes, but me and my boys play a game called Smash or Pass. It's pretty fun if y'all wanna try it."

"Let's do it. How do you play?" Junior said, rubbing his hands along the arms of the chair. "Pee, we need to look into chairs like this for the clubs. They're pretty comfortable." Preston's eyes narrowed.

Trey rushed ahead, a tight end blocking for family peace. "I'll name a famous woman and you have to decide if you would smash or pass."

He noticed that his favorite minister uncrossed his ankles and drew his burgundy leather loafers closer to his chair. Trey looked from his spiritual mentor's feet on the ebony wood floor to his equally dark face and raised one eyebrow in question. Reverend Leroy shrugged like Pontius Pilate, as if to say he washed his hands of their sins, but he wouldn't stop them. Trey swiveled his strong jawline back to their companions. Junior wet his lips and flicked his cigar at Trey to continue.

"So depending on your answer, I may ask why." His pupils moved to the right and fixed in that position, body language his father likely recognized from years of helping his son with homework. Trey's mouth formed a pinched circle and he snapped his fingers. "Okay, here we go," he said with excitement. "Taylor Swift."

"Smash," Junior said without hesitation.

"Why?" Trey asked. "I'd pass and I'm gonna tell you why."

"She's attractive," Junior insisted. "I could make a mint off her at the club if she could dance."

"She can sing, but she's not a dancer like Ciara or JLo," Trey replied.

"She's a freaking rat!" Scott joked. "If you ever break up with her, she'll write a song about you!"

"Even I know that's true," Preston said. "I'd pass." He extended his fist to his son for a pound of solidarity.

Trey threw out another name. "Tyra Banks, today. Not the height of her supermodel fame Tyra."

Junior scratched the five o'clock shadow on his cheek. "Hmmm, I'm gone hit that back then and now. She's still sexy, but obviously she's not as bad and bourgie as she was when she first came out."

"That's why I said now," Trey explained. "Yeah, me too, 'cause she's bad either way."

"We know you like 'em seasoned," Scott spoke up. Everyone looked at him in surprise before exploding with laughter. He usually abstained from their locker room talk.

"And you like 'em young enough to be your daughter!" Trey hit back, referencing the twenty-two-year age difference between Scott and his sister.

"I didn't hear any complaints last night," Scott shot back. His nostrils flared a warning to anyone thinking about piling on.

Trey and Scott trading barbs was another new thing. Scott had always been laid back and good-humored. Trey added another entry to his list of stranger things and changed the subject. The memories of Tyra softened his voice. "She was my first forever crush. I think I have about six forever crushes that I'll always love but, *ooo wee*, when she showed up on the cover of that Victoria's Secret catalog."

"Oh boy!" Junior agreed.

"Woo hoo hoo! The swimsuit issues! Remember, that Fantasy bra in 1997?" Preston offered, pumping his fists. Reverend Leroy chomped on a cube of ice, rolling his eyes around the room like he would prefer this discussion not take place in front of people outside their close-knit circle.

"'97 and 2004!" Trey added. "If real angels look like that, I damn 'sho wanna go to heaven like LaQuinesha's pig!" Trey stomped his feet on the floor as his companions doubled over in merriment, including Reverend Leroy who couldn't help laughing at that joke. "One more," he said after a few minutes. "This is an easy one. Zoey Z."

Junior shook his head side to side adamantly. "The Z girls? Unh huh, none of them sisters do it for me. Actually, I think that one is racist. I can't think of her name. She doesn't even wear black shoes." He paused, picturing the infamous quadruplets of reality television fame. Hmmm, I just couldn't though, because I know what they looked like before the filters and photoshop. Not that I don't watch that sex tape they made before they hit the big time. They got mad skills in the bedroom but, other than that, they are regular. Plus, every athlete they lure into their web gets screwed up."

"True," Preston said, "They've sent more brothers to rehab than Dr. Phil, but I'd try, man. You know every guy has had that low moment where he thinks— 'Would I?' Or even just looking something up online. You see a chick in some movie and start Googling her out of curiosity. And it's like, you know, maybe if she was wearing lingerie. Mmmm, you know."

Reverend Leroy silently studied Preston as if he were researching his next sermon on immorality. He stuffed a handful of mixed nuts into his mouth and chewed hard.

Junior puffed on his cigar, thinking out loud. "Plus, I heard she's a hermaphrodite and...." His voice trailed off.

Reverend Leroy put his hand over his eyes and groaned. "Father, forgive them." He threw his hands up in a gesture of surrender. "Y'all are my boys, but this is so out of order. I thought we were going to have a cigar, eat, and go hit golf balls. I'm not trying to get run out of my church. You do realize what you're saying is sexist?"

"We do." Preston poured a few drops from his glass to the floor. "Let the record show Reverend Leroy has condemned our lewd behavior even though he was the biggest player on the block in high school." He bared his lips in a Cheshire cat grin. "Don't think I forgot about LaQuinesha's sister!"

Now, looking more like Leroy than a reverend, he scooted lower in his seat, spreading his massive legs in the process. He pulled his glasses down the bridge of his nose, using his hand to partially block the small smile on his dark lips.

Trey felt great. He had pulled off a spiritual coup. The guys were getting along, and his father seemed almost happy for a man who had been grumpy so long no one could remember him being happy. "Last one. Rihanna."

"There's another one?" Leroy blurted.

"Yes!" voted Preston.

"Yes!" added Scott.

"Hell to the Yes!" Junior agreed.

Trey chimed in last. "That's all in favor. Ha ha. For me, I like thick Rihanna, better than skinny Rihanna though."

"Me, too," Scott said enthusiastically, scooting to the edge of his chair to reach for another meatball. His face fell when he noticed the look his father-in-law gave him

Preston looked angry. "You have the perfect wife at home. Last I heard, you need to focus on her."

"Get off his back, Pee," said Junior. "This ain't real. Besides, who are you to talk about somebody having the perfect woman at home? You married that second wife to get over Faith, then divorced her to get Faith back!"

Trey looked confused. "What? Is that why you divorced Gina? Nobody tells me anything." He forced himself not to pout, but he added a notch to his belt of resentments and felt more comfortable about his own secrets.

A waiter bearing a tray of drinks walked near the group and paused a few feet away. Junior, Scott, and Preston were in an intense disagreement about the merits of Faith and Sloane. Being a hothead tipsy on liquor, Junior stood up, waving his arms to make his point about the wonders of Faith. Preston stood to his full height a few inches taller than his brother, raising his voice to say Faith was "a less than okay mother!" When Scott heard Preston derisively reference him as an example of someone who was "henpecked," he joined the fray insisting. "The only thing whipped in here is about to be you, Preston!"

Trey stepped in the middle. "Stop it!" he hissed. "Dad, Uncle Junior, y'all chill. Security is coming. What is wrong with y'all? We're the only Black people in here." He folded his arms above his red face. "Is this who we are? C'mon guys." In this role reversal, he felt cheated. The men in his life were supposed to be paving a way for him. They were too busy living in the past to show him the future.

He growled at his father, "Quit embarrassing me. I came here trying to get your ear. I don't know why you're ghosting me, but I need that money back. Right now!" He snarled his demand. My lady found out I took it and she's mad as hell."

"You took money from your son, too?" Junior asked incredulous. "You probably owe er'body you know. You disappear with no excuses and have tantrums like a little bitch. What the hell is wrong with you?"

"It's none of your damn business what I do or when I do it, Junior. You don't own me."

"For the last time, sit your asses down and stop acting 'hood," Trey said, physically pressing his father and uncle toward their chairs.

Reverend weighed in. "We are men of God, men of standard. This behavior is not acceptable and I've had enough."

The server moved between Junior and Scott, lowered the tray, and placed the drinks on the table. "Compliments of the gentleman at the bar," he said, and walked away as if nothing unusual was occurring.

Five pairs of eyes turned in the direction of the bar. As it turned out, they were not the only Black people in the place. Raymond was walking toward them, wearing all black from collar to cuff, looking more like a deacon than Deacon Henry.

By his side, wearing equally grim attire, was Sloane's tanned but white attorney, J.D. Person. He appeared amused by the spectacle. Their body language had telegraphed the dispute he couldn't possibly have overheard over the loud music and general din. The pair came within a few feet of the group and stopped.

J.D. spoke first. "If Sloane's case goes to court, you just gave me a new defense, Preston. 'Like father like daughter' syndrome. It's not as catchy as affluenza, but I think it could go viral." He grinned and glanced at his companion, Raymond Hart. "Remind me to trademark that slogan." He extracted a business card from his coat pocket and pointed it toward Trey. "Son, why don't you take this now? If you're anything like the rest of your posse, you'll need me sooner or later."

Raymond glared at them, showing his dislike for them was as deep and wide as theirs was for him.

The part of Trey that wasn't shamefaced wanted to swing on J.D. until the man was unconscious. He assumed J.D. was alluding to the time his father jacked him up on a public highway for being disrespectful. Unfortunately, a state trooper was involved in the fray. That was the problem with a small community and a prominent mother. Every minor incident took on major repercussions.

J.D. was right, though. Sloane was a hothead. He blamed his father for that, but, like Junior, he blamed Raymond for everything else that derailed his family.

"What are you doing with this guy?" Junior asked Raymond, ignoring J.D. He wrapped his calloused palm around Preston's arm and pulled. He and Reverend Leroy were literally laying hands on Preston to prevent him from beating the Anglo-Saxon off J.D.

Raymond shrugged. "We are conducting business like civilized people. You know, people like Faith." Trey thought he saw steam come out of his father's nose.

J.D. was staring at Junior. "I know you. You were my water boy for a few years. Right?" It was a rhetorical question lobbed to blow up every man still standing.

Preston snarled. "Get that condescension out of your voice when you speak to my brother."

"Oh, I can't buy him like I bought you, Judas?" J.D. laughed. "You caused your ex-wife to lose that election, not me. She's doing Internet radio now, I hear. That's a helluva demotion. You screwed up her career royally, my man, and from the looks of those bags under your eyes, you're still crying yourself to sleep every night."

Trey watched Raymond look down and straighten his tie. The cockiness in his bobble head had dissipated. His expression said he didn't want to play this game anymore, but he already had a jersey with his name on it. He touched J.D.'s arm lightly, signaling they should leave. J.D. threw an elbow toward Raymond, stopping short of hitting him, but making it clear he would leave when he was ready.

Junior spoke calmly, "J.D., I delivered water to your firm but I was never your *boy*. Preston and I own a successful business -- but something tells me you already knew that since *your* three sons are regular customers."

J.D.'s mouth was a tight line as he stroked his double chins. His soulless eyes moved to a new target. "Reverend Carson, I'm surprised to see you cavorting with this kind."

Reverend Leroy responded, "Funny, the Pharisees said the same thing to Jesus."

Looking smug, J.D. turned to Raymond. "Let's go."

"Massah, him say move, Kunta," Preston mocked Raymond, pointing toward the main entrance. "Keep talking and I'm gonna give your mama a reason to wear black."

"Don't confuse me with your son. You don't scare me." Raymond squared his shoulders and glared at Preston. "Why don't you become a good example for a change and thank me for the drinks? Your *ex*-wife always expresses her gratitude." He accented the ex in ex-wife. "Speaking of Faith, I discovered that cocktail during our trip to New Orleans last week."

He paused long enough for his comment to register. Spinning on his heels, he led J.D. away.

Trey couldn't wrap his head around what just happened. He looked at the faces of his companions.

Scott spoke first. "I am done with all of this." Trey was surprised to see him directing his dark eyes and frown toward Preston and Junior instead of the retreating forms of Raymond and company.

Trey was the first to respond "What are you talking about Scott? We didn't start anything. They came over here."

He couldn't have been more surprised when Scott removed 3 twenty-dollar bills from his wallet, dropped them on the table and left without saying another word.

CHAPTER 18

"Ladies, it's half past the hour. I say we get started," May Bell instructed the Counsel.

"How do we start without Sloane?" Diamond asked. "Where is she, anyway?" She moved beside Faith, who stood with her back to their small huddle near the door.

Everyone looked to Faith for an explanation of Sloane's whereabouts. She heard them but she was so engrossed in her phone she hesitated several seconds before responding. She was pinching, zooming, and swiping so intently the entire group was drawn to her side by curiosity. Caught red-handed, she turned the phone to let them see a man's profile.

Gina, of all people, said, "Gurlll, keep swiping. I went out with him. You definitely do not want none of that." She took a cautious sip from her insulated cup. Her countenance conveyed the leftover exasperation of a night she'd rather forget. The familiar expression and tone made everyone but Faith giggle in solidarity.

Faith's cheeks burned with embarrassment. She'd been caught online man-hunting on church grounds. Her energy would be better spent laser-focused on her daughter's unexpected absence. If Sloane broke one condition of the terms of her probation, or that art teacher didn't recover his health, there would be nothing Faith could do to help her. The district attorney had a go-straight-to-jail hard-on for this case. He loved scandals involving high profile lawbreakers. "Uhmmm, I...," A sheepish smile puffed up her blushing cheeks.

Diamond read Faith's thoughts out loud. "We get it. You saw Raymond in New Orleans with his shorty and now you're in your feelings."

Faith gave her a 'shut up' look.

Diamond kept talking. "Speaking of, did you ever find out what's up with all the hush-hush trips to Ulysses?"

Faith's mouth fell open.

"Oh, my bad. Looks like I'm the only one who knew he has been coming here unannounced."

As only a best friend can, DK chimed in. "I knew. She tells me everything. She also told me about him and Big Booty and the poem."

Diamond made a clucking sound and appeared unimpressed by DK's report. "I saw pics from their bae-cation in Mexico on the Gram," admitted Diamond. "I love his girl's name, Eden. Isn't that unique? It's like a classy name for a stripper."

May Bell and Faith's eyes met in a mental exchange of how they felt about classy stripper names.

Rolling like a bowling ball headed straight for a pin named Faith, Diamond's unsolicited evaluation continued. "She is book and street smart. Certified bourgie!"

Faith couldn't take any more. "Spare me. I don't want to hear about him or her." Her eyes grew teary. "She is incredible. He deserves her. I guess I didn't deserve him." She groaned softly. Diamond put her hand on Faith's shoulder and squeezed. "I have completed twenty or thirty bible studies on righteousness this year, but I keep messing up. I feel like two polar opposite women are at war in my body." Faith touched her cheek to Diamond's hand and said, "That's why I'm on this app trying to get that man off my mind."

DK quipped, "The only way to get over an old flame is to get under a new one. Am I right, ladies?!" Faith puckered her lips. She was pretty sure she knew the name of DK's flame.

"Are you on Snatch.com?" May Bell asked, broadening the sensitive topic. Every eyebrow in the room went up. "I know what's up," she said matter of factly. "Pastor and I have done a lot of pre-marriage counseling over the years. We start by asking how they met; what attracted them to their significant other." She put her hand on her full sized hip. "You'd be surprised how many folks at this church met their current spouse on that site. Sometimes it doesn't work out, but you can't let fear of failure stop you from trying again. Your fairy tale ending may be one swipe away."

"Not all fairy tales have a happy ending," Gina spoke up, but her voice was soft like elevator music. Seeing the sympathetic smiles cast her way, she shook her head side to side. "Not me. What's past is past. Take the story of Hansel and Gretel. That wasn't a happy ending for the witch. Those bad kids were abandoned in the woods by their wicked stepmother. The witch takes them in, shelters them, and feeds them. In return, they push her into an oven and kill her! That's happened to a lot of sistahs. Feel me?"

That caught them off guard. Everyone howled. Gina's novel interpretation of the classic story surprised them. They were glad she finally swam into the deep end of their comradery after remaining relatively silent during the previous meetings.

"Let me see your phone," Diamond said. "Hashtag okay, IthinklikeaMillenial. Online dating is something I know a lot about since me, my two adult daughters, and most of my girlfriends are single. All we talk about is men and the games they play." She playfully bumped her hip against Faith's hip. "While we wait for Ms. Thang, we are going to find you the perfect Two tonight."

Faith was surprised. *Diamond listened to my podcast on the levels of intimacy? I would've lost that bet. She's the least romantic woman I know.* "A two? What's a two?" That wasn't in her podcast and she really wanted her phone back. If Diamond got into her photos, they would give her such a hard time. She downloaded enough photos of Raymond to fill the Louvre.

"That's who you settle for when your One is unavailable. You take the L, the loss. Call it God's will, and fall forward," Diamond explained. "I was with you from day one when you hired Raymond to work in the Mayor's office, Faith. The chemistry between you and him was instant, but you kept it professional."

Faith put her hand on her throat shielding those critical arteries; the main supply of oxygen-rich blood to her frazzled brain.

"Since we doing grown folks work, I can go ahead and say we all know you would not have had an affair with

Raymond if Preston wasn't looking for relevance in the arms of another woman while he was still married to you." Diamond glanced at Gina, the unspecified other woman, and said, "No offense."

Gina's smile was dry. "None taken. It's water under the bridge."

Faith had a flashback to Preston using that expression. The parts to her whole disembodied. The arms and legs beneath her linen jumpsuit posed in a practice manner. Her lips moved of their own accord. "Preston and I were divorced when I got with Raymond."

May Bell cleared her throat. "We're in the Lord's House, Faith. This is a truth zone. Remember, we're not brand new to your story."

Faith amended her statement. "We were emotionally separated. And Preston--" she looked at Gina and remembered May Bell's admonishment to forgive completely, not just with her words. "Preston was ready to move on, and so was I."

"Squirrel! Squirrel! Ladies, can we get back to helping her find a new man?" DK joked.

Diamond turned the phone's screen toward Faith, "What about this one? He looks nice. He water skis and there's a nice photo of him with his mother and kids." She rotated the screen vertically and the family photo filled the screen. Everyone stared at the male specimen. "By the way, Faith, I made a few updates to your bio and deleted that photo of you gardening so you don't seem so boring."

Faith chuckled and tucked a strand of hair behind her ear. "Thank you. I think." She began to reconsider her candor. She didn't want to be the center of attention at what was supposed to be her daughter's support group meeting.

Still, if they could help a sistah out.... "So historically, every guy I've dated who had a family photo on his profile had major issues with his family. He's estranged from his kids or he doesn't speak to his mother. If a guy can't play nice with his DNA, I question his ability to bond with anyone."

Diamond disagreed, despite a mouth full of oatmeal raisin cookie. "You over-analyze things, Faith. Unlike you and me, some people had horrible parents. That's why they don't talk to them. And, I won't speak for you, but my kids are ungrateful as hell. Six months ago, I installed a complete media room in my oldest daughter's garage for free. I mean the 'Dead Presidents" package that runs five figures wholesale. Acoustic panels, 7.2 surround sound with two subwoofers, leather power recline seating. The best of the best. And guess how many times she has invited me over to watch a movie?" She made a circle with her thumb and pointer finger. "Nunya. She only shows up at my house if I invite her over and I assure her there will be food served. Otherwise, I don't see her."

"Your pinwheels are good, though," Faith said, realizing she could really use a cookie, but she stopped herself as her hand reached toward the tray. DK had brought them. She said she baked them herself and she was a classically terrible baker. "Seriously, I get what you're saying. Being the parent of a young child is hard physically, and being the parent of an adult is like being in the world's longest soccer game. But Diamond, I'm pretty sure you wouldn't post a photo of you and your daughter, Sapphire, on a dating app to get a man's attention."

Diamond shrugged as if maybe she would, and a chorus of giggles followed. "I'm not trying to be a know it all. I don't know doo doo about dating, or we wouldn't be having this conversation. What I do know -- from way too much experience -- are single, middle-aged man games. Profile photos with family members or animals they've killed are red flags for me. I pass."

"Okay, what about this one?" DK grabbed the phone from away from Diamond.

Uh oh, Faith thought reading Diamond's face. She was on number two in a countdown at the A.N.G.R.Y. Space Center.

May Bell made a clucking sound. "Ladies." That was all she had to say to take the wind out of Diamond's throat. Diamond rocked back and forth on her Timberlands and shoved her hands in her pants' pockets.

Oblivious of the near-death experience she'd narrowly avoided, DK said, "Look y'all. He's stuntin' in that suit. He has a good barber. Look at that line around his edges. He's cute, too." She scrolled more as the ladies moved closer for a better view. "Here's what looks to be a recent photo of him in front of a church."

May Bell's crimson tinted nails touched DK's wrists and pulled the phone closer to her face. "Oh yes, that's Beth Israel Jerusalem Center in Dallas. I know Cantor Schwartz well, and I think Pastor has Rabbi Posner's mobile number. We can ask about this fella if you like." She moved in close. "His screen name is @HoneyBooBoo? Interesting. Diamond, take a photo of him with your phone and send it to me. They don't allow screenshots.

DK looked skeptical. "Y'all sure we wanna go that route?"

When did this become a we *thing?* Faith asked herself as she popped a cool mint between her lips. It made her mouth water like Raymond's cologne. Everything everywhere reminded her of Raymond. She'd been practicing NOT saying his name out loud since the fiasco with the Tiger King. In a way, she was glad she was with her friends being sad, rather than home alone spiritually dissecting herself.

"From what I know, Preston's overly zealous commitment to this very church was the 'other woman' when he and Faith were married. I mean before he started dating her." DK singled out Gina with her eyes. "No offense but he did meet you here. Correct?"

"Can we leave me out of this, please?" Gina asked, sounding frustrated. "Real talk. Preston was here more than he was at home. He told me as much. So can we agree I didn't break up their marriage?" The silence that ensued was not an agreement, though Gina nodded, seeming to think it was.

Ever the diplomat, Faith said, firmly. "Gina has a point. My marriage was on life support for years before it finally died." She looked at the somewhat handsome man wearing a kippah. "Isn't it strange that he's not on a Jewish online dating site, May Bell? I have not seen an Orthodox Jewish man on Snatch, B-Harmony, or Plenty of Sharks."

May Bell shrugged. "Don't get me to lying. Honestly, I know more about Torah law than Jewish dating etiquette.

Put a pin on him and I'll circle back after I do some research."

"We don't need a pin," Diamond said. I'ma vote no for Faith. Y'all know her workaholic butt is not going to the synagogue on Saturday." She put her hand on Faith's leg and squeezed it.

Faith tried not to laugh, but she had to.

Diamond twirled the backing on one of her three-carat solitaire studs. "I haven't dated a Jewish guy, but them southern Baptist boys at my church all have the same script. After about a month, they lose all that religion and start the sweet talkin'." She made her voice deeper and licked her upper lip. "So Baby, you know I love the Lord 'cause I grew up in the church. I'm a good man and I try to follow seven or eight of His commandments, but a man has needs, you know. Baby, straight up, it's not a sin if we live together in your house, drive your nice car, and eat your food. God made me this way. He understands."

The Counsel went bananas. No one could stop laughing at Diamond's dead-on impression of the typical dead beat.

Faith turned her thumbs down to a dozen more men before May Bell spoke. "My sisters in Christ, this is fun, but the spirit is telling me we should use this time for personal growth. I think sometimes we need reminders that no one is perfect, and every sweet relationship has its share of bitter."

She glanced at the wall clock. "Let's take our seats."

As they complied, she instructed them further. "While we wait for Sloane, let's try an exercise from our pre-marriage counseling manual. Everyone give five words that describe the most challenging part of being in your current relationship. Be totally honest. I'll give you a few minutes to think."

Relieved by the lowered bar for sharing, the Counsel agreed with the exercise. The mood shifted and the room seemed to brighten when May Bell smiled, making it clear she was not mad at them for playing the dating game.

Faith took the allotted time to send another urgent text to Sloane.

Where are you? Are you okay? We're waiting.

(Sloane)...

"Time's up. I'll start," May Bell announced. "Parenting. Unequal sex drives. Compromise."

"That went left real quick," DK joked. "You've excited my inner English major. This is similar to a cinquain, only we're using five words instead of five stanzas." DK tapped her fingers on the arm of the chair. "Here we go. My five words. Cooking. Finding me time. Sharing."

Faith felt some kind of way. She was happy for DK but perturbed that her friend had not mentioned one word, let alone five, about being in a relationship. She jumped in. "Toilet seats. Budgets. Picking movies." Every chin bobbed with commonality as the distinct sound of the side door chime drifted down the hall and Faith breathed a sigh of relief.

"I bet that's Sloane," Diamond said, turning in the direction of the door. She turned back to the group and asked, "May Bell, can we repeat what someone else said?" Without hesitation, everyone denied her request. "Fine," she huffed. "My five words are communication, planning vacations, and ex-wife."

"I guess that leaves me," Gina said, rubbing lotion on her hands. The floral scent filled the room. "Hmmm, I'm speaking from history, but I'll say housecleaning, trust, respect, appreciation, and fault-finding."

The doorknob turned and a full minute passed before it opened. All eyes were on Sloane who entered looking as if she'd been wrestling with a demon. Her hair was tangled, mascara streaked sideways, one eyelash missing, and a trail of tears streaked across each unnaturally red cheek. She clutched a key fob in one hand and a crumpled tissue in the other.

The absence of Sloane's ever-present cell phone and extravagant bag of the day were more disturbing to Faith than her disheveled appearance. The girl never left home without them. Was she mugged? Or was this a ridiculous excuse for being late?

They stared at her, frozen in shock as she made her way to the empty seat between DK and May Bell.

"Honey, what happened? Are you okay?" Faith's voice crossed the circle on waves of compassion.

"I'm fine. I'm fine," Sloane insisted. Faith motioned for DK to change seats with her so she could be closer to Sloane.

When Faith put her arm around Sloane's shoulder, she collapsed into her mother's embrace, gulping for air. The others started rising from their chairs, but Faith waved them off. She patted Sloane's back as she gulped tears.

May Bell held her hand. "I think we should reschedule. She's too upset. Faith, if you want to take her into my office and let her rest on the couch for a bit, I'll wait with you."

Sloane sat up shaking her head adamantly. "No, no, Aunty. I don't want to reschedule. I want to finish. I need for one thing in my day to go as planned." With strength no one in the room knew she possessed, she pulled herself together. They watched her back straighten, her eyes clear, mother eagles prepared to swoop in if her wings were not strong enough to carry her through the crosswinds.

Faith noticed Gina and May Bell clasp their hands, bow their hands, and began praying. She didn't know what to do or quite how to help her daughter. *What the hell happened?*

Sloane sniffed and turned toward May Bell. "What did I miss, Aunty?"

May Bell stopped praying. This time she looked to Faith for direction. Faith nodded and scooted her chair closer to her daughter.

"I asked everyone to state five words that describe the most challenging part of being in their current relationship. Mine were parenting. Unequal sex drives. Compromise."

"You don't have to participate if you don't want to, Sloane," DK said. "Or if you have something else you want to talk about, let us know."

Yes, that's right, the other ladies murmured. Faith made a heart sign with her hands to show her love for their love.

"I can do it," Sloane declared in a slightly stronger voice than before. She paused. No one moved. "I have five words." Her eyes filled with tears. "My husband wants a divorce."

So many questions. "What?" "Scott?" "Was he serious?" "Where's Ever?" "Did you suggest counseling?" "Is there someone else?"

She raised her hands. "I don't know. I don't know. He said something about me being a bad wife and mother. I can't believe this. I've given my life to that man. I gave up a promising career to be a stay-at-home mother."

Faith rubbed her daughter's back and avoided the looks of skepticism coming her way. It was a well-known fact that Sloane had never been anyone's employee. She went to college for a Mrs. degree, married Scott when she became pregnant, and completed the requirements for her Bachelor's degree only because her parents insisted she needed something to fall back on—should a day like this ever happen.

Faith made soothing sounds. "Honey, start from the beginning. What exactly happened today?"

Sloane looked bewildered, an expression her face had never known. Her eyebrows rose and froze in that position. Her upper lip peeled away from her teeth leaving her lower lip to do all the work as she babbled almost incoherently. "Well, before he was mad, because I was late picking up Ever from that birthday party, but his friend's mom text me that she'd bring him...and he found out I haven't been giving mom the rent money every month."

She dug her fingernails into her thighs, gulping for air. "And he said my bail bondsman came to the house. He said the transdermal thingy on the ankle monitor detected alcohol in my blood. What I'm trying to say is, I had a cocktail with Uncle Junior."

When Faith's eyes bugged, she hastily added, "And Dad. Dad was there at H.G. Sply's." Filled with remorse, she dropped her head onto her lap.

Faith couldn't hold back on the judgment. "You were in *Dallas*? *Dallas County*? Drinking with your *father*?" Faith hesitated as she processed that news.

The others looked at each other and shifted in their seats.

"Sloane, you are not supposed to drink or go outside the boundaries of Collin County!" Faith shouted. "Do you want to go to prison? How many times do I have to say it? You. Are. On. Probation. That means no drinking. Limited travel. Community service. And these sessions. What is hard to understand? All you had to do was stay out of trouble and they would have dismissed the case at the end of your probation." Torn between wrath and her daughter's woe, she started trembling from head to toe.

Sloane's eyes filled with new tears. "Mother, I'm sorry. Please. I get it." Her arms flailed. "I get it. I've ruined everything. I'm might go to jail and it doesn't even matter, because.... "

Anguish gushed though her pores, wetting everyone's eyes.

"Scott took Ever. He took my *son*."

The Counsel was quiet. A couple of the ladies consoled Faith.

"He cannot have my son and I will not give him a divorce!" Sloane protested, reversing course. "I'm not that girl. I will not be a single mother."

"Which girl are you?" May Bell said, sounding irritated. She put her finger beneath Sloane's chin and lifted her head until they were eye to eye. "If statistics are the only reason you have for wanting your marriage to survive, then you are indeed that girl, young lady. If you were as concerned about your marriage as you are about your image, we could have a real conversation this evening."

"Preach, First Lady!" Diamond said.

May Bell went on, reading Sloane like the cover of a magazine. "I don't know Scott as well as I know you, but I feel confident in saying you have taken your covenant relationship for granted. There is more to marriage than the bling and an escort." She paused to reel herself in. "Let me give you some crimson table talk. If you want your marriage to work, you need to work on it. More specifically, you need to work on *you*. Your marriage will be a better union when you become a better person."

Sloane nodded as if listening to words of wisdom for quite possibly the first time in her adult life.

"And don't think for a minute, I'm saying Scott -- or any man -- is perfect," May Bell continued.

"I know that's right," Gina cosigned.

"Leroy and I have been together over thirty-five years. We've spoken openly and candidly about our struggles to make two become one but, unlike Scott, you rarely come to church," she said, in a rare display of tough love. "Here's what you missed. For a marriage to survive, you must resiliently live out the words of Phillipians 2:3." She stopped and looked around the circle. "Paul wrote, 'Do nothing out of selfish ambition or empty pride, but in humility consider others more important than yourself.' Selflessness is not a natural product of human flesh. In fact, and this is not something we've shared widely, at our lowest point, we both had divorce lawyers."

She paused and looked at the sober faces. "I'm not blaming him completely or taking all the credit for our difficulties. The faults lie between us."

Sloane flinched at those words. She raised her hand. "Aunty, I feel pain, necessary pain. I understand I have a starring role in this failure. I was all about brands. Brands come and go. Quality matters more." She put her arm on Faith's arm. "And Mother, I owe you an apology. All these years I've blamed you for the divorce. I thought you didn't give dad enough attention so that's why y'all got divorced." They both looked at Gina who simply sighed. "I understand nothing is that simple. I was wrong." Faith accepted the apology with a kiss to her daughter's tear drenched cheek.

That epiphany was everything to Faith. She couldn't show it but she did the Stanky Leg dance in her mind.

Behind the puffy lids, Sloane's eyes filled with curiosity. "Aunty, how did you fix your marriage? Tell me what to do."

"We've had a lot of Christian counseling. We prayed and cried daily and every Wednesday and Sunday, we showed up at this church and ministered with a smile on our faces. Somehow, in giving as best we could, we received more than we deserved. What I'm saying is faking it when you don't feel like it, is an important part of making love a habit. It's not a lie to practice being a good person. Living your truth while destroying everyone around you is the lie the world is peddling, but we are not of this world."

Sloane said thoughtfully, "'Do not conform to the pattern of this world but be transformed by the renewing of your mind. Then you will be able to test and approve what God's will is—his good, pleasing, and perfect will.'"

Faith's mouth fell open. She turned to DK, "Am I going crazy? Did she just quote the twelfth chapter of Romans?"

"I don't know about the chapter, but those words are from Paul's epistle to the Romans."

Sloane stammered her reply, "Aunty May Bell, I'm listening. I confess, I haven't been listening before, but I'm soaking it in. I had a wake-up call today and I realize I need to change or I'll lose everything."

Gina paused from typing on her phone. "This is good, May Bell. I'm writing it down for all of us to have. What was that line again? Living your truth while destroying everyone around you—"

"Is the lie the world is peddling," Sloane supplied.

Faith's glasses fogged up. The room felt like a sauna to her. She fanned herself with her head. Diamond brought her a cup of water from the refreshment table. She had another cookie for herself.

"I have a final word for you," May Bell announced. "I want to stop talking, but the spirit is urging me to speak.

Sloane, go back into this fight knowing every day brings a new battle. For example, I knew I was marrying a man of God, but I never expected all of this."

She gestured around the room. "A mega-church pastor's wife? Twenty-four seven calls for prayers, financial assistance, hospital visits, city leaders wanting us here and thereafter every community crisis, twenty-thousand members with opinions about where we live and what kind of car I drive. It's always something. E-ve-ry day! There's unholy God Groupies, so called Christian women doing unspeakable things in the house of God. I wish I could show y'all video of the women of all ages in service, sitting with their legs spread wide, no panties, Brazilians shining like butter, holding up a bible with their phone number taped to it!"

Faith noticed May Bell's toes were curled in her sandals.

"That's why I say both of you must be committed and intentional. I'll never forget, one demoness was in the baptismal pool after hours with no clothes on. She had the gall to tell my Leroy Earl she needed a man like him and..." her volume dropped and she glared at Gina in a somewhat un-First Lady-like manner.

Gina dropped her eyes and mumbled, "No offense taken, May Bell. That was ten years ago. I'm not that woman anymore. I have to live with the mistakes I made, but I refuse to be confined by them."

Faith's head snap up. She gave Gina a positive side eye. *That's the best lesson I've learned in all these sessions,* she thought. *It's time to break these chains I've placed on myself. I deserve that greener grass on the other side.*

CHAPTER 19

Faith insisted Sloane leave her car at the church. When they pulled up to the dark, empty house, Sloane's resolve seemed to melt from her eyes, one gloomy drip at a time. Faith sighed and got out of the car. She paused when she realized her daughter was not following in her footsteps. She never had, and Faith realized she never would -- but maybe that would turn out to be a good thing.

She started to open the passenger door, but Sloane said, "I need a moment, please."

Faith walked into the kitchen and scanned the room. Hurriedly, she removed all signs of Ever and Scott. She put Ever's red cup in the dishwasher and placed Scott's gluten-free crackers in the pantry. She felt slightly frantic upon realizing there wasn't enough time to remove all nine hundred pieces of Ever's art from the double doors of the refrigerator. But might be more painful than their presence? A manual on possible divorces would come in handy right now, she thought. *Look at his toys everywhere. I hope he has his favorite things.* She didn't know what else to do, so she called the smartest person she knew. He didn't answer, so a voicemail would have to suffice. "Raymond, I need your help."

They hadn't spoken since New Orleans. He responded to her texts saying he was in a meeting, on a call, or driving. She gripped the phone tighter and started talking to herself aloud as she walked around the kitchen putting away more signs of Scott and Ever. "There are no signs of him on social media. I don't know if he's ill or behind closed doors doing wild things with his disgracefully nice sidepiece. Why won't he answer?"

The bright glow of the monitor made her aware she never ended the call. His voicemail was recording her talking to herself about him. She shrugged and ended the call.

Ayyy, quit being self-centered. You need to call Preston and fill him in, she thought, and quickly washed down three Advil as she heard Sloane getting out of the car.

Sloane walked past Faith and went into the family room. They ended up on the sectional, side by side, each lost in her thoughts. Sloane started crying and Faith scooted closer to her. She said nothing. As if someone were directing a scene, they silently entwined their fingers and leaned on one another.

They remained that way until Sloane ran out of tears. Faith had a tissue in anticipation. She carefully removed her daughter's remaining fake eyelash and dabbed her face dry. There was no one in any place that she'd rather be available for at that moment and tried to show it in the tenderness of each move she made. Faith moved, placed a square, gold pillow on her lap and encouraged Sloane to lie down.

Sloane looked up for the first time in hours. Faith beamed at her. Her smile was a combination of pride and compassion. She brushed Sloane's hair with her fingers and told her, "I got you. I'm always on your side, even when we don't agree. You'll always be my little girl."

"Mom?"

"Yes, Honey."

"I'm sorry. You had a peaceful life and it's been nothing but chaos since we moved in."

Before Faith could object, she added, "I mean me, Mom. No one has been a problem, but me. I haven't cooked a meal or washed a dish in two years. You hired a housekeeper to clean up behind my family and I don't even work. I've been so selfish. What is wrong with me? I spent the money Scott gave me to pay you rent. I, I, I spent it on clothes and stuff online."

"Shhh, I forgive you. Thank you, Sloane."

Her ankle monitor beeped and Faith braced herself.

"I need to recharge it," Sloane said calmly. "First, I have to say this. I know it's hard to understand, but I can't leave Scott. Not that it doesn't cross my mind daily." She removed her hand from Faith's to adjust the clip on her hair. "But, but…. Mom, I'm not like you guys. What I mean is I hope to become the type of couple and parents you and Dad were for us. Like when things were good, you know. I think that's possible."

"Of course, it is." Faith assured her. "As we mature and grow through things, we become wiser. We make strategic decisions with our words and actions. At least we should."

"Exactly. You and Dad are different now. You're calmer and kinder. And you are both dating one loser after the next."

"So is your Uncle Junior and he's never been married." Faith interjected.

"C'mon, let's be serious. He owns a jillion strip clubs, drives a Lambo, and lives in a mansion. Why on earth would he get married? You and Dad were the perfect couple for so long. I only wonder what would have happened if you two…." Faith heard a wistful sigh and watched the massive rise and fall of Sloane's chest before she proceeded, "Trust me, Mom, I absolutely am not judging. All I'm saying is what I'm not gone do is take this ring off. Maybe it's all fun and games but, single life looks a hella lot harder than marriage to me."

"No, it wasn't easy. It's not easy now." Faith took a section of Sloane's hair and started braiding it. "Honestly, I want you and Scott to live together happily. That's best for Ever and for you. Let Scott be tonight. They'll be fine and I know he won't go far because school is still in session. Tomorrow morning call him and ask him to sit down with you. Let him talk. Just let him talk. Don't get into anymore back and forth. It's time to listen. If I've learned nothing else, I learned that much."

Faith envisioned herself sitting in a classroom at Life University, revising her ten-million-page dissertation on Listening With Empathy when she realized Sloane was waiting for her to go on. "Commit everything to altering the things you don't like about yourself, not him. You cannot change another person."

"I receive that. I'll make it work. You'll be proud of me."

"I'm always proud of you. And I hope you can find the seed of love that remains. Nourish it, and make it grow strong again. But Sweet Pea--" Sloane giggled at the ancient nickname her mother used. Faith let out a deep sigh. "If you don't love Scott anymore and you're in this marriage to not be me, you will never be happy. That's not enough light for love."

Eventually, Sloane headed to bed leaving Faith lost in thought. She closed her eyes and recited a well-known scripture from the book of Proverbs her mother taught her when she was a young girl. "Do not lean to your own understanding. In all your ways acknowledge him, and he will make straight your paths." She meditated on those words a long time, then her eyes flew open. In the depths of her spirit she made a startling realization. Despite her careful planning, her children's inheritance included things that were not in her will. Things she never intended to pass down.

~   ~   ~

By 4 am, Faith had been on the treadmill at the gym for an hour. Every pore in her body was open and making it rain. If she couldn't sleep, she might as well make her insomnia productive. Her right earbud fell out again and she took that as the signal to stop the relentless pounding of her feet. She lowered the incline and slowed the treadmill for a cool off period.

She liked coming to the gym early. It wasn't crowded, and she wasn't expected to smile and be friendly. She wished she could outrun her thoughts -- but that was a marathon no human could finish.

The treadmill slowed and stopped. Draping a towel over her wet tresses, she sorted her concerns by priority. Raymond should not be at the top of the list, but oh, but he was. And what he reportedly told Preston, according to Junior, seemed so out of character. Why would he taunt her ex-husband? No one ever never *ever* needed to know about New Orleans because at the end of that trip. After all, she had arrived at DFW airport the same way she departed: alone with her baggage. Anything that happened between her departure and arrival was better left unspoken. He said he loved them both but differently. Having experienced a heart being pulled apart like a wishbone, she didn't want to do that to anyone else.

She paused the playlist on her phone and pushed aside the gut-wrenching thoughts to set her priorities in order. *Why am I even thinking about him? I need to focus on my family and my future. Raymond is not part of my future. I need to call Scott and try to convince him not to divorce Sloane. She does love him and Ever and she's changing for the better.*

Her head was all over the place. She couldn't hold one thought if it had a handle on it. She disinfected the handrails on the equipment, pondering motherhood of adults. She realized she hadn't paid much attention to Trey lately. Sloane had always consumed all the air in the room. Trey was laid back. Maybe a bit too much.

What was up with his weird girlfriend?

He rarely brought her around the family and when she came, she didn't engage with anyone. She was a mature and successful art dealer. No way she was shy. Faith didn't trust her and she didn't raise her son to be anyone's toy boy.

Maybe I should invite him to move back in now that Scott's gone. Trey could complete the requirements to become a CPA if he didn't have to work so much, but she couldn't want it for him more than he wanted it for himself. She tossed the wet towel into a hamper. She scanned the ground for the missing earbud. She got on her knees and looked under the treadmill. Nothing but dust there. Giving up, she tucked her phone in her sports bra and went to the women's locker room.

There was a woman going into the shower who had the flattest ass she'd ever seen. Thinking of asses reminded her to call Sloane's lawyer about the latest scene in her daughter's long-running soap opera. Between violating her probation and neglecting Ever, she'd given Scott plenty of ammunition if he did attempt to get full custody of their son. She shook away the thought with such ferocity, one of her earrings dislodged. *No, that is not going to happen. I'll take all means necessary to prevent another divorce in this family.*

She retrieved her earring from the top of her right shoe, grabbed her gym bag, and exited through the unlocked door at the rear of the gym. She'd parked along the wide lane used primarily for deliveries and trash pick up since she discovered it shortly after getting her gym membership. When she parked in front of the gym, she invariably ran into someone who wanted to talk about politics. *I might have overdone it today.* She was feeling the burn in her upper thighs. One leg in the car and one leg out, she dug through her purse. She heard a sound and noticed a man getting out of a dark colored car on the passenger side of her car. She screeched.

"Whoa, I didn't mean to frighten you. It's me."

She couldn't make out his face beneath the dim light, but she knew that voice like the squeak of her bedroom door. "Raymond?" She put her purse on the other seat and got our of the car..

He came closer, reaching for her with a wide smile. They hugged briefly before she pulled back, still not quite believing he was there.

"If I know you as well as I think I do, you were looking for your phone. Correct?"

"Dude! That's uncanny. That's exactly what I was doing."

He touched her t-shirt below her right collarbone. "It's right there."

So many feelings went through her at once. All she could do was giggle. "Seriously, what are you doing here?"

"You summoned me." He took her right hand and lifted it to his chest. A shock passed through her fingers and she flinched. "That surprises me every time it happens," he admitted.

"What are you talking about?"

"The jolt of energy when we touch. It's magical. I know you felt that just now." He kissed the back of her hand. His lips felt like soft velvet on her skin. "I don't think I've ever told you this before, but you're a terrible liar."

"Is that something I need to be good at?" She watched his hand caressing hers to avoid her too honest eyes confessing what was in her heart.

He moved his face closer to hers as a car slowly drove by. "It is if you want me to believe what you said in New Orleans before you left -- and in that rambling voice mail." The car braked, casting a red glow across Raymond's face. Faith turned to look at the car. It was partially blocked by the commercial waste bin on the other side of Raymond's car.

He guided her chin back to his direction. "You called for help. I chartered a plane to be here for you. I'll always come when you call."

She stepped to the side and closed the door. "That was yesterday. Everything is fine now."

"I don't believe you. Talk to me."

Faith swallowed hard and sucked in her cheeks. *Too late. I should've gotten in the car and driven away.*

His piercing gaze made her thoughts slow to a crawl. She dated tall men to avoid this exact situation. At 5'11" Raymond was an inch shorter than her, and she couldn't hide her true feelings beneath her eyelashes.

"Now you have time for me?" she asked. She intended to sound sarcastic, but there was a thread of hurt braided between the syllables. "You've been in and out of Ulysses for weeks, hanging out at the courthouse, and palling around with J.D. without telling me *anything*. We used to talk about everything, but now you're too busy with BB and—"

"What? Who is BB?"

Faith eyes darted from side to side. She smiled sheepishly. "I meant J.D." Raymond's lips were so close she smelled his breath mint and her mouth watered.

"Liar." He sighed. "Faith, I was trying to surprise you, but I forget you have your people everywhere."

She tried to wriggle away. He held fast to her hand. "Let me buy you breakfast. We can walk to the Waffle House a block away. We need to talk."

Not that word, she thought. "Raymond, I'm sweaty and I have a busy day ahead. Can we connect for lunch instead?"

He leaned closer. She prepared herself for a kiss. Instead, he reached around her to the door handle. "Get your purse. Let's go."

She complied telling herself she needed carbs. A sarcastic inner voice chided her. *Is that what we're calling it now?*

"You smell better when you're sweaty than I do after a shower. You know I don't care about a little sweat, and neither do the folks at the Waffle House." He started walking in the direction the car had taken.

She paused. Shrugged. And fell into step beside him.

The visible breath of the new day wouldn't yet appear for an hour as they were seated in a small booth in the brightly lit restaurant. The waitress handed them menus and placed glasses of water on the table.

She placed the long menu next to her water glass and put her finger on what she wanted to order. She looked at him expectantly.

"You have the most beautiful brown eyes," he said.

She smiled a thank you. "You were saying."

Raymond pushed his menu to the edge of the table and leaned forward. "I owe you an explanation. Of what I've been up to."

She tilted her head. "You don't owe me anything but having been convinced I'm a terrible liar, truth is you dodging me the past few weeks was hurtful." That time, he looked away briefly.

"I apologize. We haven't worked out the fine details, but I'm planning to move our company headquarters to this area. I applied for a Texas Enterprise Fund Grant. I told them we're deciding between here and Baton Rouge, but I'd rather be here in the Dallas area."

She lowered her eyes, mentally reviewing the evidence she'd accumulated. "Why were you with J.D. at the Cigar Bar? Trey told me he saw the two of you together." She watched him to see if his body language matched his words. Something was making her uneasy. She had a sense of foreboding she couldn't explain.

He didn't hesitate with his answer. "I retained J.D.'s firm to help me look into local tax incentives and connect with the right decision-makers. I know you don't like him, but he comes from that old, wrinkled, moldy Texas money. And he's connected. That's why you hired him to defend your daughter. Correct?"

"Touche." She felt an expression of admiration dawn on her face. That was a story she could believe. "I should have known you were doing something big. So you're thinking Texas will legalize cannabis at some point and your company will be positioned to transport it across the Bible belt. I love it. You're a genius."

He chuckled. "Always a few moves ahead of the pack aren't you?"

The waiter came to take their order. Faith ordered more food than Raymond.

"You ordered like you've been smoking some cannabis," he chuckled when the waiter walked away. "Did you start your morning with one of those tasty brownies you and Ever enjoy so much?"

"Shut up!" She laughed more loudly than him at the inside joke. "You promised never to bring that up again. And I would never eat one of those before bedtime. They are strictly for unwinding after a long day."

The waiter returned with several plates of link sausages, eggs, and waffles. Faith dived in but clearly excited, Raymond elaborated on his strategic business plan.

"Our early expansion in markets like Colorado, Illinois, and Maine have been good for business. I've plowed the profits into upgrading technology, training programs, and purchasing more top-of-the-line tractors. This is no longer a trucking business, Faith. It's transportation logistics and we are going to be very big, very soon. I mean NYSE big."

The talked and dreamed aloud for a half hour before heading back to their cars. Faith opened her car door and put her purse on the passenger seat. She felt Raymond move close behind her. She pushed him back with her hips and closed the door. She worried about body odor from her work out. She sniffed in the direction of her armpit. It wasn't great, but it wasn't apocalyptic. The two of them had left many wrinkled sheets smelling worse.

He moved close again. She put one hand on his hard chest. "So you're the next J.B. Hunt, huh?" *I have to be strong. We cannot go there again. It's wrong.*

"Something like that," he said. He glanced over the roof of Faith's vehicle in the direction of a car that passed them a few moments earlier.

She started to follow his gaze, but he closed the ten inches between their lips for a kiss. Her arms flew up as if she were going down a steep roller coaster. He wrapped his hands around her waist and pressed her against the car door with the weight of his body. Her brain tried to protest, but the rest of her body voted yes.

His fingers swept her t-shirt above the waistband of her yoga pants. The feeling of his palms on the skin of her back was indescribable. The supernova force between them was stronger than her will. He sucked her tongue so thoroughly the arches returned to her previously flat feet. Her arms went around his neck as she lost her sense of identity. Her nipples rose and orchestrated the frenetic beat of her heart. The orange-hued crown of the sun peeped over the horizon to watch her melt in his arms.

He expertly stopped her slide by wrapping one of her legs around his waist and placing a supportive hand beneath her rear. "I got you," he mumbled into the sensitive cord of her neck. He kissed her cheeks and her head fell back onto the room of her car. He thrust his hips forward and she felt his need searching for the eminent warmth of her silky cocoon. For every action he took, her body instinctively responded in manner that was equal and unopposing. Her hips and legs formed a V when she wrapped her legs around his waist and let her full weight rest on his Stone Mountain. His sigh of satisfaction warmed her ear and caused her to hold on to him tighter.

"I'm your Level One-Ten," he declared, pumping his hips against hers. "I'm your yang. I'm that guy. Tell me you love me."

The struggle inside of her resurfaced. "You don't know me," she gasped. "I'm difficult. I'm demanding. I'm a workaholic. I've self-sabotaged every relationship I've had since my divorce, including ours."

He stopped her. "Those are therapists' words. I disagree. You're not perfect. Neither am I, Faith." He lifted his head and spoke to her as if they were not rehearsing the middle of a porno scene. "I get it. You're driven and intense. You're also creative, caring, and generous to a fault. In all the years I've known you, you have only quit one thing. Don't let that one thing define our future, Baby. I'm your man and I will gladly carry you, emotional baggage and all. You belong with me."

Still staring in her eyes, he drew his finger across her abdomen until it landed below her navel. "This is the scar from the hernia surgery when you were sixteen."

She shuddered and inhaled deeply. He touched the skin behind her earlobe. "This is where you get a rash when you forget to remove your earrings before going to bed."

He drew a line down the valley between her breasts. "You worry that one day I'll notice your right nipple is one inch lower than the left." That made her giggle. "Oddly, you wash your face after your body when you shower, but first when you take a bath." She opened her mouth and he sucked it closed. "I'm not finished."

Her head bobbed when he nibbled that place on her neck that he knew made her brain short circuit every time. "I know there is an entire universe in your head where you spend a lot of the time. I understand that it's a safe, virgin space, but you can't live there and visit earth anymore."

He gently stood her up and backed away a few inches. "The world we make together is where you belong. I promise I'll be available for you emotionally, physically, spiritually, and every other way you deserve."

The love he described was like a rescue helicopter hovering above her island of regrets. She inhaled sharply, a centering breath. The flow of self-sabotaging thoughts resumed. She chose facts over feelings, saying, "You're with someone else. I shouldn't have kept in contact with you all this time. I feel even more guilty about this-whatever this is-since I met Eden.. I told myself we were just friends but you know I still care for you. I'm doing to Eden what Gina did to me. So I'm moving out of town and making a fresh start."

He looked distraught. "What are you talking about?"

"I signed a contract with Grapefruit when I got back from New Orleans. They're making big moves to dominate the podcast market." She caught herself rocking side to side and froze in place. "They promised to make me a household name." Her voice trailed off.

Raymond jerked his head back as if he were in agony. "You told me you turned that down last year."

"I did. They made me a much better offer. Guarantees. Heavy promotion. And a full team to produce the show. All I have to do is talk...and move to L.A." She twisted the band of her Fitbit around to avoid looking at him.

He cupped her chin and forced her to look at him. "That's fine, Faith. We'll make it work if that's what you want to do but we belong together. Eden doesn't mean anything to me. You're too smart, not to know that's the reason we can't stay away from each other."

"Even if she doesn't," she swallowed the embryo of hope that had arisen in her throat, "if she doesn't mean anything special to you. If I did you wouldn't have moved back to New Mexico. I need a fresh start. This deal with Grapefruit is divine order."

After years of being patient with her, he finally blew a fuse. "Are you for real right now? This is insane! Ten years! I tried for ten years before I moved. That's not love to you? Divine order, my foot." He put a fist over his mouth. Her eyes were big and soggy, watching him. "Faith, baby, baby, listen, you're your own boss. You have affiliate income, ads from major sponsors and you told me the merch Daniel put on Shopify is bringing in four figures a month in sales. What will it take to satisfy you?" She lowered her eyes. "I guarantee Grapefruit isn't the answer. Right now, you set your hours and you don't work weekends. That's what you wanted. Isn't it? Control over your career?" His voice trailed off. "Control over everything, I guess."

"Raymond. You have to understand."

"Understand what? Why would give up everything and move away from your family?" He waited for an answer. She felt the angry heat from his body as she bit her lip, fighting back the hurt.

"Answer me? What the hell is wrong with you? You are singlehandedly going to be the death of me, I swear." He started pacing back and forth in front of her. "The reason I worked with you for so long when you were in office was that I admired you. I fell in love with a woman who never quit. Now, all you do is run. You're giving up on everything and running out on us. I can't believe I wasted years of my life chasing you."

She hung her head.

"Here's what else I know," he added, breathing fire. "You think of me every time another man touches you, yet you're so afraid of failing at another marriage that you won't let me love you." Tears fell from his eyes.

She had never seen him cry before. It hurt her to hurt him again and she wanted to deny something on that list, but he'd doused it with truth and set fire to her flaws. She dug her nails into her palms and envisioned their future in flames.

The roar of a car engine erupted her thoughts.

Raymond grabbed her roughly. "Faith!"

Later, she vaguely recalled being flung aside like a rag doll, the distinctive sound of metal collapsing drowned out her shrieks. Dimly, she knew she had rolled across the gravel and landed against a parking bumper. She had struggled to lift her head and watch in stunned silence as some maniac's car sped away from the tangle of her vehicle and the Acura.

One of Raymond's shoes and the remains of a sweet potato pie were by her side. Yards away, she saw Raymond lying on the ground.

Motionless.

She ignored the daggers piercing every limb as she limped in his direction, screaming his name.

CHAPTER 20

A few miles away, the repeated chimes of the front door awakened Sloane. She slipped on her robe and walked to the stair rail above the foyer. "Mom?"

o one responded, she cried out louder, "Mom, is that you?"

"Go back to bed. It's me. I'm only here to get some things for Ever and, before you ask, no, I don't want to talk."

Sloane ran down the stairs two at a time. "Scott, I'm so glad you're here. I've been worried." She spied him with an arm full of Ever's clothes walking toward the front door. She ran in front of him and blocked his exit. He looked more bored than angry. That made her knees tremble. "Scott, I'm sorry. I was wrong to do those things. Please, talk to me."

"Sloane, please move. I have to go." He rolled his tongue around his mouth, reaching under her arm for the doorknob. He pulled his hand back and wagged a finger in her face. "You didn't even tell me Faith is selling this house. I simply cannot trust you anymore."

"Huh?"

"For sale." He spelled the word, S-A-L-E. There's a guy in the yard digging a hole for a huge sign. Why would you keep that from me?"

"Scott, I don't recall Mom saying anything about moving, but I've been in a fog, so I don't know if she did or not." She exhaled an unsteady breath. "Can we put that aside? Please, let me explain."

"I've heard enough of your explanations. You're a spoiled and selfish I want out of this marriage. I've decided whoever thought less of me for having two ex-wives won't change their opinion because I have three. That's it. End of conversation."

A lime-colored pair of jeans fell on the marble floor. They bumped heads when they both bent to retrieve them. "I'm sorry," Sloane apologized.

"Two sorry's in one day? That's more than you apologized in the past five years. I'm glad you learned a new phrase. Now, if you'll excuse me." He turned to take another exit.

Sloane fell to the ground and wrapped her arms around his calves. "Please don't leave me, Big Daddy. I'll do anything. Please, don't go and take my son. You know I love you both. Don't do this," she whimpered into the cuff of his pants leg.

With great effort, Scott removed one leg and dragged Sloane with the other as he walked toward the door. Sloane kept her right arm around his calf and grabbed the banister with her left hand. She closely resembled a washed-up starfish with limbs pointing north, south, east, and west. Scott would have to yank her shoulders out of their sockets before she released her vice grip. "Baby, please! Ten years of marriage must mean something. May I have a minute for each year? That's all I ask."

For those ten years, he'd only showed her kindness and composure, she realized. That's why she wasn't sure how to label the expression on his face at that moment. It was neither of those virtues.

He shook his leg free of her and dropped the clothes on the floor. "What, Sloane? What is there to say? You've demonstrated how you feel about me every day. You're disrespectful, disloyal, dishonest and, and, mean, and hateful and terrible in bed."

Her eyebrows went up. *Terrible in bed?* Yeah, well, she did stop faking orgasms at some point. Come to think of it, she couldn't remember the last time they had sex. Weeks? Months? He'd never believe her, but she had a headache every time. Granted, the pain started when he touched her, but that wasn't her fault. He continued with the long lists of her shortcomings.

Well hell, he's been thinking on this a while.

"Sloane, are you going to answer my question?"

Oh, hell, what did he ask? She never really listened to him in complete sentences. She homed in on keywords like "yes, Dear", "how much", and "I'll take care of it." She was confused by this new man with all these compound sentences and firm opinions. She stared at him blinking slowly. The newfound assertiveness was turning her on a little.

He loosened his tie. "Is this your impression of an owl? Speak! You've got five minutes left. I have a work meeting."

"Where is Ever?"

"Now you care where he is? The one time you picked him up this year, you attacked his art teacher. And, by the way, rumor has it he's out of the coma. You better hope he corroborates your ridiculous story." He rocked back on his heels. "Unbelievable! If that teacher wasn't as dark as me, you'd be under the jail. Black on black crime and a mama with clout is a helluva get out of jail card. I'm lucky your feral ass hasn't killed me."

She bit her lower lip and hung her head. She scooted from the floor to the steps and sat quietly. She heard her mother's voice clearly saying, *Let him talk. Just let him talk. Don't get into anymore back and forth. It's time to listen.*

She tried, but listening took too long. "Scott, I love you. I love Ever. And I'm sorry. I'll stop drinking. I mean I'll stop drinking so much. I'll get a job. I'll go to couple's counseling. I can't lose you, Bae. I love you. I promise. I'm a new woman."

"You are an insane woman, Sloane. You're not going to manipulate me into letting you have your way again. God knows I love your family but every one of you is a little cuckoo. Your father and uncle are constantly at each other's throat like a perpetual dog fight. Your mom and dad have some kinda crazy thing going on. Did you know he spends the night over here? I saw him on the couch with her and when he was leaving, he gave her a wad of cash."

Sloane was surprised. But she wasn't surprised. Those two never really ended in her mind.

"And, I wasn't going to say anything, but...Preston owes me ten thousand dollars.

Unless—" he stared at her. "I better not find out your father gave you the money and you didn't tell me. I swear I'll sue you for more than custody of Ever if that's the case."

Sloane shook her head adamantly. "Baby, no. I promise. I didn't know anything about it. I'm sorry. We'll get the money back."

"There is no we! There's me and Ever. You're on your own. And I will get every dime back."

"I think he owes my brother money, too." Sloane wiped the tears from her cheeks with her sleeve.

"That wouldn't surprise me. Nothing about this family surprises me anymore. Not your brother with his mute girlfriend or your uncle and his titty bar empire. I don't know how I lasted this long. Moving here to be close to family is a joke in every sense of the word 'close.' Hell, you never even visit my mother and that was one of your so-called great reasons for relocating. How do think that makes me feel?"

"Scott, I don't know. I didn't want to intrude. I felt I was being thoughtful, giving you some freedom to bond with your mom. I wasn't trying to send a message." He never questioned her excuses for rarely visiting his side of the family tree. Seems she was severely dyslexic in her ability to read him.

"Well, you unintentionally spoke loud and clear. It's not like she lives in Canada. She's closer than Ever's school. I love my people, too, you know. But everything has to be about you and yours." He patted his head as if putting out a fire in his brain. "And another thing…"

Oh my Lord, what's left? This list of her family's faults was longer than a list of Jennifer Aniston's ex-lovers.

He paused, out of breath and angrier than she'd ever seen him. He pinched the puckered skin between his brows. "I've had it. I'm taking my boy and my mama and we're moving back to Austin." He wagged his finger at her, a simple gesture she realized he had never done before. Then, he said the words that finally put the fear of reality TV into her heart. "You can go anywhere in the world, but you cannot go with us."

The coldness of his tone swam up her spine like a school of piranha feasting on her nerves. Taking a mug shot was literally less frightening than the absence of hope in his eyes.

Sloane agreed her family was weird, but saying it out loud was a bridge too far. She felt her tiny heart grow a vein of respect for the man whose last name and stretch marks she bore. She squeezed the hard, round edge of the steps harder. She sniffed and smelled the odor of her son on her husband. *I WILL change, but I don't know how to convince him of that. Father God, I know I've asked for too much already but please give me the right words right now.* The old Sloane would have tried again to seduce Scott into compliance. The evolving Sloane understood she had to try something new if she wanted something better. Scott yanked the door open. Sloane trailed him to his car.

"Scott?" She spoke softly with caution. This side of him was unpredictable.

He stopped fumbling with the door handle and spun around. His eyes were hard grenades on the verge of detonating. "What? What? What?!"

"Bae, believe it or not, I was up all night studying Paul's letters."

"Who the fuck is Paul?"

She drew back as if he'd raised his hand to hit her. "From the Bible," she whispered more like a question than an answer.

"The Apostle Paul? No, I don't believe you. So hurry up."

"He wasn't actually one of the original Twelve. He was transformed on the road to Damascus and he wrote most of the New Testament. This is what Paul told the believers in Phillipi." She extended her arm to show him what she'd written in red ink across the inside of her forearm. She watched him read the words she'd recited over and over all night, memorizing the map to her new best life. Then, she quoted the scripture, "'Love keeps no record of wrongs.

Love does not delight in evil but rejoices with the truth. It always protects, always trusts, always hopes, always perseveres.'" Her arm fell to her side. She dropped her head, afraid to look at him directly when she asked, "If that's true, Scott, I vow to love you a million times better. Will you please, please give me one more chance?"

Scott's face was blank, unreadable. Sloane bit her cuticle and watched for some sign of the man who had cherished her for so many years. Tears flowed from her cheek onto her hand.

When he reached to brush her tears away, she feared he might be touching her for the last time.

CHAPTER 21

"I'm here. What's the Code Blue?" Preston brushed past the housekeeper into the massive game room on the second floor of Junior's 6,000-square foot ppeared every family member and their plus ones heeded the call for a family meeting. He scanned the room, tilting his head in surprise upon spying his son's partner, Elaine, assembled along with the rest of the family.

He assessed the scene as if it were his first tour of a new listing for a single-family home. Sloane stood near the open doors to the balcony, wearing an odd combination of slippers, silk pajama pants, and a Prairie View A&M sweatshirt. He barely recognized her without her ever-present mask of makeup, artificial lashes, and perfect hair. She looked like she had rolled out of bed, fell on the floor, and got dressed in the dark while crying.

Elaine and Trey were sitting on a cushioned bench near the pool table. One of Elaine's hands was on Trey's thigh and the other strummed the bench like a keyboard. He felt his lungs fill with more tension than he had upon receiving the Code Blue text from Trey.

"Is someone going to tell me why we have gathered? Where is your mother?" he asked his children.

"She didn't respond," Trey replied. "That's not like her. When I called it went straight to voicemail. She must be at the studio. I'm sure she'll be here soon. She's known about this meeting for a week."

Preston frowned, "A week? If you planned this a week ago, it's not a house on fire emergency. Why the Code Blue? I have a million things to do today." He saw tears well up in Sloane's eyes and he moved to her side. "What's wrong, baby girl? Where are Scott and Ever?"

She hugged him tightly, crying into his chest. "I'm sorry, Daddy. I didn't want to do this to you, but Trey and Uncle Junior insisted."

He cupped her head growing more puzzled with every tear she shed. Sloane was crying as if someone died, he thought. *What did Scott do to her? I hope I don't have to punch him in his face again.* He heard a toilet flushing and water running in the bathroom behind the bar.

A minute later, Scott emerged and hurried to his wife. "Darling, what's wrong? Don't cry. It's fine. Everything will work out." He removed her from her father's embrace and held her hands. "After this, we'll go get Ever. I know you want to see him. I just texted my mother and he's fine." Sloane sniffed.

Out of the blue, Elaine said, "Can we get on with this, please? Trey and I have a spa day planned. We need to leave shortly."

"That can wait. This is more important," Trey said gruffly, putting his hand over hers to ease the sting of his words. "Bear with me, Bae. I need your support right now."

Elaine bit her bottom lip. "Okay."

Over the intercom, a voice announced, "Mr. Henry has arrived. He'll be up shortly."

Since no one was talking, Preston went behind the bar, got a cocktail glass, and poured it half full of Crown Royal. The potent liquor made a beeline to his nerves. He couldn't wait to share his good news after they resolved whatever the hell it was that needed resolving. He missed having someone special to celebrate with him when things went well.

Junior strolled into the room chest first, as if he'd just purchased the house that he'd owned for three years. DK was behind him, looking a bit like someone late on their rent. After sliding the door closed, he dramatically placed his hand over his heart and said, "DK is my lady. It's about time y'all knew. Nothing to see here." He placed his hand on her lower back, pecked her cheek and whispered something into her ear that made her smile.

"Have a seat, Baby," he suggested. His voice was silky with affection. "Sorry I'm late, fam. The traffic coming back from Houston was terrible." He sat on the low sofa next to DK. "Trey, you initiated this so let's get started."

"What about Mom?" Trey asked. "She should be here."

Annoyed, Preston grunted and drained his glass. "People, what is the problem? Why are we here?"

"G'won Trey, your mom can catch up when she gits here. Me and DK got tickets for a concert in the park, so go ahead."

Trey stood up and faced his father. "Dad, I'll cut to the chase. We are all worried about you. You've been acting strange for months. You've lost at least fifteen pounds. You seem unfocused and forgetful. Impossibly, you're more secretive than you've ever been, so nobody knows what is up with you." He paused and looked at his uncle. Junior nodded. He looked at his sister. She bounced her head up and down. He turned to Elaine who bugged her eyes. "I say this with love, but you look like hell. We are here for an intervention. You're obviously abusing drugs." He stopped talking and let that last word linger in the air like dust from a bomb.

Preston was flabbergasted. *What the hell? They think…nah, no way.* "Wait. It's not—" he started.

Junior interrupted, "Don't try to deny it, Pee. It's so obvious. And we want to help you before you kill yourself." His eyes watered. "I know I have been pushy and I don't always tell you how much I appreciate everything you've done for me, but I love you, man. You're my big brother." He paused, choked up. DK put her hand on his shoulder and squeezed. "Man, you're my hero, and I'll always be there for you -- like you've always been there for me."

Preston felt himself getting teary-eyed. He gulped the remainder of his glass and said, "Thank you, but it's not—"

"Everyone knows I'm a daddy's girl," Sloane spoke up. "I love Mom, but you get me. We see the world in the same way. We are full speed ahead, blinders on, thinking we always know what's right. But Daddy, I am learning the importance of connection and communication." She smiled up at her husband. "We have to let others in."

That's my girl, Preston thought, feeling proud of his daughter's new level of self-awareness. She was right, too, about both of them. He moved near the pool table and picked up the eight ball. He rolled it in his hands, reflecting on the moment. *I haven't had this many nice things said to me in years. I almost don't want to tell them the truth.*

"Dad, we love you and we know you will come out on the other side of this dark moment." Scott put his arm around his wife's shoulder as she nodded.

Junior took another turn. "We'll get you in a good treatment center and they can help you deal with your feelings. Help you let go of the past. You gotta know Faith ain't coming back to you."

Preston's head jerked. Before he could respond Scott piled on.

"You have to move on, Preston. Faith loves Raymond, but I think she's torn because you are still in the picture. You're hanging around and I saw you give her money after you spent the night. That's foul. Let her go on with her life."

Preston saw the looks of pity on everyone's faces. They thought they had him all figured out. He wanted to laugh and cry at the same time. "It's not like that," he said. The liquor on an empty stomach was a rookie mistake. The room was tilting. "You have this all wrong. I was repaying Faith, not giving her money."

"You need to repay Trey, then," Elaine said. "He wants to become a CPA. We saved that money for the courses he needs. What kind of father takes money from his son?"

Now she wants to talk, Preston thought. *Why is she even here? Where is Faith? Could this day possibly get any worse? I came here because I'm a good father responding to an SOS from his child.*

"And takes money from his son-in-law," Scott added.

Junior made a loud sucking sound. "And his brother. Like I said, I got chu but I need my money back."

"C'mon, Junior." Preston spread his arms. "It's not like you're hurting for money, Negro. I've always paid you back with interest, haven't I?"

"Always doesn't count when it's been three months since I loaned you fifty g's. You said it was a bridge loan to build your house. Consider that bridge burned." When Preston didn't respond, Junior turned to Trey. "I got you on the CPA courses and the exam, nephew. Why didn't you tell us that was your goal? I thought you liked working for those white folks. You never complained." He laughed. "You're my new in-house accountant until you get your CPA papers. Give your two weeks' notice. Unlike me, you can't burn that bridge. We may need them for a future venture."

"I need to make a call," Preston announced. "Sloane, text your mother and see where she is. Y'all got me all wrong. I will explain everything when she gets here." He walked onto the patio for privacy.

~ ~ ~

A few minutes later, the barn door entrance slid open forcefully. Faith walked in. She paused mid-stride upon seeing DK and Elaine at what was billed as a family-only meeting. She felt her guard go up. She had agreed to attend the intervention to protect her children from the volatile reaction she anticipated from Preston. He never liked being called on his carpet about anything. "I'm sorry I'm late, everyone. Some drunk ran into my car at the gym early this morning. He totaled it and almost killed me."

"Did you call the police?" Trey asked as Preston returned to the room.

"Do you need to see a doctor?" Junior inquired.

"What happened?" Preston asked. The three men started towards her arms outstretched in concern.

She waved them back. "I'm fine. It was a hit and run. The police were called, but I couldn't tell them much. I finished an early morning work out and I was about to get in my car when this other car came barreling toward me out of nowhere. Hopefully, they'll find him or her. Turns out, there are cameras everywhere. I'm sure they are examining all the footage." She cringed at the thought of what they'd see. "The paramedics checked me out. Bumps and bruises only. They told me to follow up with my private physician and I will."

She bent her left arm and cupped a sore spot on her elbow. Sloane cautiously walked over, led her to a chair, and put a pillow behind her back. "Alrighty. Where are we? Does he know why we're here?" She wanted their attention on anyone but her. She couldn't have explained why she omitted Raymond from the recounting. She felt a need to process the mind-numbing pain she was hiding from her family.

"Thank you for intervening," Elaine said, dryly. "Let's get on with it."

"You're here for me it appears," Preston said. "In a nutshell, my haggard appearance and stealthy moves led everyone to believe I'm abusing drugs. And," he looked at Faith, "I'm not sure if you know this part, but they think I'm standing in the way of you finding happiness with Raymond."

Faith's mouth folded in like a Cabbage Patch doll. "There is nothing between us," she insisted. "How did I get in this?"

"Why is he sleeping over and giving you money then?" Scott asked with out of character curiosity. Faith felt Sloane and Trey zoom in on her face, waiting for a plausible explanation. He had to be talking about the brownie night. She looked at Preston with a plea in her eyes.

He saved her. "You people are twisted. She was helping me with some legal stuff late one night and we fell asleep on the couch. What Scott witnessed was me paying a little on the loan she made me."

"So you made payments to her but not your only brother?" Junior wiped his face with his hand as if he were erasing all future references to loyalty between brothers.

Murmuring ensued. "Wait! Before anyone else speaks, let me explain something. I am not on drugs of any sort. I haven't been myself and I've lost weight because I have been working twenty hours a day. That's it. I'm tired, but I'm not an addict." He put his hands on his waist. "I can't even believe y'all thought that about me."

Junior pointed at Trey. "It was his idea. I thought you were lazy 'cause you sure ain't been putting in that kind of time for me."

Faith laughed aloud. She found that funny. It reminded her of something she said to Preston when she asked for a divorce.

"What's your other job, Daddy?" Sloane asked, coming to her daddy's rescue.

"You all are going to feel really bad when I tell you this, but with a little financial help from my loving family," his voice dripped with sarcasm, then lightened up "my new hotel, the Tarry Inn and Conference Center is open and off to a great start. I used my connections to book two large corporate events. As soon as their deposits clear the bank, I can pay you all with interest." His broad shoulders squared. "And another thing, Junior: I love you brother, but I'm tendering my two weeks' notice today."

"Hold up," Trey said, looking as puzzled as everyone else. "I know about the new house but, you own the new hotel, too? You're crushing it, Dad. I apologize. I read you all wrong."

"Thank you, son. That's good to hear. But what's this about a new house? I never said that."

Junior raised his voice over the excited chatter in the room. "That's on me playa. When I asked you about those carpet samples in your office. You said something about construction, and I assumed you meant a house. That's what I told Sloane and Trey."

"You didn't tell me." Faith felt a little hurt at being left out.

With his eyes still on Preston, Junior replied, "Because I don't talk about my brother with his ex-wife. You know I love you, Faith, but women don't understand about the brother code. See…" DK touched his leg, stopping him from mansplaining.

Preston jumped back in the fray. His words came fast. "I'm majority owner and it's been touch and go with the financing, so I waited to tell everyone in case I couldn't pull it off."

"That's what matters Pee, you did the damn thang. Congrats," Junior said, smiling wide. "And Trey, you just got a promotion to Chief Operating Officer of my enterprise. Your first assignment is to find us a CPA." He walked over to Preston and gave him a bear hug. "Look at my brother doing it real big. Do mom and pops know about this?"

Preston shook his head. Junior added, "They gone be thrilled. Listen, Pee, I'ma support you however I can, but you're catching me off guard with this. Before you bail, I'ma need you to train up Trey on the business. Please?"

"Of course," Preston agreed.

"Preston needs a vacation first," Faith said. "He's almost worked himself into about a," she squinted at him a moment, "thirty-two-inch waistline, which apparently is the only reason we are here. He doesn't need our assistance— bless the Lord—so I'm outta here."

"Fine." Junior agreed.

"You actually own the Tarry Inn?" Faith struggled to rise from her chair. Every part of her hurt, inside and out. She wondered if Preston knew it was Diamond's company installing the televisions at his franchise. Those two had been incompatible since Diamond functioned as her receptionist at City Hall.

Preston looked so happy. "Yes, I do. And Faith -- I know that look on your face. Don't worry. I asked the general contractor to hire Diamond's company to install flat screens in every room. We committed to hiring minority-owned businesses and her crew did a great job. Bygones are gone. I learned that from you, Faith."

Sloane's phone started ringing. "It's J.D. Person," she said. "Why is he calling?"

"Answer it," Scott ordered. "Put it on speaker."

Sloane complied and said, "Hello. Mr. Person?" The phone was moving with her trembling hand.

J.D. cultured Southern drawl filled the room. "Sloane, I got a call from the court." Sloane's knees buckled. Scott put his arms around her. She opened her mouth and moved her lips but nothing came out.

Scott asserted himself, placing his hand around Sloane's hand. He pulled the phone toward him. "J.D., this is Scott Henry. What did they say?"

Faith, Preston, and Trey moved closer, forming a shield in front of Scott and Sloane. Faith forgot her injuries and Raymond for the moment. She was glad she had come. She almost hadn't, but if J.D. had bad news, as she anticipated, she needed to be there for Sloane.

"Hi Scott. Well, it seems the art teacher..." J.D.'s voice broke up and the phone went dead.

Everyone clamored for Sloane's attention. She looked from face to face with a bewildered expression. "Call him back!" They yelled. She didn't move.

Scott gently pushed her toward Faith. "Take care of her for a moment," he stated. "I'm calling J.D. back." When he said that, the phone rang.

"Answer. It shouldn't be locked yet," Trey offered.

Scott answered with confidence in his voice and got to the point. "J.D. what did they say?"

"It's good news. The teacher confirmed that he tripped. He doesn't remember much after hitting the ground, but he said he never felt threatened. They are dropping everything. No charges, no probation, and no criminal record."

"That is good news," Scott confirmed. "We can't thank you enough J.D. We appreciate the call." He hung up and everyone went bananas.

Sloane jumped up and down in excitement. "He told the truth! The art teacher, I mean. He remembered everything. Ohmigawd, it's finally over."

Everyone was hugging it out. Junior forgot about Faith's accident and hugged her a little too snugly. She winced slightly when he squeezed her. She leaned to the side and peered behind him at DK. "I realize now there are quite a few things you kept to yourself, little brother. Nevertheless, I'm happy about this development with Sloane," she patted his broad chest. "And that development," she added, pointing at DK.

Faith removed her glasses and looked for a place to lay them. Sloane noticed and hurried to her side. "I'll take these. You'll forget them, otherwise. We'll drive you home, Mother. I saw you grimace when Uncle Junior hugged you. I know you're hurt, Queen Mother."

Faith folded her arms across her chest and shrugged her shoulders up and down like the matriarch in the movie *Black Panther*. The motion caused her to grimace again. "Thank you, Princess. You're right. I'm a little banged up." She made her way back to her chair more slowly than necessary, buying time to think. She closed her eyes and pictured Raymond on the ground bleeding. Her skin bubbled like lava. She opened her eyes and felt the world rush in with all its noise and pollution. With all its unpleasant surprises.

~ ~ ~

Faith called the police station from the back seat of Scott's car. She had two voicemails asking her to call as soon as possible. She could see Scott watching her reaction in the rearview mirror. He was acting more alpha male today. She wasn't sure why, but it was a welcome change. When she finally got the detective assigned to the case on the phone, he filled her in on their progress. When she hung up, Sloane asked, "Well, what did they say?"

Faith tugged on her seatbelt, pulling it away from her bruises. "He said traffic cameras took photos of a banged-up car speeding down Main. It's the same car from the hit and run. And they..." She momentarily lost the ability to speak. Tears rolled down her face. She put her hand over her mouth to keep herself from screaming.

Sloane was alarmed. "Mother, are you okay? You stopped in the middle of a sentence." She turned around to look in the back seat. She found some paper napkins in the glove compartment and passed them to Faith.

Faith felt confused. "—this evening. I mean the hit and run this morning. When they went to the driver's apartment and arrested him, they searched his place. The officer said his bedroom is plastered with pictures of me. Me at home in the yard. Me working out. Me at the grocery store." Faith's mind seemed detached from her body. She had so many thoughts and feelings wandering around like strangers at Union Station. "They want me to come in and bring my cell phone. They found evidence he might have been tracking me through an app on my phone."

"Why do the cops need you right now? The phone app isn't going anywhere," Scott was angry on her behalf. "I'm calling and telling them you're not coming in until tomorrow. They need to do their jobs and detect!" He bellowed.

"Calm down. It's necessary because I know the driver. He's my show producer. It's Daniel."

CHAPTER 22

A week later, Raymond was in his office re-reading the same three lines of the *Wall Street Journal's* front-page article on transportation trends when he ;oft rap on the door. "Come in."

His operation's logistics manager peeked in. "Got a minute?"

"Sure," he closed his pc and turned down the volume of the blue tooth speaker playing classical music.

"Glad to have you back in the office," she started.

"Take a seat. I needed a few days off. After the trip to Texas, I was pretty tired."

She plopped down. "I'm sure getting hit by a car didn't help."

He looked at the ceiling a moment. "It didn't." He couldn't connect the dots for how she had that knowledge.

"I know because Faith called me that morning while the medics had you in the ambulance. She texted me later to let me know you were okay. I'm glad she did, because you haven't mentioned a word about Texas since you came back."

"Oh," was all he said. That was something Faith would do. She was thoughtful to a fault.

"Yeah, she thought your significant other should know what happened and wanted me to talk you into going to the hospital. That's pretty big of her considering she's in love with you, don't you think, cousin?"

"She doesn't know how to love, Eden." He inhaled a long, steady breath but it exited in stuttered puffs of frustration. If he had a dollar for every time she refused to commit to something he wanted for both of them, he could buy another commercial building with cash. The Vikings committed some atrocious acts during their raids in the ninth century, but their custom of throwing women over their shoulders and sailing away with them held some appeal for him. Knowing Faith, if he'd tried kidnapping her back in those days, she would've jumped into the sea and swum back to France. That woman made him feel gooier than a peanut butter and jelly sandwich in the microwave. He was better off without her, he decided. There would be no going back.

"And you're the expert on matters of the heart, now?" Eden asked, dripping sarcasm. She scooted to the edge of her. "Fam, you pretending to be dating your second cousin to make the woman of your dreams jealous is pretty messed up. I went along to help you out, but I need my life back. Plus, somebody showed my mama our faux Bae-cation pics online. I had to tell her what we're doing and she is not happy. I had to listen to an hour of scriptures on deceit."

"Hey, my apologies. I'll call Auntie. It was a dumb idea and I never dreamed it would go on this long. I was listening to my friends' bad advice about making a woman realize what she lost, so they start acting right." But ex-mayor Faith Henry was everything but ordinary.

"All that planning we did for New Orleans and she said she had to stop disrespecting you and coming between *us*?" He patted his palm against his fist, painstakingly remembering every soft place on Faith's body. "That woman is a puzzle I can't solve." He sighed. "I'm out of ideas to win her heart."

"I'm not so sure you lost that bet," Eden replied. "Faith is the one who messed up. You have her heart. I believe she thought holding out on marriage would somehow prevent you from breaking it. Faith thought she could give you her body and close her heart. Real love doesn't work like that. The kind of love you both deserve includes every cell of the mind, body, and soul. Or as Faith calls it, Level Ten loving!" She smiled broadly. "BUT--I think she's finally seen the error of her ways."

"Really? What do you mean by that?"

"I mean Faith Henry is here looking for her man."

"Here? Is that a metaphor for she's mentally ready to commit? You lost me four sentences ago."

Eden laughed. "When Faith called after the accident, I told her about your B.S. scheme and warned her the next woman you put in her spot won't be your cousin who has no interest in you or children named Sodom and Gomorrah. I think she heard me. What I mean is this: Faith is literally on the other side of that door." She pointed him toward nirvana and braced herself for the updraft of his departure.

Raymond bounded out of his chair and reached the door in five long strides. When he opened it, Faith flew into his arms. As they kissed the longest kiss in the history of kisses, Junior began to sing, "I'm not living without you...I don't wanna be free...I'm staying...Yes, I'm staying...And you, and you, and you, you're gonna love meee!"

Faith's entourage included everyone who had unused PTO at the job or no job, at all: Sloane, Scott, Trey, Junior, the Carsons, and Preston, holding an impatient Ever's hand.

Raymond thought he'd died and gone to heaven's waiting room.

"Raymond, I brought everyone I love to witness my confession to you on what will be the best or worst day of my life, depending on your answer." She looked deeply into his eyes. "I love you more than anything. I want to be your wife until death does us part. Will you marry me today?"

Did that bump on the head give him a concussion? Was he hallucinating? "Are you serious?" He pinched himself. "You want to marry me right now?" He wiggled like a happy kid.

She was in his arms--waiting for his answer.

"Yes, Raymond. Reverend Leroy will marry us today if you'll still have me." The pastor held up a small bible. His wife beamed by his side. "Let's go to the county clerk's office and get a marriage license. Like Texas, there's no waiting period in Santa Fe. That's why I brought everyone here. It makes perfect sense, unless" she shuddered, "unless you don't want me. Do you, Raymond? Do you still want me?"

The warmth of Faith's breath fanned Raymond's face. Her hair smelled like a sunrise. He felt dizzy. "What about Los Angeles?" he asked her.

"We'll work that out together, my love. I'm here to prove you're my top priority. I've been a fool to think I could replace what we have with anything man-made. You fill the blanks between my thoughts."

She kissed him. "Raymond, I live because you breathe."

"And I breathe because you live." He squeezed her tighter.

"Sounds like you're starting the vows without me," Reverend Leroy joked.

"So you'll marry me?" Faith asked again.

Raymond saw goosebumps appear on her arms around his shoulders. His hands went from her waist to cradle the back of his head. He took two steps back. Faith clasped her hands in front of her. His eyes moved from her to the family and friends, who had stopped smiling. Then, he noticed his senior managers and all his employees were behind them, waiting for him to answer. Not a truck, part, or person was moving. He had been so sure about the two of them for so long, but she kept saying no. What changed her heart?

Faith's hands fell by her sides. She bit her lip. "I understand," she said and turned to leave.

Eden walked behind Raymond and whispered, "Stop overthinking. Don't you dare let her leave."

He moved quickly and wrapped his arms around Faith from behind. "Where do you think you're going?" He turned her and scooped her up in his arms. "You won't ever go anywhere without me again, soon-to-be Mrs. Hart!"

EPILOGUE

Six months later, Faith and Raymond Hart were on a sidewalk in New Orleans posing for a selfie. A video chat request from Sloane popped up on Faith's

She kissed Raymond's cheek as she moved the phone closer to accept the call.

"Hi, Honey."

Raymond chimed in. "Hey, Sloane."

Sloane was in the spacious kitchen of her new home grinning from ear to ear. "Hey, guys! Don't you lovebirds look cute in your matching red shirts? I see you made it to Nola safely, but where are you? That building is beautiful!"

"We arrived an hour ago and I wanted to come here first thing. That's St. Louis Cathedral. You should see the inside. It's amazing." Faith switched to the rear camera. "Look at the grounds. This is my favorite place in New Orleans." *This is where I threw a long shot prayer in the air last summer and I stand here today with God's gracious reply by my side.*

"I think I hear kids in the background," Raymond noted. "What are y'all up to?"

Sloane panned the room. Little boys and girls were running everywhere shooting at each other with Nerf guns. The laughing and shouting made Faith happier than the cathedral.

"Ever wanted to have a party to celebrate the full moon. I thought, why not? Scott is outside grilling hotdogs. Whoa!" A little girl ran between Sloane and the kitchen counter. She almost knocked the phone out of Sloane's hand. She caught it before it hit the ground. "Slow down, Allyson. Everyone be careful, please. No one gets hurt on my watch. Okay?"

Raymond moved behind Faith and raised the collar of her coat to cover her neck before wrapping his arms around her waist. She smiled, closed her eyes, and thanked her lucky stars.

"Get a room," Sloane kidded. "Mother, real quick. I planned to make marble cake with chocolate icing but Ever insists I make brownies. He says you make the best brownies." She wrinkled her nose. "I don't recall you baking brownies but may I have the recipe?"

Faith looked over her shoulder at her husband.

"Sloane, we must have a bad connection. I can't hear you. I'll call you later." She ended the call and they laughed out loud.

~ ~ ~

Faith and Raymond lived happily (for the most part) splitting their time between Santa Fe, Ulysses, and their condo near Grapefruit headquarters in Los Angeles.

Never close your heart.

ABOUT THE AUTHOR

Monica "Dr. mOe" Anderson is an entrepreneur, bestselling author, motivational speaker, widely published journalist, and Doctor of Dental ꞏ almost three decades, she has motivated and inspired others through her speaking engagements, media appearances, podcasts, videos, books, articles, and professional development coaching.

She has published seven books, including four novels, *Sinphony*, *When A Sistah's Fed Up*, *I Stand Accused*, and *Never Close Your Heart*; and three nonfiction books, *Black English Vernacular*, *Mom, Are We There Yet?*, and *Success Is A Side Effect*.

In 1996, she made history as the first African American columnist for the Arlington Star-Telegram. The popularity of her articles led to a weekly editorial for the *Fort Worth Star-Telegram*, a leading Texas newspaper. Her editorials have appeared in news outlets across the country. This native Texan hosted and produced a cable television program while in full time private practice.

She presents workshops to corporate, university, and civic groups, as well as, professional associations. She has lectured throughout the United States and internationally.

Her most requested topics are: Life Balance, Entrepreneurship, Cross Generational Communication Skills, and the Medical Benefits of Humor. She is consistently rated "best speaker" at meetings and conferences.

An advocate for social change, Dr. mOe incorporates her wry wit into all her activities from boardrooms to classrooms. She is a graduate of the University of Minnesota School of Dentistry and Baylor University but her most treasured credentials are mother of two, grandmother, and cancer survivor!

Currently, she is writing her next novel and working as a full-time dental consultant for a national benefits administration company. Dr. mOe divides her time between Austin, Texas and Grand Prairie, Texas.

Made in the USA
Coppell, TX
29 October 2020